A Few Hi

A Few Hints and Clews

Robert Taylor

Southern Tier Editions™
Harrington Park Press®
The Trade Division of The Haworth Press, Inc.
New York • London • Oxford

For more information on this book or to order, visit
http://www.haworthpress.com/store/product.asp?sku=5917

or call 1-800-HAWORTH (800-429-6784) in the United States and Canada
or (607) 722-5857 outside the United States and Canada

or contact orders@HaworthPress.com

Published by

Southern Tier Editions™, Harrington Park Press®, the trade division of The Haworth Press, Inc., 10 Alice Street, Binghamton, NY 13904-1580.

PUBLISHER'S NOTE
The development, preparation, and publication of this work has been undertaken with great care. However, the Publisher, employees, editors, and agents of The Haworth Press are not responsible for any errors contained herein or for consequences that may ensue from use of materials or information contained in this work. The Haworth Press is committed to the dissemination of ideas and information according to the highest standards of intellectual freedom and the free exchange of ideas. Statements made and opinions expressed in this publication do not necessarily reflect the views of the Publisher, Directors, management, or staff of The Haworth Press, Inc., or an endorsement by them.

This is a work of fiction. Names, characters, places, and incidents either are the products of the author's imagination or are used fictitiously, and any resemblance to actual persons, living or dead, business establishments, events, or locales is entirely coincidental.

Cover design by Marylouise E. Doyle.

Library of Congress Cataloging-in-Publication Data

Taylor, Robert, 1940 July 22-
   A few hints and clews / Robert Taylor.
      p. cm.
   ISBN-13: 978-1-56023-673-3 (pbk. : alk. paper)
   ISBN-10: 1-56023-673-6 (pbk. : alk. paper)
   1. Gay couples—Fiction. 2. Gay men—Family relationships—Fiction. 3. Gay men—United States—Fiction. I. Title.
PS3570.A9516F49 2007
813'.54—dc22
                                                                                    2006029406

For my parents, Larry and Virginia Taylor,
For Ted's parents, Anna and Frank Nowick,
And for Ted, the heart of this story
—and of my life.

Why even I myself I often think know little
or nothing of my real life,
Only a few hints, a few diffused faint clews and indirections
I seek for my own use to trace out here.
—Walt Whitman

No man is himself, he is the sum of his past.
—William Faulkner

Deciding to remember, and what to remember,
is how we decide who we are.
—Robert Pinsky

Acknowledgments

With gratitude to all those who have believed in me and encouraged me through the years, including my agent Malaga Baldi; my publicist Michele Karlsberg; my editor Mary Beth Madden; and all the other wonderful people at The Haworth Press. Special thanks as well to David Rosen and Robb Pearlman, Paul Willis and Greg Herren, Ian Philips and Greg Wharton—and to my friends and neighbors here in Oberlin, too many to name.

Adam comes home from the hospital, tired but not really sleepy. He looks for the cat, who is sunning herself in a chair near the front window. He scratches behind her ears, and she begins to purr.

"Hello, sweetheart," he says. "Sorry I've been away so long. Are you hungry?"

Her response is to jump down off the chair and walk toward the kitchen, tail held high. No backward glance. She knows he will follow.

Adam pours dry food into her dish and stands there watching her eat. After a minute or two, he turns.

"I'll be out on the deck for a while," he says.

She looks up and goes back to her eating.

He sits in one of the big wicker rockers and gazes down at the bay, sparkling in the afternoon sun. Death has been close to him, too close—first his father, now this—and life therefore seems very dear. With all its confusions and disappointments. So much of both.

An osprey swoops low over the water and comes to rest on a high branch of a fir tree. A loon calls from the cove off to his right.

Maybe it's the mournfulness of that call. Maybe it's the long hours in intensive care. From somewhere come thoughts of those he's loved. And those he's lost. Does it make any sense, he wonders, all this loving and losing? Can he make it make sense? He leans back and closes his eyes. He should avoid these thoughts entirely. The way he used to. You never know where they'll take you, once you start. He opens his eyes.

The bay is that deep, intense blue Adam has seen nowhere else. The mountains beyond (he knows they're really hills, but he thinks of them as mountains) are a blend of purple and green—more green when the sun shines directly on them, more purple when a cloud, round and white, drifts by. The sky is almost as blue as the water. Almost.

As he sits there rocking, a breeze blowing toward him off the bay, glimpses of the past begin to move across his mind. Of his life and Tony's. Official versions first. The old family stories told by his parents, by their parents, by Tony's mother and sisters. Then, faint but insistent, more subtle memories come creeping in. Recollections of whispers, faint murmurs behind almost-closed doors, snatches of conversations no one knew he was overhearing. Should he try to line them up, these scattered fragments? See what he can make of it all?

Better not, he thinks. Too complicated. Too painful. But . . . He sighs. If he doesn't look now, when what he loves most has been so threatened, he knows he never will. Before caution can assert itself and divert him back to the familiar safety of the surface, he plunges into the deep waters where the *real* story lies.

He goes far back, as far as he can. He sees his mother lying in bed, propped up all around with fluffy pillows. She's a small girl, maybe seven or eight, pretty in a pert, almost sharp-faced way. Her dark brown hair hangs to her shoulders in long, spiraling curls. She wears a bright turquoise bed jacket (a color she will love all her life), ruffled up the front and down the back. Somebody has taken great care to see that she looks nice, even though she's been lying in this bed for almost a year.

What she has is not entirely clear. Scarlet fever? Rheumatic fever? Maybe even tuberculosis. Nobody says. Many families would have laid it all out by now, labeled it, let naming the disease take away some of its power. But not this family. One of its strictest rules is that nothing unpleasant is ever a suitable topic for conversation. And their concept of what is unpleasant is a broad one, with most of what happens to the human body well within the boundaries. Certainly, nothing so personal as a long illness is the business of anybody outside the walls of the house, and one way of keeping a chattering little girl from talking about it is not to tell her. So they don't. In some ways, though, none of this really matters. The crucial thing here is not the precise medical diagnosis, but the fact that the treatment her doctor has recommended is a solid year of rest in bed.

Irene had always been an active little girl, running here and there, eager to be in the middle of whatever was going on, which led to anxious conversations between her parents, after this illness struck, about how they were going to keep her still for so long. They needn't have worried. She's taken to the bed like a duck to water. The first few infectious weeks were a bit hard on her, it's true, as she was such a social child, used to the constant comings and goings of a large extended family. But even during this time—especially during this time—she has never been alone for a minute. One or the other of her parents is at her side day and night. They've worked out some equitable arrangement under which her mother sits with her while her father goes to see about a rental property or an oil lease or to do some fishing, only to be relieved by him later in the day so she can go off to a DAR meeting or to the grocery store or to church. For the entire year, one of them is with Irene all the time, sitting in a chair, sleeping on a cot.

These arrangements can't be easy for Irene's father to manage, because his wife has never learned to drive. This might have something to do with eyesight or physical coordination or apprehension, but more likely it's a conscious choice. An outward manifestation of an inner view of herself: she does not drive; she is driven. Usually, until now, by her husband, who has willingly—certainly uncomplainingly—assumed the responsibility for seeing that she gets to wherever it is she wants to go. He gives every indication of approving of the way his wife sees herself, as something of a matriarch, even at such a young age. This is reflected in their wedding picture, which sits in a silver frame on the breakfront in Adam's parlor. The two of them stand side by side, in the stiff, formal pose of photographs of those days. He looks stern and a little uncertain. She looks matronly, already, with her wire-rimmed glasses and her hair pulled tidily into a bun on the top of her head.

The room Irene lies in, at the front of the house (in which Adam will spend many a summer night), is a bright, sunny room. Windows on three sides, one looking north onto the front porch, a full wall of windows looking east across the front yard, and one looking south toward the long, narrow driveway. The handsome, two-story rock house, in the leafy, charming little town of Weatherford, is set far back from the street. Its wide, vivid green lawn is tended carefully, and daily, by Irene's father, along with the large vegetable garden out back and the flower beds all around, in which jonquils and irises and roses bloom as the months go by. The huge pecan tree in the front yard shades this bedroom all through the spring and summer but keeps out only some of the intense Texas sun. So rather than being a 'sick room,' gloomy and dank, this is a happy room through which passes, after that initial quarantine, a stream of visitors—school friends, aunts, cousins, members of the Presbyterian church out to do their Christian duty by visiting that sweet, bedridden little Kendall girl. A chance to see inside the fine Kendall home, one of the nicer ones in town, to be served tea in a tissue-thin porcelain cup poured from a tea service of solid silver—these cannot be thought of as primary motivations for the decision to pay a call.

The only exception to the almost perfect unanimity of her parents' lives has to do with going to church. Her father continues to attend the Baptist church, which is too raucous and unrefined for her mother's tastes. Her mother's Presbyterianism, in addition to being the true religion, is more decorous, though certainly no less fervently believed.

As the result of either mutual agreement or the natural division of labor practiced in those days, her mother is in charge of setting the religious tone of their home and of seeing to the proper Christian upbringing of the two children, Irene and her much-older brother. Therefore, her mother takes advantage of these long hours at her daughter's bedside to tell stories from the Bible, stories both beautiful and pregnant with meaning: Abraham and Isaac (do as God commands), Moses and the Red Sea (don't mess with the Almighty), Mary and Martha (a woman's place is in the home), the Parable of the Talents (to he who has, and tends it well, shall more be given). This God of hers is demanding when it comes to prayer, church attendance, and the avoidance of liquor, cigarettes, cards, motion pictures, and the taking of His name in vain. But He is also quick to give comfort to those who obey and truly believe.

Her husband, though, is taciturn, the way he believes menfolk ought to be. He is wary of chatter, particularly with such a young girl.

When his turn at the bedside comes, it is his daughter who does most of the talking. His way of showing love and approval is not to say what he feels but to give tangible evidence of it. The car his wife rides in is new and black and shiny. Their meat and milk stay cool in one of the first iceboxes in town. Her closets are full of the silkiest dresses Fort Worth and Dallas can supply. Hats of many styles and shapes sit in boxes on shelves, and gloves of fine cotton and soft kid lie in rows across a bureau drawer. His daughter has dresses with stiff petticoats, shoes of gleaming patent leather that buckle around her ankles, and dolls with real hair and eyes that open and close. A colored woman comes two or three times a week to keep the house spotless and the clothes ironed.

Irene's mother is proud, not only of the position she occupies at this moment, but also of where she's come from. A sense of heritage, that most Southern of passions, is strong in her. And a passion it surely is. Her family: Five stalwart, Presbyterian, Scotch-Irish brothers who reached the shores of South Carolina early in the 1700s, in plenty of time to marry and provide soldiers to fight in the American Revolution. Her part of the clan moved on to Mississippi, where they prospered and then saw it all crumble during the War Between the States and its harrowing aftermath. Her grandparents, deciding to make a new start, traveled by covered wagon to the hills of East Texas, where they prospered yet again. Her father had become a respected doctor, and she herself had gone to college, one of only a handful of women in the state to do so in those days, to study to be a teacher.

Through the years, she has carried on an extensive correspondence with many of these relatives across the South, in particular the cousin in Mississippi who will go on to become a lion in the U.S. Senate. So if she is proud, she has much to take pride in.

And Adam's father? He's much farther west, hundreds of miles from Weatherford, at the southern edge of that endless Texas Panhandle that almost pushes its way through Oklahoma and on up into Kansas and Colorado. Adam sees him out behind a small rectangular wooden house on a dirt street, in a fenced-in corner of the yard, tossing feed to a few busily scratching chickens. He's twelve or so, young Samuel Hunter, who, of course, is called Sam. He's an appealing boy, everybody says so, with his handsome face and ready smile, although he's worked too hard and seen too much to really be called a boy anymore.

He's gregarious, in that hearty way so many Texans are. He falls easily into conversation with practically anybody, tells a good story, whether about a baseball game he's helped to win or a fish he's caught, and he's respectful and attentive to his elders. His mother has seen to that. But he's also something of a loner, partly because of the nomadic life his family has led, in which friends get left behind with disconcerting regularity, partly because, even at this young age, he likes his own company. Oh, he loves his family with a fierce loyalty, especially his mother, who is sometimes too distracted by the pressures of her own life to love him back the way she'd like to, and his big brother, three years older and very much worth looking up to. But still, there are times when Sam is most comfortable, most at home, inside his own mind.

Unlike Irene's, his family seems to have come out of nowhere—or, better yet, from everywhere. He has no lineage, no pedigree to speak of, not a grand one at any rate. His only really memorable ancestor is his father's grandmother, a full-blooded Cherokee from Oklahoma, the almost certain source of the thick black hair and dark brown eyes Sam will later pass on to Adam.

Sam's family has roamed from the Texas side of Texarkana, where he was born, on into Arkansas, then all the way over to New Mexico, clear across on the *other* side of the state. They lived for a while in Clovis and Portales before coming back to Texas, to the tiny town of Slaton up here in the Panhandle. The house they live in now sits right beside the two-lane highway that cuts straight through the middle of town. Sam's grandfather, on his mother's side, owns a loudly clanking cotton gin just across on the other side of the road. Sam's father runs a little cleaning plant up on the main street of town, which is actually just the highway with the traffic slowed down for a couple of blocks, and his mother, when she isn't cooking and scrubbing and hanging out laundry for her husband and four kids, alters clothes and makes buttonholes for other people.

Slaton. Only fifteen miles or so from the bustling county seat of Lubbock, it seems to exist in a space and time all its own. The land here is flat, flatter than the flattest image you can construct in your mind. A tabletop, the one that occurs to most people, doesn't capture the feeling of it at all, not really. A tabletop is *supposed* to be flat; a carpenter or a planing machine has worked hard to make certain there are no bumps or indentations. Land, though, to anybody who hasn't lived in Slaton, is expected to have *some* variations, some little hills that industrious colonies of ants have struggled year after year to pile up, some small nick where a can of motor oil has fallen off a rack and left its mark.

Not in Slaton. Nothing rises, nothing dips. Everything stays exactly on that even line that stretches unbroken from here to the horizon, and on beyond. At this time, the 1920s, the air is crystal clear. So clear that Sam has the feeling, out there throwing feed at his mother's chickens, that he can see forever, though of course he knows that isn't so because he can't even see Lubbock and that's just down the road a piece. But he *feels* like he can see a hundred miles. And for all those miles, there's nothing there.

Except for when the dust storms come. Then he can't see past the end of his nose, assuming he was crazy enough to keep his eyes open *to* see, which he isn't. All he—or anybody—can do when one of those big clouds of dust, a mile high and fifty miles wide, comes boiling across the flat plains directly at him, all dark brown and mean and angry, is to go inside the house, or the barn, or the cotton gin, and lie down someplace with a wet handkerchief across his mouth and nose and wait for it to go roaring by. Sometimes, when the storm is a reasonable size, it might be only half an hour, maybe forty-five minutes. But when the cloud stretches clear to Kansas, gathering speed and dust as it comes, it can last all day. No work gets done on those days, everybody hiding like they are behind whatever cover they can find. No cotton gets picked, no trucks full of plump white bolls pull up at his grandfather's cotton gin. When workers don't get paid, of course, neither do their bills. Sam often sees his father, then and other times too, quietly counting up the income from his cleaning plant, to see if it's likely to last to the end of the month.

The wind doesn't always blow quite that hard, but it always blows. Hardly any days go by that the air isn't moving in one direction or another. Like everybody else, Sam has gotten so used to it that sometimes he isn't quite sure if it's blowing or not, so he checks the windmill and sees that sure enough it's spinning around to beat the band. Or he looks out across the endless rows of short, dark green cotton plants whose topmost leaves will be bouncing and swaying—a lot or a little depending on how strong the wind is that day.

The surest sign, the one all the kids like best, is the tumbleweeds that roll across the hard-packed front yards not much grass ever manages to take root in, out onto the highway, and up against the wire fence on the far side. There they join the forty or fifty others already piled up from yesterday and the day before, clustered in a tangled heap, taking a rest from tumbling for a while, till the wind shifts to the other side of the fence and sends them rolling back across the highway, back across the yards, and off into the fields somewhere.

Are there new tumbleweeds coming along all the time? Sam sometimes wonders, inquisitive as he is about everything. Or do the same ones just keep rolling from one side of the Panhandle to the other, year after year after year?

The worst of the wind, though, worse even than the dust storms, if that's possible, are the tornados. Every spring they come, predictable and unpredictable at the same time. Predictable in that he knows for sure they'll be coming, but unpredictable in that he never knows when or where. They're the quirkiest of all Nature's quirky tricks. He'll watch a front come roaring in—everything in those wide empty spaces seems to roar—dark ugly-green clouds racing ahead of it, hail more often than not, big as golf balls usually but sometimes the size of oranges, smashing into roofs and denting any cars left out from under a carport. Lightning starts to flash, jagged and angry, far off and then close by.

All that noise and hoopla is just to set the stage, though. The main event is waiting in the wings. First everything gets still, stiller than the bottom of a deep well or the inside of a cave, as still as the land is flat. The air that's no longer moving sideways presses straight down on top of him, so thick and heavy he can hardly breathe. And green. Getting greener by the minute.

Then he sees it, the dark bluish-black funnel, thick at the top and angling down to a delicate, almost dainty tail that whips and skips and jumps around, flicking a house here, leaving the next four or five untouched, smashing another down the block, sideswiping the one across the street, hurling a tractor through the side of a barn, picking up pieces of straw as carefully as a monkey picks fleas, and lining them up, each imbedded three inches deep, in the bark of an oak tree, whose branches are so undisturbed the acorns don't even fall to the ground.

Usually he doesn't get to watch the twister do its dance because his mother herds him and his older brother and two younger sisters into the storm cellar out in the backyard, a long cement cylinder like half a sewer pipe, with thick cement ends and a room dug underneath, where he can't see which way that fickle tail is headed but where he can still feel the ominous weight of the thick green air.

The rest of the time, always, always, over this flatness, when clouds or dust don't obscure it, there's the sky. An immense blue bowl turned upside down. So huge the world seems to be nothing but sky, the point being to make clear the magnificence of it and the insignificance of all the tiny creatures struggling along down below. Other places, people make special trips to vantage points from which to 'see' the sun set. A hillside, or a balcony, or a clearing. Out on these plains, evening *is* the sunset. From wherever a person might be, he can watch everything above turn from blazing red to gold to the deepest rose. No house or tree (of which there are maybe ten or twelve in the whole town) is big enough to offer the slightest obstruction. The sun, like the wind, goes where it wants to, and there is nothing man, in his puniness, can do to interfere with its progress across the sky.

That, along with whether the rains come or not, whether crops flourish or fail, whether a tornado hits your house or a neighbor's, is up to God. He will provide, but only if He so chooses. All-knowing, inscrutable, quick to anger, hard to please, He sits up there in that limitless, splendid dome of a sky and looks down and judges. And He has created, in Slaton, the perfect place to be able to do that, because there is nowhere to hide. No mountain crevasse or thick forest or garden even in which a person can conceal his nakedness and his unworthiness. All that he is, forget pretending, is exposed, same as the rows upon rows of cotton and the highway that goes off, mirages of puddled water sparkling every hundred yards or so, straight as an arrow toward the horizon. Like the sun beating down, God's gaze is relentless. He allows two choices, and two choices only: believe or be damned. Young Sam, like all the devout Methodists in his family, believes.

Time shifts. Sam is older now, fifteen or sixteen. He's quite a bit taller, still slender, strong and athletic. Good at lots of sports—baseball primarily—just not quite as good as his older brother, who's better than almost anybody else for miles around. Sam loves his big brother Nathan, though, looks up to and admires him, so being second-best bothers him only a little. Besides, in the area of the mind, he's the one who's out front. He's even more inquisitive than before, the wheels in his head straining against the sticky mud of incomprehension that surrounds him and keeps threatening to bog him down.

His teachers try hard, he'll grant them that. They want their students to learn, of course they do. It's just their vision of what there is to know that seems limited. They focus mostly on answers, dull and predictable. Easy to memorize. Sam cares more about questions—the kind that keep getting bigger as you explore them, not narrower.

Especially structural ones. How do tall buildings, the ones he's seen in pictures, stay standing up? Never mind just the tall ones, how does *any* complex building stay upright? His grandfather's cotton gin, for example, so high and wide. Adam sees Sam sitting inside it, for hours, staring up at the intricate framework of metal struts and beams supporting other beams. It has to do with distribution of weight, Sam understands that, and the inherent strength of individual joints and members. But what are the secrets? How can you be *sure* a beam is not too wide, or a joint is strong enough, to bear all that weight? Before you go to the trouble of putting it all up? And how do you determine how much weight there's going to be, angling the way it does down one strut and out onto another? He wants to know. That's the crucial thing. He wants to *know*.

And not just about buildings, though they're the things that fascinate him most. Also birds, how they fly so effortlessly, and what makes a hawk able to see a tiny little prairie dog from way up high in the sky, and what kind of understanding lets it dive unerringly, allowing for the direction and speed of erratic gusts of wind, to the exact spot where the prairie dog is standing, sniffing the air and looking all around in every direction except for that one part of the sky through which the hawk is hurtling, claws extending at the last moment, ready to clamp on that prairie dog and carry it back to her babies probably fifteen, maybe twenty miles away, however far it is to the nearest tree big enough for a hawk to build its nest in.

Or people. He has lots of questions there. Why it is they find such complicated ways of dealing with each other, when simple, straight-forward ones would be so much easier on everybody. What it is that happens to his father, when things get to be too much for him and he disappears for a while and comes back unrecognizable, all blurry-eyed and blurry-tongued, so that his wife has to hustle him off to bed and then pretend everything is fine, just like it always is. "Only a little headache, that's all, you know his nerves aren't all that good." And what it is that's going on, at times like this, inside his mother's head, behind the eyes she makes intentionally blank and the mouth she tightens up into a little circle. She would never say, Sam is sure of it, so he would never ask. But he wonders.

And he dreams. About other places, not so small and dusty. Not so hemmed in by lack of understanding. He's seen some more of the country by now, a bit. Here in Texas, and New Mexico before that. And Arkansas, back when he was young—now *there* was a spot to remember. The hills were green, birds sang in the woods, and the streams were full of fish. Not like here. He feels restless. He wants . . . something. He's not at all sure what it is or where it might be. But it's out there, all right. He does know that. Off down the road somewhere.

He stands beside the highway, watching the fancy cars and big powerful trucks go whizzing by. He loves the wistful, plaintive sound they make: eeeeeeeeeEEEUUUuuuuuuuuuuuu. eeeeeeeeeeeeeeEEEEUUUUuuuuuuuuuuuuuu. He wants to grab onto that sound and let it pull him to wherever it is it's going.

— 4 —

Downtown Fort Worth: back in the days before suburbs when factories sat near the center of town and employees could walk to work from neighborhoods close by. On this day, though, at this factory, the heavy steel gates are chained and padlocked, and clusters of workers are standing around in the street out front. The crowd, growing larger by the minute, hovers between anger and resignation. A brooding sense of restlessness, of agitation, is so thick you can almost reach out and touch it. The barely audible hum of their conversation is punctuated now and then by a shout or the irritated rattling of the chain-link fence.

A few blocks away, another group is lined up two abreast, down along the street and around the corner. Those at the front of the line are knocking, hard, on the door of a bank whose shades are still drawn in the middle of a workday morning. The 1930s have arrived, like a slap across the face, bringing with them a kind of hardship nobody is remotely prepared for.

These are frontier people, after all, tough and self-reliant, and they aren't used to things being so out of control. They don't question the acts of Almighty God, of course, Who moves in ways too mysterious for man to even try to comprehend. Floods, droughts, tornados—you just do your best to prepare yourself and then ride them out. The ordinary problems of everyday living, though, have always been things to be managed, one way or another: by rolling up your sleeves and getting a grip on them, by sinking an axe into them, by plowing them up, paving them over, taking aim and shooting at them. But *this* one ... Well. This one is different—elusive, shifty, inaccessible, its perpetrators off someplace where nobody can get at them and force them to make things right again.

Out at the edge of town, where the highway crosses the railroad tracks, a few men are sitting under some live oak trees near the freight yard, waiting for dark. It'll be easier then to sneak into a boxcar without anybody noticing, although their sitting here like this is a clear advertisement of their intentions. Other men are standing along the side of the highway, spread out at intervals, thumbs pointed one way or the other.

This wandering has become its own justification, a throwback to the days of the real frontier, not so long gone, when anybody could change his life—for the better, was the idea—merely by moving on. Now, in these perplexing times, a person may not know *what* to do, but he still has the memory that *doing,* whatever that might turn out to be, is a whole lot preferable to sitting around waiting. That seems un-American somehow, lying back and letting fate roll over you. A person may not be able to control the direction of his life, that's been made abundantly clear these past few years, but he *can* control his feet, and they might as well be taking him someplace different, where it's just possible he'll find a way to get a handle on things again.

On up the highway twenty miles or so, in Weatherford, is Irene's house. Here there is stability, or what passes for it during the turbulent '30s. No one in this house is thinking of moving on. Irene is a teenager now, and her father continues to provide for her and her mother, not lavishly by any means, but comfortably. He does this by being shrewd and fair, at the same time, and in pretty much equal measure. The tenants in the houses he's bought and fixed up to rent now pay him with whatever they can lay their hands on. Instead of giving him money, which they don't have and which he would have a hard time finding a safe, productive place to put anyway, they bring him corn from their fields out back, tomatoes and black-eyed peas and squash from their gardens, chickens and an occasional turkey or duck freshly killed and plucked, the hind quarter of a hog.

He has his own vegetable garden on a terrace at the rear of his house, which flourishes year after year under his watchful eye. He has plenty of venison from deer he's shot, a quail or two and some rabbits, cut up and put away in the frozen-food locker downtown, and he takes advantage of his favorite pastime to bring home strings of perch and bass and sometimes a catfish as big as the bathtub. He's always been a pay-as-you-go man, never cared much for borrowing, so his debts, now in particular, are few. He sees the relative security he has maintained in these perilous times as proof of the wisdom of his faith in thrift, self-reliance, and the willingness of God to help those who help themselves.

His wife contributes to their well-being by calling on the frugalness that is as much a part of her makeup as her appreciation of nice things. She stands out by the garage, in a simple housedress and sensible shoes, making lye soap in a big washtub. She sits in her sewing room cutting large rectangles out of feed sacks and hemming them up into dishtowels, or in her easy chair by the window in her bedroom sticking a lightbulb into a sock and darning the hole in its toe. She stands in the kitchen in late summer, boiling jars and filling them with vegetables of all kinds and jams she has made and watermelon-rind preserves. And she tells her daughter, "Remember, two squares of toilet paper at a time, no more. You can be clean enough without being wasteful."

That daughter, Irene, has grown up to be a lovely young woman. And a lively one. Her face is never still, eyes constantly on the move, eyebrows going up and down, maybe even sideways, mouth smiling, frowning, pouting, smiling again, hands tracing intricate patterns in the air. And she talks from morning to night. Her lungs have never been the same since that long year in bed, and when she is too excited or unhappy or distressed, her bronchial tubes seize up so tight she can barely breathe. People around her have learned to be careful about what they say, and how they say it, so as not to be the cause of one of those terrifying fits of wheezing.

But she doesn't let a lack of air or a difficulty in replenishing it keep her from saying the hundreds of things that race through her brain. "Well, you know," she says (then and often through the years to come), "I was vaccinated with a phonograph needle, so there's not a blessed thing I can do about it."

Such a barrage of words could present a problem, could be too much for some listeners to handle. But Irene has a secret weapon that saves her: charm. She has charm to burn. She bubbles over with enthusiasm, stopping when she needs to to catch her breath, then wading back in with fervor undimmed. Still, in the midst of all this talk, she manages to give those she's with the feeling that she's listening as well, and sympathizing with what she's hearing.

Adam sees her sitting with a group of girlfriends, all of them chattering away, spurred on, it seems, by the high level of energy she carries with her and with which she charges the air around her. They're all talking, all nodding, all drawn into a close bond of affection and mutual understanding. And, she will tell her mother after more than one of these gatherings, each of them has heard every word all the others have said. If pressed on the point, she can recite details to prove it.

Irene has a knack for remembering things that matter to other people—birthdays and anniversaries and even the days on which relatives or close friends of the family have died. She loves sending cards and everything involved in the giving of gifts. Thinking (for weeks) about what to give, shopping, buying, wrapping (in exactly the right paper with just the right color of ribbon), delivering the present in person, and waiting breathless (for a happy reason on these occasions) to see the look on the face of the recipient. She is rarely disappointed, since she has an unerring ability to choose well.

Christmas, of course, sends her into spasms of delight. Cards, gifts, decorations, anticipation—all the things that feed her soul rolled into one happy season. Here she is, on a Christmas Eve. She is sixteen at least, maybe seventeen, and she is radiant. Only part of her attractiveness, Adam can see, comes from the pleasing arrangement of her features. What raises her to specialness is the light that comes from inside, up into the capillaries of her cheeks and out through her eyes.

She goes from the kitchen, where she has been helping her mother put the final touches on the meal, to the dining room, where she straightens a fork and moves an iced tea glass a little to the left and counts the serving spoons on the sideboard, to the living room, where she lights the candles on each side of the sleigh and reindeer prancing across a bed of evergreens on the mantel. The doorbell rings, and she runs to let in the first of the guests, then more. A good many aunts, a few uncles, piles of cousins, in they pour, presents under their arms, laughing and shouting. She hugs them all, puts their coats and hats on the bed in her room, fits the new presents into the heap under the tree. Occasionally, she has to go off by herself to get her breathing under control, but she comes right back, smiling, to make sure everything is proceeding the way she thinks it ought to be.

After dinner, she organizes the move into the living room, adults on the sofa and chairs and piano bench, young people and children on cushions or on the floor. Her mother and two aunts, coming from the direction of the kitchen, are the last to arrive. Once everybody is settled, she starts handing out the presents, commenting on each one— "what pretty paper," "feels awfully heavy," "wonder what this big one could be." That accomplished, she calls the name of each person in turn, clockwise starting to the right of the tree. One will open a present, then the next person, then the next, on around the room, so everybody can see each object as it comes out of the wrapping. She insists on this part of the ritual. Everybody here must have a turn in the spotlight.

This Christmas, as has been true throughout these difficult years, the gifts are simple, many of them handmade. Knitted sweaters, crocheted doilies and antimacassars, carved wooden toys, Mason jars filled with plum jelly or green beans or pickled okra. Those presents that have been store bought run toward the useful—socks, underwear, fishing tackle. But even so, a few unexpected gems have managed to creep in. A book or two, several brightly colored scarves, and a cameo, passed from Irene's grandmother down to her.

Everybody is delighted, or professes to be. The point, many of them can be heard to say, is the giving and receiving, not the amount that's been spent, the chance to share in the warmth and good fellowship of such a large, loving family. Here, in this room, the air thick with the smell of evergreen and candle wax and the slowly fading hint of roasted turkey, who could doubt it?

— 5 —

The story of how Sam and Irene met is a familiar one to Adam, told over and over, with great pleasure, by both his parents. They are at college, at Texas Tech in Lubbock, just up the road from Slaton. Sam is a senior, and Irene is a freshman. Adam can see them there, right where the story always puts them, in the Student Union. Irene is drinking a Coke and laughing with a group of her friends. Talking nonstop, of course.

Sam is sitting two tables away, alone, watching her through a rolled-up piece of paper that he holds to his eye like a telescope. She senses that she is being observed, turns, and looks directly at him. He keeps the paper telescope trained on her for a few seconds longer, then lowers it. She sees a handsome face, coal-black hair tumbling onto its forehead, impudent brown eyes, dark and impenetrable, a self-confident smile. The young man lifts his left eyebrow and tilts the right side of his smile a tiny bit farther upward. She is lost. And he knows that she is lost.

They fall so rapidly in love that casual dating seems like a waste of time. In less than a week, they go from not knowing of each other's existence to spending every possible moment together. He walks with her between classes whenever he can, carrying her books along with his. They go to church, his church, every Sunday morning and to choir practice every Thursday evening. Many other evenings find them sitting at a table in the Student Union, drinking Cokes, leaning toward each other, lost in conversation. The surest possible sign of the depth of her love is that she lets him do most of the talking.

That's the official story, but there's more. The hidden part. The important part. Underneath their decorum—the politeness with which he opens doors for her and holds her chair while she sits or stands, the demureness with which she tilts her head and lowers her eyes—is a seething sexual attraction. Adam hasn't heard this from anybody, of course not, but he's as sure of it as he is of anything he *has* been told. Never mind their strict upbringings, never mind her occasional struggles with getting her breath, these are lusty young people, suddenly aware of appetites they never knew they had. That nothing in their past, certainly no hints from their parents, has prepared them for.

The desire they feel for each other is obvious to both of them, but the ways of expressing it that are allowed in these more-restrictive times—hand holding, tight embraces, good-night kisses near the doorway of her dorm—only serve to intensify their frustration. The most immediate effect of the strong moral code of the day is to send their hormones racing. To their delight, they stumble upon a satisfying middle ground. Being sincerely religious, both of them, they come to see this most secular of passions in spiritual terms. To be this strong, and to seem this *right,* their love must have been predestined.

Besides, Irene sees in Sam's life all that's been missing from hers. Travel, excitement, new places, new people. The opposite of the sameness and stodginess she's grown so tired of. Just look at where all he's lived, where all he's *been.* Once she's hooked up with this bold adventurer, she will shake herself loose, kick up her heels, and see the world.

Sam's first visit to Irene's home is a revelation. Here, laid out before him, is what he's been searching for as long as he can remember—comfort, ease, stability. Her parents have lived in this same house for twenty years. Twenty years! Imagine. And they are the epitome of what a married couple ought to be, the husband firmly in control, the wife, though supremely self-assured and a force in her own right, content to be the kind of supportive helpmate God put women on Earth to be. Their frosty politeness Sam sees as one more indication of proper breeding, so much more dignified and appropriate than the loudly inclusive hugging and backslapping of his own family. He looks around and thinks, yes. He and Irene will settle in someplace, put down roots of their own, and be at peace.

Her parents have other ideas. Who *is* this interloper? This nobody? Her mother looks for pedigree. Her father looks for soundness and reliability where finances are concerned. Both are disappointed. When, some months later, Sam does the required thing and goes to Irene's father to ask for her hand, her father says no.

He might have been more understanding, Irene's father. He might have seen in this outwardly brash but inwardly uncertain young man a slightly different version of himself at the same age. He too had created himself out of limited resources—and he too had aimed high. He, a clerk in a general store, had wooed and won the daughter of the town's most respected physician. Mightn't the parallels in the two stories, pointed out to him by Irene, have given him pause, caused him to soften his heart toward his daughter's suitor? They might have, but they didn't.

No. It's clear to him that the two sets of circumstances are not remotely the same. Soon after he married the doctor's daughter, he *bought* that general store. And then another, and another. He was already on his way up in the world when he courted so far above himself. Irene's young man, on the other hand, is a charlatan. Her father knows the type. They rely on affability and good looks instead of hard work and a keen sense of how money gets made. And held on to. No, this is an entirely different matter from his own marriage. He'd known what he was about, even then—just look where he's arrived. Irene's young man wouldn't recognize opportunity if it walked up and hit him with a two-by-four.

His answer has to be no.

Once again, Sam finds a satisfying way of reconciling religion and what appears to him to be essential for his own happiness. He sees the adamant opposition of Irene's parents as a test, a hurdle put in his path by—whom if not God?—to find out whether his resolve is firm enough, his love as strong and undying as he believes it to be. Isn't the Bible full of stories about how God tests the faithful with seemingly insurmountable obstacles, giving the prize only to those who persevere and will not be defeated?

As for Irene, honoring her father and mother, a commandment as powerful as "Thou shalt not kill" in that time and place, is all well and good up to a point. She is not, however, accustomed to being denied the things she really wants. And she really wants to spend her life with Sam. Who wouldn't? He is such a prize—tall, dark, handsome, just as he ought to be, intelligent, ambitious, witty. In her circle at college, there isn't one young woman Irene knows of who wouldn't give her eyeteeth for a glance from him. But he has chosen Irene. Declared his love in words that approach poetry. She'd be a fool to let him get away. If her parents insist on being difficult, she'll just stop breathing for a while. Then we'll see.

Irene, her father's own daughter, is determined in this, and her determination carries the day. Plans for the wedding proceed, and quite a lavish affair it will be, in keeping with the family's position in their little town. Irene stands patiently for hours, being fitted for a beautiful white satin dress with a long, long train. The Presbyterian church is reserved, bridesmaids are chosen and outfitted, a huge cake is baked, mountains of food are prepared, flower shops all across town are emptied. Into this flurry of activity walks Sam, all unsuspecting.

For Irene's father, no more accustomed to defeat than his strong-willed daughter and no more pleased at the prospect of having to accept it, has one more arrow in his quiver. Late on the evening before the wedding, sitting through the rehearsal and the dinner that followed it having strengthened his resolve, he calls Sam outside into the backyard and says firmly, in that abrupt, take-no-prisoners way of his, that it's not too late for Sam to change his mind, to show the strength of character Irene seems to lack and break off this unsuitable match.

Sam knows what this is—one last test by God of the depth and constancy of his love. He will not be found wanting. He says no. He won't give up the best thing that's ever happened to him. Irene's father shakes his head, to indicate that he wishes it could have been otherwise. "Well, then," he says, "if that's your final answer, I want you to know there's no way I'll be a party to something as wrong as this."

That next day, a bright sunny Saturday in August, Sam Hunter, young and vulnerable in spite of all his bravado, in a church where doing things properly is a religion almost as sacred as the love of Jesus, stands near the altar, surrounded by masses of flowers, his mother and father ill at ease on the front pew in clothes that are too new, his big brother beside him to witness his humiliation, and watches his bride walk toward him, all alone. No father walks beside her to give her away.

6

They easily leave all this behind, though, as they pile into Sam's secondhand coupe and drive down to the Texas coast for their brief honeymoon. Brief for lack of time—Sam is about to start a new job—and lack of money. But to Sam and Irene, it doesn't seem as if they lack for anything.

After driving around Port Aransas looking at possibilities, they settle on one of a little cluster of cottages. The curtains are torn, the linoleum is peeling, and the mattress is lumpy, but who cares? Their pleasure in each other is so complete that they believe the cottage to be charming. Even so, they don't spend *all* their time inside it. They go for walks most mornings and afternoons, carrying their shoes and squeezing their toes into the sand along the tide line. They eat shrimp two times a day, skipping only breakfast. And, in the evenings, as they sit on a bench looking out at the Gulf, where a three-quarter moon sends sparkles across the top of the waves, he sings to her. Irish lullabies in a high, clear tenor that makes her shiver it's so beautiful.

Then they go back. To Abilene, a strange-sized place. Too many people to be just a town, but not really substantial enough to be called a city. A strange, in-between sort of place. Sam starts his job at Mid-Texas Steelworks full of enthusiasm, and Irene sets to work making something of the house they've rented. Neither endeavor turns out well.

Sam listens carefully, grasps what he is told right away, and is diligent in his work. But he can't believe what he is seeing. He may be fresh out of college, but he still knows a lot more about structural engineering than the old fogies running this company. The job they've all been hired to do is to check the architectural plans for large buildings and then provide the steel—in exact amounts and milled to his company's exact specifications—that will be needed for their construction. Sam, every bit of twenty-four by now, can tell right off that the way the other workers and the supervisors do these things is all wrong. He can do the detailing work faster and more accurately than any of his co-workers, and he could manage the whole place far more efficiently than most of those in charge. He tells them this, and they are not pleased.

Sam is genuinely astonished. Why wouldn't those in charge want to adopt his suggestions, when they are clearly better than the procedures now in place? But not only do the foremen not want to do things Sam's way, they won't let him do them that way either.

His problems at work are the central fact of Sam's life, and he wants Irene to be as upset by them as he is. She's too busy fretting about the size of their house. It *is* small, true enough, but no smaller than the houses Sam grew up in. And *they* had accommodated six people. This one is being lived in by only two. With a baby on the way, granted, but how much more room can a little baby take up? Sam can't understand why Irene doesn't see that the house, the biggest they can afford right now, is perfectly adequate. His lack of understanding irritates Irene to distraction, and 'affording' things is not something she is used to considering. But, true to her family's strict code of silence when unpleasantness arises, she says nothing. She'll talk about everything else—the weather, clothes, food, people she's met in the aisles at the grocery store—but not this.

All ill feeling between them ceases at nighttime, however, when they go to their bedroom, turn out the lights, and do that marvelous thing they've discovered, which is even more satisfying than they could ever have suspected back in their heavy-breathing, kissing-outside-the-dormitory days. Here they are truly joined together, him inside her, arms wrapped tightly around each other, the outside world and its aggravations forgotten for as long as their joining lasts.

Until Irene begins to feel nauseous most mornings, and ponderous and out of sorts the rest of the time. Nobody has told her that pregnancy would be this tiresome, and the relentlessness of her discomfort takes her by surprise. One night, she tells Sam no, it's too hot and she's too tired. Then the next night. And the next.

It's Sam's turn to be irritated. The one beautiful thing in his life, the thing he's looked forward to every day, the thing he's put up with Irene's quirkiness in order to get, is now being denied him. Well, he won't allow it. He's the master in his own house, and she *will* submit. "It's your Christian duty," he tells her, his shoulders thrown back, his feet planted firmly on the floor. But she does not reply. She simply widens her eyes, gasps for breath, and leaves the room. No discussion. No resolution.

This unexpected breach intensifies the stubbornness of each of them. Even on those nights when Irene is relaxed enough to miss the feel of Sam's arms around her, she doesn't dare reach out to him. She'd just have to go through the bother of cutting him off all over again. And when Sam looks across at her and the smooth lines of her face fill him with tenderness, he doesn't dare move nearer and touch her hair. She would only close up inside herself and leave him feeling lonelier than ever.

Sam takes a lesson from Irene and turns to illness for solace. He comes home from work early one afternoon with a 'bug.' Irene is overcome with concern, fluttering around—heavily and awkwardly, of course, but fluttering nonetheless—making him lie down, taking his temperature (which registers just a hair above normal), putting a cool washrag across his forehead, gently rubbing his temples. When, by the next week, he is well enough to go back to work, she is so thankful for his recovery they make love four nights in a row.

7

Adam has arrived, two years after his sister Carolyn. He is born in Abilene, but not long afterward, his parents begin planning their move to Fort Worth. Pearl Harbor has been attacked, the United States is at war, and hundreds of thousands of young American men are marching off to boot camp.

Not Sam. He's a married man with young children, so his contribution will be helping to design and construct a mammoth new cargo plane, the B-36. The move to Fort Worth is so he can be near Consolidated Vulte, the company in charge of this high-priority mission. All very straightforward and patriotic, yes?

Adam—the man, not the baby—isn't so sure. Vague whispers, about how things weren't going so well with the job in Abilene, how Sam had gotten on the wrong side of his superiors, trouble Adam's memory. And the house they move to in Fort Worth. There's that to consider. How they happened to live in such a nice house, Adam feels certain, is far from straightforward.

In his mind, he hears Irene and her father talking on the phone, during the day while Sam is at work. Her father owns a number of rental houses in Fort Worth, barely twenty miles from his home base of Weatherford, and he helps her decide on one that will have plenty of room for her whole family. Irene talks with her father about this peculiar concept of 'affording' things. He suggests a monthly rent only slightly higher than what they've been paying in Abilene—for what Irene knows is twice as much house. If this is what 'affording' things means, it's not nearly as awful as Irene had feared.

Sam is not fooled. As soon as he sees the house, he knows what's going on and is secretly irate. Irene's father knows that Sam knows and is secretly pleased. But politeness reigns, as always, and the matter is not discussed.

That house. Roomy, full of light, grassy lawn out front, big back-yard surrounded by a tall hedge, with swings and a seesaw and a sandbox in the corner. Adam's first memory—the first one he knows for sure is *his* and not reconstructed from what he's heard—is of that house. And of a violent electrical storm. He has no idea how young he was, he couldn't have been more than three, but he was still sleeping in one of those large cribs with wooden bars all around and one side that goes up and down. He remembers standing up holding on to those bars looking out the window at a night sky full of lightning. He's so terrified he screams and screams.

His mother comes running in, picks him up, sits in the chair beside his bed, and holds him close. The more he screams, the closer she holds him. Suddenly his father lifts him out of her arms and carries him through the living room and into the front yard. The sky is vast, and the lightning streaks across it and down toward the earth. Adam screams again, and Sam holds his son above his head, straight up toward the sky. Adam stops crying.

They stand there a long time, Adam high above Sam's head, both of them looking up at the wildness in the sky. When his father's arms get tired, he lowers Adam down. He turns Adam toward him and winks. Adam starts to laugh. Then Sam does too. They stand there, his father's arms around him, lightning ripping apart the sky above them, laughing.

– 8 –

Why Sam stopped working at Consolidated Vulte is one of the murkiest areas of the Hunter family story. He was asked to do something morally repugnant, says one version, the one Sam likes best and chooses to keep on believing. Asked to cut corners. Pad costs. Somehow give the government, and therefore the war effort, less plane for its money than it deserved.

Or (the version Irene prefers and hints at, never tells directly, whenever someone tiptoes up to the subject) Sam once again thought he knew better than those in charge, spoke out too forcefully, ruffled feathers, refused to go along when going along was clearly the prudent thing to do. However it comes about, whether he leaves on his own or is asked to go, the leaving adds more pressure to that already building up inside Sam's head. The safety valves are plugged or somehow refuse to open, and his mind gives way. He has a nervous breakdown, that catch-all term in those psychologically more-innocent times for a wholesale retreat, a severe inability to cope.

And he does this here in the midst of Irene's family, champion copers from way back, people for whom male weakness is the ultimate affront, to be looked at askance and pitied. Worse yet, after the shock treatments, those repeated attempts to jump-start Sam's batteries and get his motor humming smoothly again, where does he come to rest? For *his* year of lying in bed? In a small upstairs room in the home of Irene's parents. The loony in the attic right in the heart of enemy territory, where he is seen to, clucked over, subjected to daily Christian charity. And all the time, the constant rebuke "I told you so" hangs unspoken in the air, dangling from the ceiling of every room and peeking out from behind every piece of furniture.

Adam can hardly bear to think of it.

And the family? Irene and her three children—the last of them, Dwayne, has just been born—have moved to Weatherford to be near Sam. Into another of the houses owned by Irene's father. Rent-free. Charity all around.

Looking back, Adam feels the weight of the anxiety pressing down on Irene at this turn of events. Three young children to care for, one still an infant. Her husband pale and unreachable in that upstairs room. No job. No income. Certainly no savings. Who will pay the bills? Who else? The one she's always been able to turn to, rely on.

With her father's help, they manage, although that year is a long one for all of them. In time, however, Sam gets better, leaves his little sanctuary, and comes home. To pleasure and disappointment. The two pleasures are Carolyn, who is only seven but has been pulling more than her weight around the house while Sam has been gone, and Dwayne, his husky, robust, bright-eyed baby son. The disappointment is Adam, who appears to have inherited his mother's lungs. He is skinny, sickly, unable to breathe properly much of the time. His sister taught him to read while she was learning in first grade, and now that's all he seems interested in doing. He doesn't play outside like the other little boys, that just sets off fits of wheezing. He sits in his room instead and reads. At five, for heaven's sake. Sits and reads. A big disappointment.

Here, Adam can call with certainty on his own memories. He remembers the tightness in his chest, the terror when too little air makes its way into his lungs and he thinks he's going to die, the tent made from towels placed over his head into which damp medicated air is pumped, late-night visits by a worried doctor. Most of all, he remembers hating it.

— 9 —

Another move. To San Angelo. Adam's fourth home in seven years.

Why was that? Why did they leave Weatherford and go back out to West Texas? Adam sees his father behind a desk, in the office he's rented in Weatherford. On the second floor of a building down on the courthouse square. Now that he's well again, Sam has decided to act on one of his best ideas yet. He's excited and full of plans. He'll combine his two interests, his two loves, architecture and engineering, and will design both the shape and the internal structure of buildings. Private homes would be the ideal application. People will come to him, and he will create it all, from start to finish. But these people, the doctors and lawyers and bankers who can afford to build houses to their own specifications, don't appear to share his enthusiasm for the idea. Some of them come by to consult, a few, but then they go out and hire architects to do the architecture and engineers to do the engineering. Short-sighted stick-in-the-muds, thinks Sam. Their loss.

After a couple of years, though, even he realizes his idea has failed to catch on, and the family moves yet again. To San Angelo, where Sam has rounded up a job with a construction company about to build a large dam. Into a house not owned by Irene's father.

With some astonishment, the adult Adam remembers how his life changes in this new place, goes off in a whole new direction. Somehow, that funny little kid with his mop of coal-black hair, who's spent his time watching and listening when his nose wasn't in a book, senses something big. It comes to him, from where he doesn't know, that although moving around so often has its disadvantages—a feeling of restlessness, of being uprooted just when you're getting used to things—it does have one definite advantage. You can leave past mistakes, past impressions, past ways of being behind you. Leave them

29

the way you leave houses, friends, neighborhoods. How you've been seen before doesn't have to be how you'll be seen from now on.

Soon after he arrives in San Angelo, Adam finds to his delight that one of the things he's left behind is his asthma. It's gone, and will not return. A drier climate? Different sorts of pollen? Maybe. It doesn't matter. What does matter is that, in this new place, Adam remakes himself, an act of will astonishing in one so young. He turns himself into a little boy—at last.

He doesn't give up his books entirely, he loves them too much for that. But he saves them for the nighttime under the covers with a flashlight when he's supposed to be sleeping. He starts spending time outside, after school and on weekends, alone usually, over in the vacant lot across the street from their house. With his lungs so miraculously restored to him, he runs for hours through the mesquite trees, throwing rocks at horned toads and snakes and chasing the rabbits that pop out from behind bushes. This tangled-up, overgrown city block is a neglected hunk of nature, completely empty of manmade structures, except for one: a huge water tower, round like a petrified hot-air balloon, perched high up in the air on four massive legs, reachable only by a steel ladder up one side, which looks impossibly narrow against so much bulk.

That enormous silver mushroom sits there gleaming, brooding over the neighborhood, beckoning anybody with an ounce of adventure in his soul. The Hunter children are forbidden to go near it, absolutely, unequivocally forbidden, and so much as setting foot on the ladder is too unthinkable an offense for a punishment even to have been named. The switch Sam keeps up over the kitchen door is sure to figure in it somewhere. But Adam doesn't care. Once he's gotten out into the world, run around amongst the mesquite trees for a while, begun to believe in the strength of his thin arms and skinny legs, the lure of the water tower is more than he can resist. Had he wanted to. But resisting is not uppermost in his mind. Getting to the top is.

He plans it carefully, for a Saturday more likely than not, when his father has gone bowling, his mother has taken his little brother with her to run some errands, and his sister is off with her friends. These details the adult Adam has to assume, but of one thing his memory is certain—the boy Adam does this thing alone. He doesn't want anybody along to tell him he's doing it all wrong, or to say it's too difficult and they should turn back, or, to be completely honest, to share in the triumph.

Adam sees himself, a gangly kid in shorts and a T-shirt at the foot of the ladder, looking around to be sure nobody's watching, looking around again. All he has to do is get started. If people see him halfway up, what can they do? They'll have to climb up after him. He'll say he didn't hear them yelling. They can gather in a crowd and wait for him to come down. Arrest him. Take him to jail. Switch him till his skin comes off. But it'll be too late. He'll already have been up there.

Adam watches himself put a small foot on the first rung. Then another. And another. He doesn't climb fast, he's not *that* strong. And he stops every few minutes to catch his breath. But he keeps going. Up and up. The adult Adam can see, as clearly now as then, the view as he climbs. He can look out over everything, past downtown, past the highway, past the river his father will dam. He glances down only once, at the tiny trees and little play houses. A twinge of fear shoots between his legs; his stomach turns halfway around; his palms get sweaty, slippery. Hard to hold on. He grips with one hand, wipes the other on the back of his shorts. Grips with the dry one, wipes the other. No problem. He just won't look down any more.

Up he goes. Slowly up, looking out at miles and miles of nothing. Up he goes. Is he afraid? A little. But too excited, too determined for it to matter. He reaches the gigantic silver water tank, immense, warm to the touch in the afternoon sun. Other kids have bragged about getting this far, touching the bottom of the tank. Bragged as if that was something to be proud of. Not Adam. It's not enough. He's going up and over, to the very top.

He rests a minute and continues on. Slowly. A step at a time. He does his hand-wiping routine again and continues. Up. Up. Up. Then over, almost level with the ground. A little more. A little more. He's there! He's done it. He can see forever, far off to the horizon, all the way to New Mexico probably. He wants to raise his arms and shout. But more than that he wants to hold on. So he just smiles, satisfied and proud.

Going down is easy. He looks straight out and never, ever at the ground. One step at a time, slowly, confidently. One step at a time.

When he gets to the ground, nobody is there. Nobody has seen him, no crowd has gathered at the bottom to wait, nobody's father has taken a switch down from over the kitchen door. No punishment. No verification either, come to think of it. But that isn't necessary. Not at all. Adam knows he's done it.

After the dam near San Angelo is completed, there's no more need for the engineers, and Sam is out of a job. Full of ideas as ever, he decides to try going into business for himself once more—but not as an architect or an engineer. He has fond memories of learning, as a child at his father's side, how to run a cleaning plant. He'd been a heck of a presser back then, and probably still is. The little place not far from their house that's just gone on the market may be the very thing he's been looking for.

But . . . where will the money come from? He has no savings, no collateral. No experience that would satisfy the skepticism of a bank or a savings and loan. What to do? There's only one answer. Only one person around with the means to bring this endeavor, a guaranteed success, to fruition. Sam asks Irene to ask her father. He would do it himself, of course, he says, but the answer would be 'no' right off the bat. He's sure of that. Irene can do it, though. Her father has never liked to refuse her anything. Has he?

Irene agrees. She calls up her father, pleads, wheezes a bit, pleads some more. "It's for me and the kids," she says, "really. It's for us. Maybe this *will* be the thing that finally works. Wouldn't it be wonderful if it was? And it might be, you know. It really might. Sam's all excited about it. Says he just *knows* he can make a go of it. So please. Give us all this chance."

Her father is silent for a long, long time—Irene somehow has the wisdom, and finds the strength, to keep quiet—and then says yes. "I'll do it," he says. "But Sam has to sign a note. This is a business proposition, not a gift. Sam has to agree to interest, the going rate, and regular payments. And he has to repay the whole thing. On time. No excuses."

"Of course," says Irene. "Of course he will."

Sam signs the note and buys the cleaning plant. Adam has never seen his father so enthusiastic. Sam supervises the fixing up of the somewhat rundown little building. He does a lot of the painting himself, has some nice linoleum tiles put in out front, and helps the two men who deliver it hang the sign he's ordered—'Samuel Hunter, Cleaning and Pressing, Overnight or While U Wait.' Sam, so proud of the place he could pop, wishes his father were still alive to see it. Irene's parents come for a visit just after the plant reopens, the family all goes by for an inspection visit, and her father is clearly more impressed than he had expected to be.

Sam and his three employees—a woman up front at the cash register and two men on the presses with Sam out back—get along just fine. They work hard. And there's plenty of work to do. For a while. The number of customers increases, levels off, then starts to decline. A fancy new cleaning plant, filled with the latest equipment, has opened up not five minutes away. A whole block of plate glass and neon and chrome. They advertise on the radio—all the time, seems like— and have put up some colorful billboards around town. Two-for-the-price-of-one specials. Quantity discounts. Free delivery. People start going there, just to see what it's like. Pretty soon, they get into the habit.

After a while, Sam has to let one of the pressers go. Then the woman. Dwayne started first grade this year, so Sam asks Irene if she could help out at the cash register. Just till the business gets back on its feet. She says yes. She will. She's pleased, she says, that Sam would ask.

Pleased? She's more than that. She's thrilled to death. It's not the kind of career Irene would have chosen for herself, but Adam—well, anybody who looks at her—can see that she loves being out there in the working world. She's delighted, though hardly surprised, by the speed with which she learns how to fill out a job slip. How to mark a spot or a stain that needs special attention. How to locate a customer's clothes right off. Even the sound of the bell that rings when the cash register drawer springs open is exciting to her. And chatting with the customers, naturally, is right up her alley. Some of the regulars, she tells Adam with a 'what else?' smile, have gotten to where they count on spending a little time shooting the breeze with her whenever they stop by.

Irene works clear through that next school year, Carolyn, now twelve, taking over the running of the house. Cooking. Cleaning. Looking after her two younger brothers from the time school is out till Irene can get home from work. Adam and Dwayne do their share of the chores. What Irene has to tell them when she gets there is not good. Fewer and fewer of the regular customers are sticking with them. And she can't remember the last time a new customer dropped in.

All three of the kids go off to Weatherford to spend the summer with Irene's parents, so she can keep on working full-time. There, Adam learns—by eavesdropping on hushed conversations with relatives who stop in for a visit—how horrified Irene's mother and father are at this unexpected turn of events. The very idea of *their* daughter standing behind that counter, in that dreadful part of town, being pleasant to who knows what kind of people!

When the kids go back home to start school, Adam finds that things have gotten worse while they've been away. His father has had to let the second presser go and is doing all the cleaning work himself. But it's no use. Debts are piling up. Suppliers are sending warnings. Irene's father hasn't been paid for six months. He's losing patience, Irene says, even with her.

"I guess," says Sam at last, "we'll have to just call it quits."

He sells the plant right after Christmas, for much less than he paid for it. He gets enough to pay off his creditors, but not Irene's father. Almost immediately, he is hit with a 'bug.' A severe one that sneaks up on him. He takes to his bed and isn't able to get out of it till well into March.

11

Slowed down but not defeated, Sam moves his family to San Antonio, where his big brother has lived these many years. The job Sam finds here, doing structural detailing for a big, well-established steel company, is the one that lasts. Maybe Sam, into his forties now, has begun to lose the zeal that fueled his earlier attempts to make the work he did fit his own image of it. Maybe the chemistry between him and his bosses is somehow right this time. Maybe he's grown tired of the nomad's life. Whatever the reason, he settles into a comfortable, nonconfrontational groove—and stays there.

Irene, too, falls into clover. Her volunteer work with the local Girl Scout organization is so highly regarded they offer her a full-time job. Managing all the activities in the southeast quadrant of the city. Out of nowhere, they offer *this* to her. Adam knows it's the answer to a prayer she's been offering up all her life—that someday she'll find a way to actually use her brain and her talents—and she is ecstatic. Sam is not. He says no. Absolutely not. What will people think? That he can't take care of his own family? No. Her place is at home.

Pushed to her limit, Irene defies her lifelong commitment to the avoidance of confrontation. Adam sits in his room, listening to them out in the kitchen, amazed that she's actually saying something like this to her husband.

"Now wait just a dadgum minute," Adam hears her say. "You didn't seem to think that when you needed me so bad. To help try and save that little cleaning plant of yours. Did you?"

Silence.

"Did you?"

Sam appears to be stumped. Adam expects him to say 'no' again, but he doesn't. He says nothing. Is it an underlying sense of fair play, suddenly blossoming? A sense that, although this thing she wants is unnatural, she may be right? Adam doesn't know what causes it, but his father stops saying 'no.' He doesn't say 'yes,' but he stops saying 'no.'

So it is that Irene begins driving off downtown every weekday morning, beautifully dressed, the way she's always wanted to look. She spends her days surrounded by capable, intelligent, talented women, all of whom respect and admire her. And are eager to tell her so. She loves it.

As it happens, Sam is also respected and admired. For the speed and precision with which he works. For the diligence that keeps him at his desk while others are wandering off to the snack bar or the coffee machine. For his obvious intelligence. It's the best set of circumstances ever to have blessed the two of them. Yet even here, they find a way to keep happiness from overtaking them.

One thing in their lives cannot change. Sam insists on it. Irene must be home to serve him his supper. Every night. Promptly at 6:30. He would prefer 6:00, the time they've always eaten, till now. Always. But he gives in. *Way* in, it seems to him. She has to drive clear back out from downtown, after all, so he lets her have this extra half hour.

Usually it's enough. Usually, she can wind up her committee meetings. Make the last of her phone calls. Get preparations in order for the next morning's activities. Usually.

The evenings when it doesn't work—when meetings drag on or last-minute emergencies arise or traffic comes to a standstill—these evenings all follow a pattern. Irene comes rushing in to find the rest of the family already sitting around the kitchen table. Carolyn has fixed the meal, as she does most nights. Adam has set the table. Dwayne has helped Carolyn serve. Sam has been sitting, silent, staring directly at his plate, since 6:25.

The other three have almost finished eating by now, but Sam's plate is still two-thirds full. He's been nibbling at what's on it from time to time, but mostly he's just pushed it around, from one side of the plate to the other. He doesn't raise his head as Irene comes clattering in, smiling her nervous smile, rattling on about the traffic on San

Pedro, or the sudden rainstorm, so heavy you couldn't see, or the woman she *had* to talk to who didn't get to the office till nearly five.

She sits, puts a few spoonfuls on her plate, eats, chatters, eyes darting from Sam to Adam to Sam to Carolyn to Sam to Dwayne to Sam. She fills what had been a totally silent room with her laughter and her talk.

Sam does not look up, does not respond. For two or three, maybe five minutes, he continues to push his food around his plate. Then he gets up, not looking at anybody, and leaves the room. Irene stops her rambling, fork poised in midair, trying her best to hang on to her smile. She does not succeed. She puts down her fork, wipes her mouth with her napkin, and stands up.

"You kids finish your supper and then start in on the dishes," she says. "I need to go check on your daddy."

12

The first time Adam goes anywhere by himself is the summer he's fourteen. He's taking the bus to Clovis, New Mexico, to spend a few weeks with three of his cousins. Their mother is his father's sister, and at the last family reunion, she'd said, "Let Adam come stay with us a while. It'll be fun for the kids."

Adam thinks going off alone is the best idea he's ever heard of. He has to change buses in Amarillo, though, and his mother is afraid he'll get confused and end up who knows where? "You keep a sharp lookout so you know when you're coming into Amarillo," she says, "and be sure you get off." "Yes, Mother, I will." "You have to wait for an hour and fifteen minutes, then you take the bus that says 'Albuquerque.' Got that?" "Yes, Mother. I've got that."

It doesn't seem to Adam like something he can't handle, and sure enough it isn't. He gets off in Amarillo and finds out where the Albuquerque bus will be leaving from. His suitcase will be put on for him, so all he has to do is wander around the station till it's time to go. The most interesting place he can find is a little store off in the corner that sells magazines, newspapers, toothpaste, candy, and paperback books. The books are lined up in tall rows on a wire contraption that spins around. It squeaks when Adam touches it.

Adam glances through a couple of books, one about a sea captain's daughter who gets captured by pirates and another about how to grow tomatoes and zucchini. He creaks the rack around, and a book way up at the top catches his eye. He takes it down. The title says *Men Behind Bars,* and the picture on the cover shows two prisoners standing in a cell facing each other. Behind them is a door made of steel. Two bunks hang off the wall, one above the other. The shorter man is blond; the other has black hair. Neither of them has a shirt on, and the artist has drawn the shape of their chests with loving care. Something in the way they're standing makes Adam know they aren't planning to hit each other.

He flips through the book and stops at a place about a third of the way through. As he begins to read, his skin gets prickly. A group of prisoners is being led into a shower room by a guard. The guard closes and locks the door, then stands there with his rifle. The men undress and go and stand under the showers strung along both sides of the room. One naked man, big and brawny, drops his bar of soap. "Bend over and pick it up," he says to the smaller man next to him. The smaller man bends over, but he doesn't pick up the soap. They don't care if the guard is watching or not.

Adam can't believe it. What's a book like this doing in a bus station? He figures whoever put it here thought it was about crime and punishment, not this kind of stuff. Adam flips again, and the book opens at another place just as steamy. In this part, a man in an upper bunk waits till the lights go out and then moves quietly into the bunk below. The man who climbs down is the one with the black hair. The one in the lower bunk is the blond. My god, thinks Adam. Oh, my god. He expects the book to burst into flames right there in his hands.

When it doesn't, Adam realizes he has to have it. So he can learn all the things it can teach him. But how? He doesn't want anybody to know he has it. Not anybody. For that to be, he would have to swipe it, like he did that pocketknife from Ben Franklin's. Charlie Ferguson had dared him to, one summer when Adam was in Weatherford with his grandparents, and he did. It was the easiest thing in the world. He just slipped it into his jeans and walked out.

But then he couldn't sleep. Night after night, he tossed and fretted, wishing he'd never done such a thing, thinking about the fiery pits of Hell. Finally one afternoon, when he was sure nobody else was around, he went into the room where his grandmother was sewing. She looked up.

"I swiped a pocketknife, Grandmother," he said, "and I can't sleep."

She motioned him to come over by her. When he did, she put her arm around his shoulder.

"From where?" she asked.

"Ben Franklin's."

She nodded. "And what do you think you ought to do?"

"Give it back?" he said.

She squeezed his shoulder.

"Will you do it for me, Grandmother?" he asked. "Please?"

"No, Adam, I won't," she said. "You have to walk back down there and do it yourself."

The man at Ben Franklin's was very nice, much nicer than Adam had expected.

"It was brave of you to come in like this," the man said, "all by yourself. If you promise never to do it again, not ever, we'll just let it drop."

"I promise," Adam had told him. So there's no way, now, he can swipe this book. He'll have to buy it. And somebody in the world will know he's got it.

He looks over at the cash register. Behind it sits a middle-aged woman. Her brown hair is braided and coiled at the back of her neck in a bun. She's reading a magazine through little wire-rimmed glasses. Why does it have to be somebody's *mother* minding this store?

The only thing Adam can do, if he's going to have the book, is walk up and hand it to her. "What do you think you're doing with this kind of filth, young man?" she will say. She'll adjust her glasses and look at him hard. "Wait a minute," she'll say. "I know you. You're Irene Hunter's son Adam. I'm going to go call her up long-distance this very minute and tell on you." She'll come out from behind the cash register. "Elmer," she'll yell. "Get out here and keep an eye on this Hunter boy while I go to the phone." A heavy man in overalls and dusty boots will come out of the back room and stare down at Adam, his eyes all glittery with contempt, his hands twitching, aching to do their Christian duty and knock Adam across the room.

When she hears, Irene will sigh, lean against the kitchen doorway, and put her hand to her head. "Oh, no," she will say into the phone. "Not Adam. Not my Adam."

Is it worth all that? Adam wonders. Is one book worth all that shame and distress? He thinks of men bending over in shower rooms.

Of the black-haired man climbing down to be with the blond. Worth it? You bet it is.

Adam's father has given him ten dollars, for whatever Adam may need during the trip. He picks out another book, a guide to butter-flies, and puts it on top. He takes both of them over and sets them on the counter. His heart is beating so wildly he can hear it. The woman lays down her magazine, looks at him, and smiles. She rings up the books and puts them in a sack. Adam hands her the ten-dollar bill, and she gives him back his change. She smiles again.

"You enjoy your books, now," she says. "You hear?"

— 13 —

It's along about now that Irene begins making Adam her confidant. The receptacle into which she can pour her dissatisfactions and frustrations. Her parents don't want to listen anymore—she's made her bed, let her lie in it, seems to be their general attitude at this point. They will still love her, of course they will. Comfort her when they can. Her father will gladly give *her* whatever she needs. But having to hear all those repetitive details? That's another thing entirely. Enough is enough.

Irene turns to Adam.

He wants not to know these things. They're too perplexing, too painful. But he also wants not to disappoint his mother, whose life has been one long series of disappointments. She's given him so much, hasn't she? All his life. And now that she needs him, he wants to run the other way? Besides, where would he find the words to tell her to stop? He's had no experience with doing such a thing.

Hardest to absorb, by far, for Adam are the suspected infidelities. Irene's hints, though heartfelt, are vague and full of innuendo. What is it his father is supposed to be doing? Paying attention to other women is the best Adam can figure. Women who find his father attractive and don't mind letting him know they do. Apparently, his father goes ahead and says nice things back to them. Talks with them at church suppers when he ought to be concentrating on Irene. Dances with them when he and Irene go out, most often with Sam's brother Nathan and his wife Roberta.

Adam is confused about all this. These are the things he does with the girls he meets at church or at school. He pays them compliments, he dances with them, he even holds their hands sometimes. But none of it means anything. It's what he's expected to do, he knows that, but it doesn't arouse any deep emotions. Does it in his father? It must.

There must be more to it, like in some of the books he's read and most of the movies he's seen. Where people go through agonies of jealousy and guilt and recrimination, for reasons Adam can only conjecture about. A man-and-woman version of what the black-haired prisoner does with the blond. Lying together naked with somebody who's supposed to be off-limits. Is *that* what his father's been doing? Adam can't imagine how he would go about asking.

Besides, in books—and in the movies, certainly—it all gets brought out into the open. More often than not. People yell about it for a while and then leave. Or they yell and decide to stay. Or they yell and kill each other. Whatever it is, they *do* something. They don't just talk about it to other people. Talk and talk and talk and not *do* anything. Adam is hard-pressed to see the point in that.

Sometimes he almost wants to discuss with Irene his own dilemma, the things he's feeling and has no way of getting a handle on. See if maybe she can help him understand. There'd be a point to *that,* all right, should she by some miracle be able to. But he doesn't dare. If his mother is this wound up about what she's afraid her husband might be doing, think how distraught she'd be if she got even a whiff of what Adam wishes he could *definitely* do. If he only knew how.

For all these reasons, Adam doesn't ask any questions. Doesn't ask her to stop. Doesn't volunteer any information. He just listens. Listens and nods.

14

Adam gets his degree in journalism from Texas Tech and finds a job right away. On a weekly paper, *The Canyon News,* in a town a hundred miles or so north of Lubbock. He'll work here for almost two years before his mother forwards him a brief letter from his draft board.

The job isn't much to brag about, he thinks at first. No big-city daily, with politics and crime to report on. Just the ordinary doings of little old Canyon, way up in the Panhandle where nothing ever happens. But being here has taught Adam something important—that everybody has a life. Everybody, every insignificant-looking person you bump into, has a life. No matter how small the town. No matter how ramshackle the house. No matter how limited the horizons. Each person in this funny, out-of-the-way place gets up in the morning hoping for the best. Praying that things will turn out all right. Wishing for a big break—or even a medium-sized one. Or that a pain will go away. Or maybe just that they'll make it through the next day without things getting any worse.

Adam likes them, these small-town people. And they like him. The paper's editor, a hard-working man with a kind heart and a sharp tongue. The chubby, round-faced woman who runs the boarding house where Adam lives and where he eats most of his meals. The muscular young construction worker who just last month, as a volunteer fireman, went in and pulled an old woman out of her burning house. Adam interviewed him, took his picture, and struck up a friendship.

Out of high school for two years, Cory still lives with his parents in a small house on the north side of town. "Let's drive up toward Amarillo and see if you can buy us some beers," he says one morning when he stops by the newspaper office. "I'll pay my share, a course, but you'll have to go in and get 'em."

"Fine," says Adam.

"I get off at five. Come on by the house 'bout five-thirty."

"All right."

Cory's mother answers the door. "He's still sittin' in the tub. Tryin' to soak off all that grime. He says go on back and chat with him while he finishes up."

Dear god, thinks Adam. Go on back?

He goes.

When he knocks on the door, Cory says, "Come on in."

He goes on in.

"Flip down that toilet lid and sit a while. This feels too good to get out of just yet."

"Rough day?"

"Lord, yes. Pourin' cement. You wouldn't think that'd get you so dirty. But it does. You ever pour cement?"

"No."

"No, I guess not. Well, don't ever take it up, just to find out I'm right."

"I won't."

They talk for five minutes, maybe ten. Adam is having a hard time concentrating.

"So," says Cory. "I guess I've lolled around here long enough." He stands up.

Holy sweet Jesus, thinks Adam.

From the waist up, Cory is tanned a deep rich brown. From the waist down, he is snowy white. And so beautiful Adam feels weak.

"Hand me that towel?" says Cory.

"Sure."

"Come on in my room while I get dressed. Then we'll go see about those beers."

After the beer run to Amarillo and, during the next few weeks, a couple of trips to Dairy Queen for hamburgers, Cory suggests a double date at the drive-in. His steady has a girlfriend Adam can take.

Cory and Tommie Sue are in the front seat, Adam and Marcia in the back. As soon as the lights go down and the first picture starts, Tommie Sue turns to Cory, his arms go around her, and they are deep in a kiss. To Adam's surprise, Marcia does the same. She turns toward him, picks up his arm and puts it around her, and pulls his head down to hers. Her mouth opens, and her tongue pushes against his.

My god, thinks Adam. No preliminaries. Straight to the heavy stuff. He has the fleeting memory that he's been looking forward to seeing this picture. But . . . never mind. This is familiar territory for him—soulful kissing, hands all over each other, unbuttoned blouses. It's not what Adam would have preferred to be doing, but he's done it enough that he can keep up appearances.

Adam and Marcia give it their best, hands and mouths busy all the time. Adam can tell from the sounds up front that Cory and Tommie Sue are doing the same. Then, all of a sudden, Adam is conscious of Cory's presence in a whole new way. He realizes the two of them are facing each other—Adam has turned to his left, Cory to his right. All that separates them is a foot or two of space and a few inches of vinyl-covered front seat. Adam's perception shifts again, and it seems that Cory is in his arms, holding him tight, their tongues dancing around each other. The muscles of the back Adam is caressing aren't soft any more but hard. And the hand holding on to his neck is rough and strong. The afternoon at Cory's house comes into sharp focus in Adam's head. Cory's naked body as he stepped out of the tub. That's the body Adam is holding. Adam tightens his arms and moans. Cory, up in the front seat, gives a little moan in response.

My god, thinks Adam. He knows! In *his* mind, he's holding me as surely as I'm holding him. Bright lights come on for intermission, and the spell is broken.

The petting through the second picture is lackadaisical, for all four of them. Marcia and Tommie Sue are in a rotten mood as they head for home, picking a fight with each other and ending up not speaking. The good-night kisses are brief and perfunctory.

On the way to Adam's boarding house, he scrambles around in his brain for a way to acknowledge what has happened. Both of them are aware of it, Adam is sure of that. If so, then Cory is just waiting for

Adam to speak. To reach over and touch his arm. But why doesn't Cory say something? It's his town, his territory. Why doesn't *he?* Scared, of course, thinks Adam. Well, no more than me. God. No more than me.

When they pull up at the curb, Cory starts to switch off his engine, but doesn't. He turns toward Adam and sighs. It's now or never, thinks Adam. He sits looking at Cory. Cory sits looking at him.

"Heavy evening," says Cory. "All things considered."

"Yeah," says Adam.

"That Tommie Sue is one tough babe."

"I'll say. And Marcia's not far behind."

Cory nods and laughs. "I'm glad you got to have a good time, too."

"Yeah," says Adam. The sparks between them have all gone out. Adam reaches for the door handle.

Well, he thinks. I guess it's going to be never.

15

Adam hates boot camp from start to finish, but . . . somehow he has a compulsion to be good at everything, even here. It doesn't matter how bizarre or horrifying a thing is. Tossing grenades, shoving bayonets into straw dummies, seeing who can crawl the fastest while live machine guns fire over your head. He keeps trying to be the best at all of them. And a lot of the time he is.

He ends up third in his class, so when the assignments are posted, he gets a plum. Special Services at Fort McNair, a beautiful little post in the southwest corner of Washington, DC. The row of mansions that stare out across the tree-lined river are home to some of the area's most exalted generals. Down at the end of a perfectly manicured parade ground is a huge ornate building that houses the War College.

Adam's job is to help take care of some tennis courts, a putting green, a gym, and a swimming pool. He and his boss, an easy-going captain named Melcher, like each other right away. Adam is so grateful to have such a soft job—especially considering all the other things he could be doing—that he throws himself into it with a vengeance. He organizes, files, anticipates, learns the things that need to be done before Captain Melcher has to mention them to him. The captain responds by giving Adam the most coveted of the work shifts, Monday to Friday, seven-thirty to four. No nights. No weekends. This means Adam has time of his own, to go places, do things.

But doing things means having friends, and he can't imagine where, in a big, strange, hostile-seeming city, he can go to meet people. People as far from the Army as he can get. Walking around town one Saturday afternoon, he stops and stares at the dark gray imposing walls of what the sign out front says is a Methodist church.

He smiles.

The service the next morning is amazing. The sanctuary is big, light streaming in through stained-glass windows high up. The music is glorious—pipe organ, huge choir, soloists with wonderful voices. Paid to sing there, he finds out later. He's never heard of such a thing.

One of the announcements during the service mentions a coffee hour afterward to which everyone is invited. Lots of young people are there, some of whom come up and invite Adam to the Young Adult meeting that evening. Naturally he goes, and soon after he arrives, he has maybe twenty new friends. Nice friends. His mother would be proud. "You like movies?" they ask. "You like going out to eat?" "You play bridge?" "Yes." "Yes, I do," Adam keeps saying.

He dates a couple of the women and, at the Sunday night gatherings, strikes up conversations with some of the men. On a double date one Saturday evening, he gets to know a man he's seen at church a time or two, a law student named Richard Gorham. Richard is tall and handsome. Elegant, Adam thinks, with his dark wavy hair, his carefully tailored suit, and his enormous sense of self-assurance. Over dinner, Richard talks most of the time, with great authority. About constitutional law and the revolution in civil rights that is just getting under way—and that Richard is sure will succeed, eventually.

Adam, the Southern boy, is fascinated. Civil *rights*? A fair deal for colored people? He's never laid eyes on anybody like Richard in his life.

After dinner, the four of them go to a concert at Constitution Hall. During intermission, the others talk about how the National Symphony really isn't one of the country's top orchestras. Getting better, you understand, but not really first-rank. Adam thinks it's great— the music, the people he's with, everything.

Richard is driving, so he drops the two women off at their apartment on Q Street and then takes Adam down to Fort McNair. As Adam is getting out of the car, Richard says, "How about dinner next week? Just the two of us?"

Adam is astounded. This sophisticated man who can talk about *any*thing wants to have dinner with *him*?

"Sure," says Adam. Casual as can be.

"Sure," as if it happens all the time.

Before long, dinner once a week is dinner two or three times a week. Richard is far too busy to cook much for himself, he says, and surely Adam doesn't mind getting out of the mess hall as often as possible. "Absolutely not," says Adam. By watching his pennies pretty closely, Adam is able to afford it all right. *Just,* but . . . all right.

The Saturday-night double dates become a tradition, almost like a ritual. They take the two roommates from Q Street, Pam and Suzy, most often. But not always. Sometimes Richard asks a classmate, who brings along one of her friends.

Richard's idea that Adam start staying over at his apartment on Saturday nights seems perfectly reasonable. It will save Richard the trip all the way down to McNair. Which means they can stay out later if they want to. This sounds good to Adam. He isn't sure if it's allowed or not, but Captain Melcher says, "No problem. Go ahead and enjoy yourself. Just leave a number where you can be reached."

Adam is amazed that Richard, still a student, has his own apartment, all by himself. Adam could barely afford the dorm room at Tech. He puzzles over this and ends up assuming Richard's parents must be wealthy—or at least very comfortable. But he doesn't consider it appropriate to ask.

At the apartment, Richard sleeps in his big double bed in the bedroom, and Adam sleeps on the couch in the living room. Adam likes to stay up late after they get in, talking with Richard for a while, listening to music, wandering into the kitchen to get a snack if he feels like it. Usually, after Richard has said good-night and gone to his room, Adam folds out the couch, switches on the lamp on the end table, and lies there in his underwear reading. Once he's turned out the light, though, and settled in, he thinks, every time, about Richard, stretched out, naked for all he knows, barely—what?—twenty feet away? He can't conceive of the amount of courage it would take to walk into that room. Neither of them likes to get up early, so they are late for church more often than not. But they prefer sitting in the balcony anyway and can usually sneak in while everybody's singing a hymn.

On one of those Saturday evenings, all through the bridge game at Pam and Suzy's, Richard has been talking about his new recording of

Norma. He's excited and can't stop mentioning it. One of the duets by Joan Sutherland and Marilyn Horne, in particular, is "just magnificent." He talks like that. "Just magnificent." The others will have to hear it sometime, he says. Adam gets his chance later that night.

He and Richard sit on the couch—not yet unfolded—and listen. Adam is in a kind of trance. He hadn't known singing could be this beautiful. He leans forward to pick up his wine glass off the coffee table and sees, out of the corner of his eye, that Richard has put his left arm, the one nearest to Adam, across the back of the couch. Has, ever so casually, draped it there. Adam takes a sip, sets his glass down on the table, and leans back—an inch or two closer to Richard. He has the feeling that some sort of dance is beginning. With very precise steps. Choreographed, like a ballet. This one does this. Then that one does that. But Adam doesn't know the *moves.* He's suddenly frightened. Not of what may happen. He's been *praying* for that. He's afraid he'll make the wrong move and mess it all up.

They sit there, those two voices soaring in perfect harmony, Richard keeping time with both his hands. When the duet is over, he drops his right hand into his lap and his left onto Adam's shoulder. Adam edges a bit closer and leans his head against Richard's chest. He feels Richard shudder, just a little, which comforts Adam somehow. He closes his eyes and listens to Richard's heartbeat. It's so loud it drowns out the music. Richard reaches over to turn Adam's face up toward his and kisses him softly on the mouth. Of course, thinks Adam. Of course. Why haven't we been doing this all along?

Those next few months, Adam and Richard can't seem to get enough of each other. They make love every time they're together. Two or three evenings a week and sometimes twice on Saturdays, when one of them will wake up in the night and reach out for the other.

Then, so slowly that Adam isn't aware of it at first, their paths start to go off in different directions. As Adam becomes more passionate, Richard becomes more wary. Their lovemaking slacks off to maybe once a week, then not even that. Adam wishes they could talk about it, but doesn't know how to make that happen.

"What's wrong?" he asks, a time or two.

"Nothing," says Richard.

Adam wants to force the issue some way or other, but, as usual, he backs off. The thought of losing even the little they have left fills him with sadness.

After a while, Richard stops answering his phone. Maybe he's studying even harder, off at the library. Or maybe not. However it happens, Adam has to wait for Richard to call, and the two of them spend their first whole week apart in more than six months. From then on, it's just going through the motions. Their evenings together every couple of weeks rarely end up in bed. And when they do, the excitement is pretty much all Adam's.

Adam hates what's happening. He hates having to lose something so wonderful that he's just now managed to discover. But most of all, he hates his own stupidity. His lack of any sense of how to get them back to where they'd been.

Then time runs out. Adam's orders come for Vietnam. Out of the blue. A couple of weeks to wrap things up at Fort McNair. Get everything in order for his replacement. Then home for a short visit and straight over.

Even worse than the shock of going off to war is Richard's reaction. He is relieved. To be fair, he's also concerned and worried, and he says all the right things. But Adam can see that underneath all that is relief. He won't have to keep dancing around with Adam—this do-si-do he's clearly grown tired of.

16

"I just don't see how I'm going to make it through this next year,"
says Irene. "It *is* a year, you say? A whole year?"

"That's what they tell me," says Adam.

"But where will you *be*? What will you be *doing*?" She knits as she
talks, her excess energy going directly into the needles, which clack
against each other, hard and loud. She throws the yarn around them,
then clacks them together. Clack. Clack. Throw. Clack. Throw.
Clack. Clack. Throw. Adam is hypnotized.

"Do you *know*?" she asks.

"Know what?"

"Where you'll *be*. I don't think I'll be able to cope if you're out in
some jungle somewhere."

"It seems pretty likely, doesn't it, Mother? That I will be. I'm in the
Infantry, after all. Taking care of that swimming pool was just a
fluke."

"Don't say that, Adam! For goodness sake. Infantry. The word
scares me to death."

"Me, too," says Adam.

"But it's different for you," says Irene. "For you military boys. You
know how to handle those things."

"Do we?"

"Well, don't you? Now, don't scare me even more by making me
think you *don't* know how to handle it."

Clack. Throw. Clack. Clack. Clack. Throw. Clack. Throw.

"Yes, Mother. They did teach us. The best they could. I'll be all
right. You'll see."

"But how will I *know* you are? That's what worries me the most.
How will I *know*? You'll have to promise to write me every day. So I
can keep myself together."

"That's not a very good idea," says Adam. "Don't you see? Expecting a letter every single day. If the mail gets held up, for whatever reason, you'll think I'm dead."

"Be careful what you say, Adam, for pity's sake!" Clack. Throw. Clack. Clack. Throw. "Don't use words like that. They scare me."

"Dead?"

"Just stop it. Let's talk about something else. Should we do some more laundry, do you think? You want to be sure you have enough underwear and T-shirts."

Adam's father has a different concern. He and Adam go off to the golf course, for Sam's regular Saturday outing with his big brother Nathan and two of their friends. Adam pulls his father's little two-wheeled golf cart around the course. He loves the walking, the breeze in the tall trees, and watching his father and uncle, far better golfers than the other two players, fight it out to see who will win. During all the years they've both lived in San Antonio, the brothers have kept a running tally. Nathan was three strokes ahead when today's game began.

The lead seesaws back and forth between them, the other two men struggling to keep up. Sam plays brilliantly the last four holes and wins by two strokes. Now Nathan is ahead by only one. On the way home, Sam is clearly proud of his accomplishment and pleased that Adam was there to see it. But he has something else on his mind.

"I want to have a little talk with you, son," he says. "While we're alone."

"Sure," says Adam. "About what?"

"Being extra careful . . . you know . . . with the women over there."

"Ah," says Adam.

"Now, I don't know how much . . . well . . . experience you've already had. I . . . realize things are different now from when your mother and I were growing up. You kids . . . You *young people* have different ideas about what's okay before you get married. And you've been off on your own for a while. Up there in Washington and all. But I just . . ."

He takes a couple of deep breaths and swallows hard.

"I just want to tell you to be careful. I haven't been off to war, as you know, myself. But I heard a lot of stories from guys after they came back. And . . . two things happened, seemed to me. They caught things that were hard to get rid of. And they . . . they picked up bad habits they couldn't correct, once they were home again. They got to thinking that finding . . . well . . . satisfaction, outside of marriage, was an all right thing to do."

"And you think it isn't?"

"Of course I think it isn't. Why do you ask?"

"No reason," says Adam. "Just curious."

They're nearing home, so Sam pulls into a drug store parking lot and shuts off the engine. He turns toward Adam.

"You're old enough now that we can talk honestly, don't you think? Man to man."

Adam wants to say, *"No, I'm not. I'll never be that old."* But instead he says, "Yes."

"Well . . . ," says Sam. "I've had the feeling, through the years, that your mother was telling you things about us. She and I. About . . . how we were or weren't getting along. I was right, wasn't I?"

"Yes."

Sam nods. "Then you must know that, even though things haven't been perfect, we've at least tried. And we've never been unfaithful to each other."

"No?" says Adam, and immediately wishes he could take it back.

Sam cocks his head to one side and narrows his eyes. "No," he says. "We haven't. We've had our misunderstandings, like everybody else. Some worse than others. But we've stuck it out because that's what we thought we ought to do. And because we didn't have any experience with anything else to lead us astray. So that's what I'm trying to impress on you now. Just a little piece of advice before you go. Don't let yourself have experiences you can't handle. With the women over there. That will give you wrong ideas about how to act, once you get back home."

"I won't do anything like that, Daddy. I can promise you I won't."

Sam nods again.

"Good," he says. He reaches down and starts the engine.

– 17 –

Each step Adam takes, the jungle closes in behind him. He stops, holds his breath, and stands perfectly still, but he can't fool it. It keeps on closing in. His knee tries to bend, pulls upward a couple of times. No use. His foot wants to stay right where it is. God, he knows how it feels. The thought of going on terrifies him. Who knows what's out there? Hiding. Waiting for him to come stumbling along. But just as unnerving is the thought of standing still. He will rot. On this very spot. The water dripping off of everything will soak into him and rot him from the inside out. Or else he'll take root. Send down shoots into the ground and grow branches out of his head. Maybe that's what these trees are. Guys who've been too scared to go forward. Or moved too slow.

The jungle is alive. He's always known that. Not alive, like you expect plants to be. Sitting there making chlorophyll. But ALIVE. Watching. Biding its time. Looking for that opportunity when your attention wavers and it can grab you. Make you part of it forever. Jesus!

That thought gets Adam going again.

He looks from side to side as he moves slowly forward. The light filtering down through the canopy makes everything an eerie, ominous green. Except for the thick red mud underfoot. Green leaves, green bark, green vines. Shit. Even his hands, holding his rifle out in front of him, look green. The only sounds he can hear are his boots sucking as he pulls them out of the mud to take another step.

Just let it stay quiet, he thinks. Please. Please. Just let it stay quiet. Just one more time.

This is it. His last patrol. It's hard to believe. Eleven days and he'll be headed home. God. Eleven days. All he has to do is make it through four more. That final week in-country nobody gets a dangerous assignment. Unwritten law. He'll sit around base camp, smoking and waiting.

Four days. Four days. His mud-sucking footsteps count out the cadence. Four days. Four days.

Rifle fire! Off to his right. His head snaps up. Christ! This is no time for daydreaming. He freezes. More rifle fire. Two bursts. Another. Then the rattle of a machine gun.

"Over here—quick!" yells Sambo, his squad leader. "You three go right. You two off down that way. Alfie and Gaucho, stay with me. Keep low, for Christ sake!"

Peterson and Ratso run to the right. Adam follows. Rifle fire dead ahead. The machine gun again, to his left at ten o'clock.

"Anybody see 'em?" Sambo yells behind him.

"Hell, no," Gaucho yells back. "When do we ever?"

Adam moves cautiously through the thick vegetation. An explosion to his left. Jesus! Grenade? Mine? He can't tell.

"Medic!" somebody yells. "Over here! We got two hit."

Adam creeps forward, cursing the mud. In the dim light, he can barely see his friend Vinnie, bent over a blood-stained body with only one leg. Adam kneels beside them.

"Peterson?" Adam asks.

"Yeah," says Vinnie, pressing a handkerchief hard onto the stump that is left. "He's hanging on. Ratso, over there . . ." Vinnie cocks his head. "He's bought it."

"Shit," says Adam.

The medic rushes up and kneels down. "I'll take it," he says. "Thanks."

"No sweat," says Vinnie. He wipes his bloody hand on the back of his pants.

"Come on," he says to Adam. "Sambo's over here."

They move slowly off to the left. Sambo and three others are crouched beside a log. Adam and Vinnie join them.

"We're movin' back," says Sambo. "Too many of 'em. Looks like a company, Martinez says. I've called in air support. We gotta get outa here pronto."

"Peterson's hurt bad," says Vinnie. "And Ratso's dead. Doc's seeing to Peterson."

Sambo nods. "You two and Martinez go help bring 'em back."

"Roger," says Vinnie. "Let's go, you guys."

Vinnie and Doc carry Peterson on a makeshift litter. Adam and Martinez carry Ratso's body between them. He's heavy, and his head keeps bouncing from side to side. A bullet whistles past Adam's ear. He ducks and crouches lower.

"Come on, dammit," he says. "Let's *move.*"

"I'm with you," says Martinez.

They've gone only a hundred meters or so when a jet whines overhead and an explosion follows right after. The ground shakes as bomb after bomb hits the area they've just left.

Back at the clearing where they landed that morning, Adam watches a medevacchopper carry Peterson and Ratso off toward base camp. He stands there, looking up at the empty sky. A big orange sun is setting behind the trees.

Well, he thinks. One more down. Three to go.

The line Adam is standing in is a long one, stretching across the runway apron on the air base at Tan Son Nhut. They've been waiting here almost half an hour, but nobody's complaining. They all hold one hand and then the other up to their foreheads, trying to block out the blazing sun. Even though dark wet patches are spreading along the sides of their khaki shirts under their armpits, everybody is laughing and whooping and calling out to buddies farther down the line.

"Hey, Polack!"

"Yeah?"

"You short?"

"Fuckin' A! I'm so short I gotta jump up to see in a basement window."

"You call that short?" yells a man just ahead of Adam. "I'm so short I could fall off a dime and still break both my ankles."

Chuckles and whistles ripple up and down the line.

"Now *that's* short."

Adam holds a fresh cigarette to the butt of the one he's just finished. He watches three men climb up on the wing of the big TWA jet parked a little ways out in front of them.

"Hey, Sarge," Adam says to the man standing behind him. "You're Air Force. What do you reckon the problem is?"

"Engine. They sent for a replacement part earlier. Now those guys are putting it in."

"How long's that gonna take?"

"Another half hour. Forty-five minutes."

"So why're they leaving us stuck out here on the tarmac?"

The sergeant stares at Adam. "I don't believe you, Corporal. You been in Nam a fucking year and you can still ask a dumb-ass question like that? Your brain's gone all mushy, sounds like, from the strain."

"Sorry, Sarge. I guess I was just making conversation."

"Well, don't. It's too hot."

Adam smokes three more cigarettes while the men on the wing take off a metal panel, tinker around with something inside, and screw the panel back on.

"All right, listen up," yells a lieutenant at the foot of the portable stairway. "Let's start moving in, single file. Head for the rear of the plane, and fill in every seat, back to front."

"Fuckin' A," somebody shouts, and soon the whole bunch of them are yelling at the top of their lungs. "Fuckin' A!"

The line starts to move, slowly at first, then more steadily.

"So long, shithole Vietnam!" somebody yells. The rest chime in. "So long, shithole!"

Adam is close to the front of the line, so it isn't long before he's climbing the stairs. The inside of the plane seems dark after the glare outside, and it's probably thirty degrees cooler.

A young stewardess with green eyes and red hair smiles at Adam.

"Welcome aboard, soldier," she says.

"Thanks," says Adam. He smiles back.

Toward the rear of the plane, the man in front of Adam slides into the aisle seat of a full row. Adam throws his duffel into the overhead rack and takes the next window seat forward. The Air Force sergeant behind him heads for the window across the aisle.

Good, thinks Adam. It would've been a long goddamn flight with *that* asshole next to me.

A PFC with an airborne patch on his sleeve sits down beside Adam. He looks over and says, "Hi."

"Hi," Adam says and sticks out his hand. "Adam Hunter."

"Patrick Murphy." He shakes Adam's hand.

Adam stares out the window at the line of men getting shorter and shorter. Once they're inside the plane, a much smaller group of men comes out of the terminal building, walks across the tarmac, and starts up the stairs.

"Christ," says Adam. "Would you look at that?"

"What?" asks Patrick, leaning toward the window.

"Officers. They've been sitting in there nice and cool all this time."

"So what else is new?"

They both laugh.

"Where do you go from here?" asks Adam.

"Fort Bragg. Well, home first, then Bragg. You?"

"I'm out. I go off the plane, get processed at the base in San Francisco, and I'm through."

"Wow. Congratulations."

"Yeah, well . . ."

As soon as the officers are settled in at the front of the plane, a sexy voice on the loudspeaker talks about oxygen masks and life preservers, while the redhead demonstrates. Adam puts out his cigarette, and the plane moves onto the runway and takes off. Adam looks around. Christ. Everything is so clean and orderly—and so quiet. He can't remember a place ever being so quiet. He looks out the window at some puffy clouds down below and can feel more than hear the churning of the big engines just ahead of him.

"What would you like to drink, Corporal?"

Adam looks up. A blonde stewardess with an even bigger smile than the redhead's is standing beside a cart.

"Dr. Pepper. You got Dr. Pepper?"

"Of course."

She puts ice into a little plastic glass, pulls the tab off the can, pours a little into the glass, and hands the glass and can to Adam.

"For you, Private?" she asks Patrick.

Adam takes a sip and looks back out the window. He takes another sip and starts to shake. First his foot, then his leg. He tries to control it, and does all right at first. But then his shoulders start to shake.

He feels Patrick's hand on his arm.

"You all right?" asks Patrick.

"Yeah," says Adam. "I really am. I just . . ." He tries to smile. "It's . . . silly, isn't it? I mean . . . I just never thought I'd actually be doing this."

"Going home?" says Patrick. He nods. "I know what you mean. I wasn't so sure myself a couple times, I can tell you. But . . . we're on our way. It's okay now."

"Yeah," says Adam, tensing his leg to make it be still. "It's okay now."

— 19 —

San Antonio. Home. But Adam is at loose ends. Nothing interests him for long. He takes a book out of the library, and gives up after fifty pages. He tries listening to records, and finds he's impatient with the same old songs. It's early September, so the grass doesn't need mowing anymore, and after he's pulled the last of the weeds and cut off the dead flowers, there isn't anything else to do outdoors. He smoked his last cigarette on the plane from San Francisco—his mother doesn't know he ever started—and being without them is hard. He can't figure out what to do with his hands.

His sister and brother are gone now, married with lives of their own. His parents head off to work after breakfast, before Adam gets up most days. He fixes himself some cereal, washes all the breakfast dishes, takes the grocery list around the corner to the store every two or three days, and, at least once a week, hangs up and brings in the laundry. Big deal.

He starts riding the bus into town and wandering up and down the streets. He likes the bustle of people moving past him—until he realizes *they* all have someplace to go. Even so, it's better than just sitting around.

The sidewalk in front of Frost Brothers is crowded. As Adam strolls along looking at the elaborate displays in the windows, he gets bumped a good bit by those in a much bigger hurry. The mannequins seem strange to him—vacant eyes, hair like spun straw, fingers curved out at odd angles. He jumps! Noise overhead. Loud and out of nowhere. He looks up. Two fighter jets scream across the sky. They are long gone, but he still hears the screaming. It's him.

He glances around. People are staring and edging away from him. His face is hot. He feels himself wanting to scream again, but he holds it in. He turns and goes back the way he came. A path clears, and nobody bumps into him any more.

— 20 —

Church on Sunday mornings is like a time warp. Nothing has changed. Adam could be ten years old. It could be 1950 all over again. No, not over again. Still. The '60s haven't happened here. No assassinations. No dead bodies spilling their guts out in rice paddies.

Everything in this carpeted, padded place is calm and placid. People smile. People pray. People lift little cups of grape juice to their lips. They drink. They pray again. They sing. They smile.

My god, thinks Adam. Where the hell have they been? Don't they *know?*

The choir stands and smiles and sings. Bright faces beaming above starched white robes. Rosy-cheeked, contented faces. Dammit, thinks Adam. *Dammit!*

Somebody has turned up the heat. Sweat pours down Adam's sides. He pulls out his handkerchief and wipes big drops from his forehead. His father turns and frowns at him. Adam looks around. Nobody else seems to notice how hot it's getting. They're all cool and calm and happy.

The collar of Adam's shirt starts to shrink. He's having a hard time breathing. He loosens his tie. His father frowns again. A funny kind of buzzing hums in his ears, and he can't hear the choir. They aren't going on and on about Lambs of God any more, just opening and closing their mouths. Sometimes the men. Then the women. Then all of them at once. Open and close. Open and close. And always that buzzing in his ears.

His collar has gotten so tight he feels dizzy. His forehead is dripping, and his shirt is soaked through. He can't breathe.

He stands up. Faces swing around and stop smiling. His mother wrinkles her forehead and makes a little hiss.

"I can't," he whispers. "I gotta get out of here. I can't . . ."

He bumps along the row. He hits old-lady knees wrapped tightly in nylon. Bony male knees pushed way out so they can trap him.

"I'm sorry," he whispers. "I'm sorry."

They stare up at him and don't smile.

Adam gets to the aisle and runs toward the back door. It's warm outside, warm for this time of year, but not as hot as inside the church. At least out here there's air to breathe. He unbuttons his collar and feels blood rushing back to his brain. He takes off his jacket. He's headed down a hill. He takes off his tie. He feels better. Walking so fast makes a kind of a breeze, and he stops thinking he's about to faint.

He doesn't know which way he's going, and he doesn't care. Away. That's all he cares about. Away.

They have no idea. None of them has the least idea. Are they crazy? he wonders. Or is he? Maybe all of them. Maybe none of it means a blessed thing. Getting killed. Coming home. What's the difference? Maybe it's easier *not* to come home. *Not* to spend the rest of your life wondering why you're here and all those others aren't.

He turns a corner, walks up a block, turns a corner. Buildings go by, fuzzy, hazy. Reflections in windows flicker in the corner of his eye.

What's the point? he thinks. What on earth's the point?

Guys dropping out of helicopters. Running around. Falling down. Bleeding. Noise and smoke. Everybody dropping, running. Smoke and blood all over. For what? Jesus. For *what?*

So people can ignore it. Pretend it never happened. Not ask you. Not want to know. Smile and sing and ignore it. Jesus.

No, that's not true. Not ignore it entirely. Ignore what it really was, all the blood and smoke and noise, but pray about it anyway. Pray in that rising and falling, singsongy voice that winds its way up to heaven. Prayers to protect this one and that one. Our boys. As if that did any goddamn good.

Or did it? Christ! What if that *was* what made the difference? If so . . . then . . . what? Then all the ones that died were bad in some way? Not worthy? Or somebody forgot to pray for them that day? Just when they needed it most, everybody was too busy? Nobody cared?

They were atheists? Or Buddhists—or worse? What? Whose fault was it? The ones who died? The ones who didn't pray? Whose?

He keeps turning corners and walking as fast as he can. Maybe he's going in circles. What difference does it make?

Does it matter? Any of it? The chaplains sure thought it did. They'd taken their duties very seriously. *Their* faith had never seemed to waver, though everybody else's did—a good bit.

"Comfort ye thy children," they would say, *"in this their hour of peril."* Dear lord, thinks Adam. Is that *really* what they believed was going to happen out there, when peril came flying at us out of the jungle? Bullets with our names written all over them? That comfort would come descending on a cloud to make us feel better as we got blown apart? Not likely. Not goddamn likely.

In the end, we were all alone out there, he thinks. All of us, all alone. Not even comradeship, a helluva lot stronger than comfort when you get right down to it, was powerful enough to overcome that. We were alone, no matter how many other guys there were around us. We walked through those rotten jungles alone. A valley of the shadow of death if there ever was one. We took the bullets alone. We died alone. Nothing could overcome that. Not families, with their letters and their missing you and loving you. Not congregations, with all their smiling and praying. Nothing.

The Hunters' church is across town, a long way from their house. Late in the afternoon, Adam starts to concentrate and heads in the direction of home. It's almost dark when he walks in through the front door. The TV is on in the living room. A football game. Adam's father is sitting in his big easy chair watching. He looks up, his face hard.

"Just where do you think you've been this whole afternoon?" Sam asks.

"Around," says Adam. "I'm not sure where all."

"You've worried your mother to a frazzle. And me, too, I might add. What were you thinking of, upsetting us like that?"

"You?" says Adam, half shouting. *"You?"*

His mother walks into the room from the kitchen.

"Adam, sweetheart," says Irene. "You look awful. Where's your nice new coat and tie?"

Adam looks at his empty hands.

"I don't know," he says. "I . . . somewhere, I guess."

She rolls her eyes and clicks her tongue. "We're not giving in to this kind of foolishness, you might as well know that right off. You're home now. You're safe. You've got to pull yourself together and start acting like a normal human being. Not go wandering around feeling sorry for yourself."

Adam's arms are trembling. He clenches his fists, and they stop.

"You want something to eat?" asks Irene. "I'm fixing grilled-cheese sandwiches."

"I'm not hungry."

"But you've got to eat something, Adam. Goodness sakes. You can't go all day on just a bowl of . . ."

"Jesus Christ!" says Adam. "Aren't you listening? I told you I'm not hungry!"

Sam is up out of his chair. "Don't you dare use language like that in this house, young man. Ever. Especially not on the Sabbath."

Adam is trembling again. His parents are standing there, looking helpless. He sees the confusion in their eyes.

"I'm sorry," he says. "I'm tired, and I . . . I guess I don't know what I'm doing. I'll just go lie down for a while."

Irene nods. "Good idea. I'll set aside a couple of sandwiches and grill them for you later on."

His father pats him on the shoulder. His mother kisses his cheek. He goes to his room and shuts the door.

For the first time in his life, Adam feels rich, and it gives him a sense of freedom he's never known before. The Army, in what turned out to be a hopeless attempt to keep the Vietnamese economy from exploding, had tried to make it worthwhile for those serving there to save their money. Ten percent interest, compounded monthly over the whole year. Some of the others hadn't seen much point to it, but Adam had been happy to comply. Everything was being provided, after all—where he slept, what he ate, what little entertainment there was in the way of occasional movies, and live singers and dancers from time to time. Beers were ridiculously cheap.

Since he'd had no girlfriend to buy clothes or jewelry or perfume for and had been careful to stay away from the high-stakes card and dice games, his paychecks had rolled pretty much intact into the Army's bank. He hadn't been paid much as a corporal, but he's still come home with more money than he knows what to do with.

He's decided to go back to Washington. Texas is too . . . he isn't quite sure what. Not confining, exactly. It's far too big for that. But something like it. When he's thought of where else, he's always landed on Washington, the only place in the country outside of Texas he's ever lived. Besides, being there again—without the Army to contend with—is appealing to him. He knows the city, reasonably well. He has friends there. And, so far as he knows, Richard is still there as well.

Adam heard from Richard once in Vietnam, about halfway through his tour. A brief letter: "Hi, soldier. How's it going? Busy here. Gotta rush. Take care."

But, still . . . Richard could have changed his mind, couldn't he? Mellowed some. It's possible. Adam still feels a powerful emotion—

longing mixed with physical desire—every time he thinks of Richard, so he figures it's worth a try.

Adam goes around to the local car dealerships and spends some time test-driving Mustangs and Thunderbirds and Pontiac sport coupes. In the end, though, his basic frugality wins out, and he buys a sensible dark blue standard-shift Chevrolet. Even paying cash for it takes less than half of his well-stocked bank account.

His parents tell him they're sorry he has to go, and Adam is sure they mean it. But it's also clear to him that after their initial delight at having him home alive, they've found dealing with what he's going through more than they can handle. So he piles some clothes and a box of books, a new stereo, and all his old records into the trunk of the Chevrolet and drives off toward Washington.

He stays in a motel in Arlington for a few days while he looks for an apartment. He goes in and out of a number of them before he finds one he loves—in the basement of a row house on Capitol Hill, just south of Lincoln Park. The minute he sees it, he knows he wants to live there. It's little—small living room, with fireplace, tiny kitchen, small bedroom, tiny bath—but it feels like home. He puts his name on the list of those who are interested, and he's the one the landlords call. The size of the apartment means he doesn't need much furniture, so, once again, there's no need to dip very far into his bank account.

He feels settled and happy and goes out to look for a job. A woman at an employment agency tells him the government is giving hiring preferences to Vietnam vets. Fine, thinks Adam. A little quid pro quo. He goes from one personnel office to another till he finds a spot in Public Affairs at the Department of Transportation, writing news releases. Not a particularly gripping way to make a living, but interesting enough. And the pay is good. Time, Adam thinks, to get in touch with Richard.

But Richard isn't at the old number anymore. Adam calls Pam and Suzy. Pam answers.

"How wonderful to hear from you," she says. "You're home safely then."

"More or less," says Adam. "Home, anyway."

"Poor Adam," she says. "We've been seeing such graphic things on the TV recently. It must have been just dreadful."

"It was."

"Richard has been awfully upset that he lost touch with you somehow. He's wondered I don't know how many times if you were all right."

"Yeah. Well . . . I was on the other side of the world, don't forget, so I guess letters had plenty of chances to go astray."

"That must have been it. So . . . are you passing through?"

"No, I've moved back here."

"With the Army?"

"No. I'm out now, thank heavens. I've found a job with the government. DOT."

"How nice," she says. "Welcome to the ranks of the civil servant."

"Glad to be there, I can tell you. Very glad, in fact. You still see Richard, then?"

"Oh, yes. As often as I can. You know how much fun he can be."

"Yes," says Adam. "I do."

"We're not an item or anything right now, though I must say I wouldn't mind if we were. We just go out for an evening—dinner and a show or a concert—every so often."

"Good for you."

"You haven't talked with Richard yet, I gather."

"Not yet. He wasn't at the number I had."

"Well, of course he wasn't. I should have realized. Right after graduation, he landed a job with a law firm downtown and moved out of his apartment into a nice big house. I can give you his number."

"Thanks. I'd appreciate that."

"Home or office?"

"Home would be better."

Adam calls three nights in a row and all the next weekend. No answer. Late on Monday night, Richard picks up the phone.

"Adam, you old devil! Pam said you were back in town. Why didn't you give her your number so I could've called?"

"Didn't think of it, I guess. So, how *are* you?"

"Couldn't be better. Sitting on top of the world. I've landed my dream job, can you believe it? On the corporate law staff at Safire and Lowell. You must know how prestigious *they* are."

"Well. With a name like that, they'd have to be. Is it the Cabots the Lowells talk to, or only to God?"

Richard laughs. "Not to junior attorneys, that's for sure. I'm tempted to genuflect when either of the Lowells walks by."

"Wouldn't hurt," says Adam.

Richard laughs again.

"And," he says, "I've moved into a beautiful old house up by the cathedral. Me and two other bachelor attorneys at the firm. You'll have to come see it, though we're hardly ever here."

"Sounds great. I'd *like* to see it sometime."

There's a lull.

"Well, well," says Richard, after a second or two. "Good old Adam, back among the living. When can we get together? Start catching up?"

"I doubt I'm anywhere near as busy as you are, so you tell me."

"I *am* really pressed these days, you're right. You were lucky to catch me here tonight. Big merger to get all the papers drawn up for. I'll be working late all this week, but maybe . . . hold on a sec. Let me go grab my appointment book." A pause. "Here we are. Nope. Dinner, brunch, cocktail party this weekend. No good. How's next Thursday? No, better make it Wednesday. No, Thursday. I'll just have to juggle a little. How's next Thursday?"

"Fine. Whatever's best for you."

"We can meet someplace interesting for dinner. You have your own wheels?"

"Yes."

"Oh, good. Then how's La Fonda?"

"Okay by me."

"La Fonda at 7:30 Thursday. I'll have my girl make reservations. In my name."

"I'll be there."

"Oh, and Adam . . ."

"Yes?"

"*Just* dinner, Adam. That other stuff's all over. You'll go home to your house, and I'll come home to mine."

Adam has been sitting at a table in the restaurant for half an hour when Richard comes rushing in, cheeks flushed, handsome as ever. Adam stands up. Richard shakes his hand, pats his shoulder, and sits down.

"Cabs! They're the bane of my life any more," says Richard. "You *never* can find one when you need one. And rainy days, forget it. I spend hours just getting from place to place. But . . ." He grins. "I bill the time to the clients, so the firm comes out ahead. What's that you're drinking?"

"Ginger ale."

"Ginger ale! No good. Not with paella. We'll split a pitcher of sangria. Waiter? Camarero? Over here. A pitcher of sangria right away. Grathias. So, tell me all about yourself, Adam. You look terrific. Tan and fit."

"We were outdoors a good bit of the time."

Richard laughs. "What a card you are. 'Outdoors a good bit of the time.' I'll bet you were. Was it really awful?"

"Yes. Really awful."

"Did you kill anyone?"

"Several, yes."

"Ours or theirs?" He laughs again.

"Theirs."

The waiter comes with a pitcher and pours sangria into two tall glasses.

"Paella for two, por favor," says Richard. "Heavy on the clams. Well, cheers!"

They clink their glasses.

"So where'd you go for R&R?" Richard asks.

"Bangkok."

Richard whistles. "Great city, so they say."

"It was all right."

"Well, *you're* certainly lively tonight." Richard sips his sangria.

"Sorry. I didn't mean to . . . I . . . I've been looking forward to see-ing you, a lot. But . . ."

"You're stumbling around, Adam. But what?"

"But now that we're here, I'm feeling . . . frustrated. I . . ."

"Oh, dear." Richard puts down his glass. "This isn't going to be one of those emotional evenings, is it? I'd hoped we'd gotten beyond that sort of thing."

"*You* may have, but I . . . It's just . . . I have no idea where things stand . . . with us. And I . . ."

Richard looks around to see if anyone is close enough to listen. No one is. He leans forward and lowers his voice anyway.

"I thought I made myself clear on the phone. That's all over, Adam. It's history. If you came back here hoping to rekindle any of that old stuff, you're wasting your time. Why did I not write you more often over there? Because I didn't want to encourage you, in any way. All that is finished, Adam. Do you hear me? It *has* to be. That's kid stuff. All right, maybe, when you're young and full of hormones. But we've got to grow up now and get on with our lives."

"That's exactly what I'm *doing*. Getting on with mine."

"By coming back to DC and looking me up? By trying to suck me back into that foolishness I've put way behind me?"

"Wait just a goddamn minute!" says Adam. "Who sucked whom?"

Richard glances frantically over his shoulder. Adam grins in spite of himself.

"Seems to me," says Adam, "we both did plenty of sucking. Quite happily, if I remember correctly. In the beginning, at any rate. And who's the one that got us started, huh? Not me! I didn't have the faintest idea it was possible till you showed me how."

"Sure," says Richard. "Blame it all on me. How was I to know you'd be such a romantic, and think it could just go on forever? Get real, Adam. Come to the party. Wake up and smell the coffee." He takes a long drink of his sangria.

Adam looks straight into Richard's eyes, but Richard turns away.

"I used to be scared of it, too," says Adam. "Like you. When we first met. But then I found out what fear is really like. And, believe me, compared to that, this is nothing."

"*Scared* of it," says Richard. He looks directly at Adam. "Of course I'm scared of it. Anyone with any brains is scared of it."

"I'm not."

"Oh, you. Of course not. You're the last person I'd expect to be sensible about all this."

Adam shakes his head. "Our conversations just pass each other in the night, don't they?" he says. "Here I am talking about affection, and caring, and you're talking about sensible. What's sensible got to do with it?"

"It's got *every*thing to do with it. Can't you see that? No, I guess you can't. You think you can create a lovely world out of hope and not much else, and then actually go live in it." He shrugs. "I could almost admire that—*almost*—if it weren't so naive. But . . . believe me, Adam. That world you're looking for doesn't exist. Not now, not ever."

"How can you be so sure?"

"How?" Richard laughs. "By the bitter experience of people who forgot the rules, that's how." He glances around again and leans closer to Adam. "A man in our firm—this was before I got there, but they still talk about it, whenever some new faggot joke is making the rounds. Anyhow, this man was exceptional, they say. About to make partner. Everyone admired him. But he pulled into one rest stop too many. A plain-clothes cop hauled him in, and bam! He lost everything. Job, wife, home, kids. Everything. I've come too far and done too well to ever take a risk like that."

"So that's what I am to you?" says Adam. "A risk?"

"A very big—and a very dangerous—one."

Adam nods. "I see. Then . . . if that's not possible, what is?"

Richard's face softens. "Dinner. Movies. Talks, if you can keep off that other subject. We can be friends, Adam. I'd like that."

"Would you?"

"Of course I would. We've been through a lot together."

Adam laughs.

"No," says Richard. "You know what I mean. We got close during those months. I was closer to you than I've ever been to anyone in my life. Oh, I don't mean *that* way. Well, not *just* that way. But in under-standing. I was able to let myself relax and feel . . . comfortable."

Adam smiles. "Comfortable," he says. "Well, that's something."

Richard smiles, too. "It was for me."

"So . . . what is it, exactly, that you're offering me?"

"Friendship, Adam. A very worthy thing. I'm offering you my friendship. Can't you just let that be enough?"

"It's not what . . ." He looks away, then back at Richard. "I'm not sure," he says. "We'll have to see."

The waiter sets a wide, steaming dish of paella in the center of the table.

"Yum," says Richard. "Muchas grathias." He reaches for Adam's plate and starts to serve. "Bangkok," he says. "Very pretty, from the pictures I've seen. Where did you stay?"

– 22 –

There isn't a specific moment when Adam decides this arrangement is all right with him. He just goes along with it, and the subject doesn't come up again. He and Richard go out to dinner a time or two, listen to the National Symphony, see a play at Arena Stage. Each time, they arrive in separate cars—or a car and a cab—shake hands good-night, and go home alone.

Adam is doing well at work. He has a flair for writing news releases, he discovers. Big deal, he thinks. Like being national tiddlywinks champion. But he enjoys the people, appreciates the order and tidiness of desks and suit coats and indoor plumbing. He even finds gasoline emissions and interstate highway construction to be interesting in their own way. At least that part of his life, he thinks, is well under control.

One lazy afternoon, he's sitting with six of his co-workers in a conference room. The Secretary of Transportation will be going out to California, and the advance team has swung into action. Adam is helping to prepare the briefing book—items of particular interest to Californians the Secretary wants to be able to speak intelligently about. Talk drones around the room, and Adam jots down a note every now and then.

The door swings open and *bangs* against the wall! Adam shouts and leaps to his feet, knocking his chair over backward. He drops quickly to the floor, out of harm's way. The room is totally silent, except for his own heavy breathing. Startled faces stare down at him. He clenches his fists tight to keep his arms still.

"Sorry," he says. He gets up, dusts the lint off his trousers, picks up his chair, and sits down in it.

"Sorry," he says.

The latecomer finds herself a seat. Faces swing back toward the director of public affairs, who moves to the next item on the agenda.

— 23 —

After they've been out to dinner one evening, Richard asks if Adam wants to see where he's living. Adam says sure. He wonders if Richard's roommates will be around, for protection, but they are nowhere to be seen. Aha, thinks Adam. Doesn't want them to meet his fairy friend.

The two of them walk around the enormous two-story, five-bedroom house, Adam says things to indicate that he is impressed, and they end up sitting on the couch in the living room talking and listening to music. Something lyrical and soothing. Lush strings, with an oboe here and there. Richard stretches his legs out onto the coffee table, leans his head back, and closes his eyes. The hand with no wine glass in it keeps time to the music.

Yes, thinks Adam. This is what Richard was talking about. Times like this. Relaxed and . . . comfortable. He looks at Richard's face for a long time, glad that Richard's eyes are closed so he doesn't have to look away. It's such a familiar face. The only one in the world Adam has kissed every inch of. The strings repeat their lovely melody, and Adam's hand rests lightly on Richard's hair.

Instantly, Richard is sitting up. "No, Adam. Don't do that."

Adam pulls his hand back into his lap.

"I thought you understood," says Richard, "or I would never have brought you here."

"Understood what?"

"That I can't afford to let you touch me like that. Ever."

"I don't intend to spend my life not touching *anybody*," says Adam.

"Then please. For god's sake. For *my* sake. Go find yourself someone with less to lose."

"Find someone? Where?"

Richard laughs. "What do you mean, 'where?'"

"I mean *where*? Where are there any others? You and I are the only ones I know of. For sure."

"Leave me out of it," says Richard. He moves toward the far end of the couch.

"All right, then," says Adam. "*I'm* the only one I know of! Where the hell are the others?"

"You really don't know?"

"Of *course* I don't know. How on earth would I *know*?"

Richard sits there, smiling and shaking his head. "Jesus. You people from the sticks. Bars, Adam. The people you're talking about go to gay bars."

"Where?"

"Southeast, mostly. You live near Lincoln Park?"

"Yes."

"Not far from there."

"Show me."

"What, now?"

"Right now."

Richard laughs again. "Well, why not? I guess I owe you that much."

They go in Adam's car, Adam following Richard's directions. Down Connecticut to 17th. Toward the Tidal Basin and left on Independence. Right on South Capitol. Left into a dingy, dimly-lit industrial area. Cars parked all along the streets. A glaring neon sign up ahead. Adam stops across the street.

"This is the one where I've had the best luck," says Richard. "Well, *used* to have. Called the Lost and Found. Appropriate, I always thought."

Adam watches for a minute or two without speaking. A group of three men, laughing and waving their hands, goes in. Two men come out and walk, arm in arm, down the dark street. Adam puts his car in gear and circles the block over to South Capitol. Richard chats as they drive, but Adam doesn't hear much of what he's saying.

When they stop in front of Richard's house, Adam turns and says, "Thanks."

"Don't mention it." Richard opens the door, gets out, and leans down. "I'll give you a call."

Adam nods. Richard closes the door and stands there on the sidewalk. Adam pulls away and doesn't look back.

24

The next night, just after ten, Adam parks near the Lost and Found. He sits for a while, waiting for his heartbeat to slow down. When it refuses to, he gets out, locks his car, and walks toward the entrance anyway.

As he nears it, a group of five men are coming toward him from the other direction. Two of them glance at Adam and look him up and down. One of them smiles and says, "Hi."

"Hi," says Adam.

Each one hands something to the man at the door. Adam looks at the wall. A sign says, "Cover: $5." Adam takes out a five-dollar bill and gives it to the man. The big room inside is dark, except for the brightly lit dance floor, where rotating beams move back and forth across hundreds of heads and shoulders. All male.

My god, Adam thinks. Look at them. *They've been here waiting all this time.* Waiting, yes, he discovers. But not necessarily for him.

Even though he's self-conscious and ill at ease, he watches, and he learns. Where the lines form at the bar. What steps are most popular on the dance floor just now. Where the restrooms are. That it's better to sit down to pee, since the frank and open stares at the urinals make it hard to get a flow started.

He listens, fascinated and amused, to conversations the likes of which he's never heard before. And he waits. At one-forty-five, he's still waiting. He's talked to nobody, and nobody has talked to him. He decides to go on home. He's feeling so frustrated he starts to jerk off, lying there in the dark alone, but he stops. Might as well save it, he thinks. Tomorrow could be my lucky night.

And it is. Summoning up all his courage, Adam walks over to a man with a beard and asks him to dance. The man says yes. Then another man asks Adam to dance, and *he* says yes. Adam stands at the edge of the dance floor for a while, waits in line for another drink, and strikes up a conversation with a veterinarian from Cheverly. They end up dancing three songs in a row, two fast and one slow.

"You planning on staying much longer?" asks the vet.

"Not really," says Adam.

"Want to come by my place for a quickie?"

Adam laughs.

"I gotta be in the office by seven-fifteen tomorrow is why."

"A quickie would be very nice," says Adam.

25

His new discovery fills Adam with conflicting emotions. He loves the act of sex itself, and while it's happening feels no guilt whatsoever, only excitement and more pleasure than he had any idea was possible. Afterward, however, when he's alone and quiet, he feels guilty about his lack of guilt. What his mother—or, god forbid, his grand-mother—would make of all this is too staggering a thought to even contemplate.

He's able to push these intrusions aside without too much difficulty because of another, even more unexpected discovery: he is at home in-side himself for the first time in his life. This is who he is, and he's not alone. He's one of thousands. Millions, probably. And, astonishing as it seems to him, given where he's come from, being one of them is all right with him.

Even so, he's bewildered by the passing parade that seems not to want to slow down. A history professor one night, a mechanic the next. A real estate agent, a hairdresser, a senator's aide, and one smooth-skinned, heavily muscled Marine MP Adam is sure he will never forget. There *is* something thrilling about so much variety, he has to admit, but the lack of continuity, of the chance to get to know the person he's doing such intimate things with, leaves him feeling restless and out of sorts.

Then he thinks of Richard. Plenty of continuity there, and on Adam's part, at least, something like love—but very little pleasure. Suddenly, pleasure without continuity doesn't seem like such a bad deal after all.

Richard is still calling every once in a while. "I'm kind of busy right now," Adam tells him each time.

"Maybe next week," Richard says.

"Yeah, maybe. We'll see."

Cruising at the Lost and Found, Adam soon realizes, is something of an art, with elaborate rituals of advance and retreat that most of the other patrons take very seriously. In fact, for some of them, this maneuvering seems to be the whole point of being here. Not for Adam. His only concern is the end result—somebody to be with and hold close for a while.

Assuming the costume, however, is no problem. Adam digs out some T-shirts and a faded pair of jeans, and buys a pair of construction boots. Now, not only does he feel as if he belongs, he looks as if he does as well.

As the nights go by, Adam keeps on watching and listening, and tries hard to adapt to the atmosphere of urgency disguised as nonchalance that seems to him such a waste of time. Logic tells him, though, that if waiting for somebody to come to him is going to take so long, he can speed things up by going to them. This directness of purpose, more often than not, keeps him from feeling rejected when one of them says no. He just moves on and starts looking again, until somebody says yes. And, with perseverance, somebody always says yes. This method, he finds, is most likely to succeed late at night, when so many of the most desirable possibilities have already paired up and those who had been lofty in their indifference earlier in the evening are feeling some panic at the thought of going home alone. Adam starts showing up between midnight and one.

He falls into a fast decision-making process that depends entirely on first impressions—maybe, maybe, no, no, no, maybe, yes. The factors involved, he works out one night when he can't sleep, are height (six feet and above), shoulders (broad but not massive), chest (its shape and strength perhaps the most important thing of all), and virility (the more obviously masculine the better). Blond hair and black hair each have their attractions; he is drawn, at different times, to both. Regular features are a plus, startling handsomeness an irresistible temptation.

This night, a Saturday, the place is packed. Hardly an inch left on the dance floor, long lines at the bar, every corner and passageway filled with male bodies. Adam finally manages to get a rum and Coke and pushes his way toward the dance floor. As he passes, he bumps an arm and feels the man's drink spill onto his wrist. He looks up and says, "Sorry." The man smiles and says, "That's all right." He's about to say something more, but Adam keeps going.

At the edge of the dance floor, Adam stands a while, sips his drink, and watches the dancers. Those with nice chests wear tight-fitting T-shirts, those with well-developed ones wear skimpy tank tops, and those with sensational ones wear no shirts at all. Adam moves in time to the music and concentrates on looking at the bare flesh.

As one song ends and another begins, a pretty young man in a light yellow tank top comes toward Adam and picks a drink up off the little counter that wraps around the pillar holding up the roof.

"You're a great dancer," says Adam.

The young man smiles, warmly enough, and says, "Thanks."

"Ready to go again?" Adam asks.

The young man takes a swallow, sets down his glass, and says, "Now I am." He reaches for Adam's hand and leads him out onto the dance floor. They prance and turn through the next two songs, touching every once in a while, but not even trying to talk over the pounding din of the music.

As the second song ends, the young man smiles and shouts, "Thanks!"

"Thank *you!*" Adam shouts back. "Have you got plans for later?"

The young man hesitates, looks at Adam, seems to turn alternatives over in his mind, and says, "Some other time, okay?"

"Okay." As Adam watches the yellow tank top moving away, his eyes catch those of the man whose drink he'd spilled, who's now standing at the edge of the dance floor across the way. A tall blond, he's wearing a blue-striped Oxford button-down and beige slacks. Not at all the usual Lost and Found attire. Adam glances at his feet. Sure enough, he has on loafers with those little leather tassels. Adam is grinning as he looks back up. The man raises one eyebrow and smiles.

A definite maybe, Adam thinks, as he heads toward the pillar where his glass may still be. It isn't. He waits in line at the bar for another drink. As he turns toward the room, a man standing beside him says, "You've been to San Juan, then."

"No," says Adam, smiling. "Why?"

"I thought that's where most people learned to drink rum and Coke."

"Well, not me," says Adam. "I'm kind of new to drinking and don't much like the taste of most things. But . . . I grew up with Cokes, so this was the easiest one to get used to. Actually, I'd probably drink it with Dr. Pepper if they had it."

"Aha," says the man. "Fascinating."

"What are *you* drinking?"

"A Tanqueray martini. They've finally gotten some respectable liquor here, after a number of us complained loudly enough."

Adam glances down. Tight T-shirt, faded jeans, and drinking something with a fifty-dollar name. He shakes his head.

"So where'd you learn to drink that?" Adam asks.

"Marbella, I believe."

"Where's that?"

Adam sees the man trying not to smirk.

"In the Mediterranean," he says. "Could you excuse me?"

He turns away, leaving Adam wondering what to do next. He suddenly feels very sad.

"Hi," says a voice in Adam's left ear. He looks up. It's the man in the Oxford button-down. Adam feels a wave of relief. "Hi, yourself," he says.

"Having a good time?" the man asks.

"No," says Adam.

"Me neither. Why don't we just get out of here, then?"

"Great idea!" Adam puts his almost full glass on the bar and starts pushing his way toward the front door. Halfway there, he looks around.

The man reaches for his hand. "Right behind you," he says, holding on. He lets go when they near the door.

Outside, the air is cool and refreshing, almost cold. In the bright lights of the entryway, Adam looks up at the man's face. It's nice looking. Not stunning. Not carved out of marble to be worshipped by lesser mortals. Just reassuringly attractive, with warm, amused eyes. Nice looking.

"Thanks," says Adam.

"For what?"

"For rescuing me."

The man laughs. "I was afraid you'd be whisked away before I could manage it."

"God! I'm glad I wasn't."

The man smiles and nods. "Me, too."

"I don't know what I was thinking of," says Adam. "I should've just latched onto you in the first place, instead of going through all those tired routines. 'Marbella,' for Christ sake! Have *you* been to Marbella?"

The man laughs again. "No, I'm happy to say." He holds out his hand. "Tony Marchak."

"Adam Hunter." They shake first, then just stand holding hands.

"I've never known anybody named Marchak before," says Adam, wanting not to let go of that strong, soft hand.

"Now you do."

"Yes."

"Can we go to your place?"

"Sure," says Adam. "It's real close. Maybe five minutes."

Tony gets his car and follows Adam's. Adam rolls down the window and points to a parking place just down the block from his apartment, then goes around the corner to find one for himself. He runs back to where Tony is standing on the sidewalk, waiting. As soon as they are inside, Tony bends down and kisses Adam, hesitantly at first, then hard. Adam puts his arms around Tony and pulls him tight against him.

Afterward, they lie in Adam's bed, his head on Tony's shoulder, their legs intertwined. Adam moves the hand resting on Tony's chest up and down, lightly ruffling the mat of blond hair he finds so exciting. Tony turns and kisses Adam's forehead.

"I don't really feel like going," Tony says. "Could I stay here with you? Till morning? I think I'd like . . ."

"What?"

"—waking up beside you, I guess. You know what I mean?"

Adam feels himself grinning. "Yes," he says. "I do."

He nestles in closer beside Tony. They lie quietly for a while.

"I've dreamed about this . . . god, how many times?" says Adam. "But it's never happened before."

"What's that?"

"This. Making love so . . . passionately, and then lying close together feeling . . . I don't know . . . feeling safe."

Tony tightens his arms and kisses Adam's forehead again.

"*Never* before?" he asks.

"Nope," says Adam. "Not like this."

"I find that hard to believe. I mean, you're such an attractive, sexy man."

Adam sits up and stares at him. "You think so?" he asks.

"I know so. Don't you?"

"God, no. I'm just a very ordinary person who scores on persistence and not much else. You have no idea how many guys I've talked to who kept looking over my shoulder trying to figure out how to get away. Like that idiot with the martini."

"Their loss," says Tony.

"Well, *they* certainly didn't think so."

"You really have so little confidence in yourself?"

Adam laughs. "Heavens, no. That's not the problem at all. I've got plenty of confidence in myself. I know pretty well what I can do and what I can't. Talk about expensive liquor and moonlight in Marbella? That I can't do, and nothing in the world's going to make me pretend I can. Attract the gorgeous guys with the bare sculptured chests? I can't do that either. I've tried, and I can't. I don't have anything to offer that they're interested in."

"Is that what you want? One of those gorgeous guys?"

Adam looks down at Tony's face. At his smooth broad shoulders and strong arms. "No," he says quietly. "I want this. I want somebody like you. Somebody smart and interesting and . . . easy to be with. I want to stop jumping around on dance floors and drinking drinks I don't like and going to bed with people I'll never see again. All that feels wrong to me.

"I . . . I've thought about it a lot recently, running around from place to place. And I've realized that what I want, more than anything, is to come home every night to the same man. Sit across the supper table and talk about things we both care about. Work together to make everything all right. And, most of all, to know for an absolute fact that I'll have his arms to curl up in every night for the rest of our lives.

"I'm not at all sure if I can have that. Maybe it's not what anybody else is looking for. But you asked."

Tony pulls him back down and holds him close.

Long after midnight, on a Tuesday that has turned to Wednesday, the phone wakes Adam out of a deep sleep. He's too groggy to be startled or concerned.

"It's Richard, Adam. I have to see you."

"Richard?"

"I'm sorry to call so late, but I've got to come over. Right now."

"Now?"

"Look. Just pull yourself together, and I'll be there as quick as I can. Half an hour?"

"What time is it?"

"Doesn't matter, does it? Now that we're both awake. Half an hour." He hangs up.

Adam switches on the lamp and looks at his bedside clock. 2:45. Jesus, he thinks. He goes to the bathroom, comes back, pulls on the clothes he'd left piled on a chair, and stumbles toward the kitchen to make himself some coffee.

The doorbell rings. Richard is standing there smiling. But his face is drawn. He takes off his jacket and hands it to Adam, who hangs it on the coat rack beside the door. Richard is wearing a crisply starched white shirt. To Adam's surprise, he smells strongly of aftershave. At three in the morning? thinks Adam.

Richard reaches out, puts his arms around Adam, and tries to kiss him. Adam turns his face away.

"What's wrong?" asks Richard.

"I have no idea what's going on here," says Adam, removing Richard's arms and stepping backward.

"Isn't it obvious?" says Richard. "I . . . love you, for god's sake. I . . ." He swallows hard. "I've tried to fight it—you know I have—but I can't anymore. I see now I was wrong to ever think I could.

I love you, Adam, and . . ." His face seems to pull in on itself even more tightly. "And I want to see if we can figure out a way to be together."

"Dear lord in heaven," says Adam. "'See if we can figure out a way'? That's the most romantic thing anybody's ever said to me."

"Don't give me a hard time, Adam. I'm doing the best I can."

"I'm quite sure you are. Want to sit down?"

"I think I'd better."

Adam goes and sits in the big easy chair by the fireplace, leaving the loveseat for Richard. Richard sits far out on the edge of it, as close to Adam as he can get.

"Well?" says Richard.

"You're amazing," says Adam.

"In what way?"

"Did you honestly think I was just sitting here waiting for you to work up enough courage to love me?"

"I . . ." Richard shrugs. "Yes, I guess I did. Although that seems like a harsh way of putting it."

"Harsh?" Adam laughs. "Then how would *you* put it?"

Richard takes a deep breath. "These last few weeks have been hell for me. Not seeing you. Barely talking to you. I . . . I thought you were playing hard to get. I mean . . . showing up out of nowhere again and then disappearing like that. I . . ." He runs his fingers through his hair. "I figured you were trying to make me realize what I was missing out on. What I was about to lose if I didn't get on the stick. And it worked. Boy, did it work."

He reaches for Adam's hand. Adam moves it away.

"Jesus *Christ,* Adam! Don't keep doing this to me."

"Then don't keep making it necessary."

"Didn't you hear what I said? I love you, goddammit. I want us to . . ."

"I heard you, Richard. Loud and clear. But it's not going to happen."

Richard's face looks stricken. His eyes widen. "Why not?"

"Because it's too late. Much too late."

"Shit," says Richard. "You've found someone else."

"Yes."

"Shit!" Richard hits the arm of the loveseat with his fist. "But how? Where?"

"Where? Right where you showed me. Don't ask me how."

"The L and F," says Richard in a low voice. "The fucking L and F."

"Yes. The fucking L and F."

"But . . . what about us? You and me?"

Adam feels like laughing again, but he holds it in. All but a little smile. He sees Richard flinch.

"There isn't any 'us'," says Adam. "There never has been. I didn't know that till recently, but I certainly know it now."

"Couldn't there be, if we tried?"

"Maybe. But we're not going to."

Richard looks at the floor. "You love this guy?"

"Very much."

"And he loves you?"

"I believe so, yes."

Richard looks back up at Adam. "But, wait . . . you can't have known him for more than a few weeks."

"Three."

"And yet . . . you feel certain enough to . . . ?"

"He's moving in here week after next."

Richard's eyes glance involuntarily at the door to the tiny bedroom. Adam feels a little pang in his chest, but he refuses to give it room to take root.

"So that's it?" says Richard.

"I'm afraid so."

Richard puts his head in his hands. Adam has a strong urge to reach over and touch him, but he resists that, too.

Richard looks up. "So what am I supposed to do?" he asks.

"I haven't the slightest idea."

"We can still be friends, can't we? Go out for dinner or a movie every now and then?"

"I don't think that's a good idea."

"Why not?"

"Well, it wouldn't be fair to Tony, for one thing."

"Tony!" Richard's lip curls when he says it. "I hate him."

"That may well be. But it doesn't change a thing."

Richard stares with such intensity that Adam has to look away.

"You . . . want me to go, then?" says Richard.

"Before too long, yes. I have to work tomorrow. God! Today."

"Any chance we could . . . you know? Just once more? For old time's sake?"

"No chance."

Richard sighs, gets up, and walks to the door. Adam follows him. Richard turns.

"Could I . . . hold you, though? Just for a second?"

"Sure," says Adam.

They put their arms around each other, Richard trembling a little, Adam determined not to.

Richard pulls away, grabs his jacket, jerks open the door, and is gone.

— 27 —

And Tony's family? His life? How he got from there to the Lost and Found? Adam reconstructs this the way he's done with his own family history, from stories he's heard through the years and his own sense of what must have happened.

The thing that's clearest to Adam is that his parents and Tony's could not be less alike. Tony's have led very different lives in a very different part of the country. Older than Adam's parents by a generation, they came to the United States just after the turn of the century, separately and a few years apart, from Russia.

Tony's father, a tough, keen-witted, no-nonsense young man, skipped out just ahead of the authorities, in his case a contingent of the tsar's local constabulary. What he had done—whether it was revolutionary, or obstreperous, or merely an attempt to get enough to eat—he never said. Nor how he got the money for his passage. Once he set foot on the shores of America, he never looked back. Then was then; now is now.

The bureaucracy at Ellis Island helps him do this. As he passes through the high-vaulted, noisy, confusing room in which immigrants are processed, Sergei Martwiaciak not only gains a future, he also loses his past. He stands in a seemingly endless line that moves, inch by inch, toward one of a long row of desks. The man sitting behind this desk—his hair mostly gone, his eyeglasses so thick they ride low on his nose, his nerves in tatters, what patience he may once have had now only a dim memory—moves those who come his way right along. Approvals, rejections, bright new lives, forced returns, separations, reunitings, they're all in a day's work for him. He has the power to decide, and decide he does. Quickly. Efficiently, he would say. Brutally, those on ships headed back east would agree.

He sees no reason to refuse this sturdy young man with alert and watchful eyes. Hearing what he says, however, is another matter. The huge room with its bare metallic surfaces rings with the echoed fragments of a hundred conversations. What comes out of the young man's mouth simply adds to the din, making no sense whatsoever. And what he has written down is even worse, those wiggly lines that bear no resemblance to proper letters. "Steven Marchak," the official writes, once on the entry papers and again in his ledger. He hands the papers to the young man and waves him through. The young man looks at the papers, asks a woman beside him what they say, smiles, and becomes Steven Marchak.

All alone on the lower east side of Manhattan, no family to either rely on or have to answer to, Sergei, now called Steve, makes his own way. He's seventeen, eighteen at the most, but far older in the ways of the world. His cockiness stops just this side of arrogance, so people like him. Maybe he really *does* know what he's doing, they think, so some of them give him a chance to prove it. Those who do are well rewarded for their confidence, especially the tailor who decides to teach him to make suits. Sergei/Steve learns fast, works hard, assumes responsibility, picks up the slack of slower workers, comes early, stays late, speaks okay English, better all the time, is an employer's dream.

He's short and a little round, but so full of life and his own sense of himself that the young Russian girls in his neighborhood are crazy about him. A couple of the Italian girls up the street, as well, look a bit longingly as he passes by, but it's a Russian girl, a pretty one who's come to work for the tailor, way at the back of that endless room sewing on buttons, that he asks to marry him. Tony's mother Elena, it turns out, has other plans.

– 28 –

Elena came to America earlier than Steve, by three or four years, from another part of Russia. The part that's gone back and forth between Poland and Russia so many times everyone has lost count (but the circumstances of which no one has forgotten—or forgiven—make no mistake about that). When she doesn't like the Russians she is with, Elena tells them she's Polish, and switches to that language to prove it.

She came when she was eleven, with her mother and younger brother, to join her father, who had come even earlier to establish a place for them. Everyone around her seems to like this new country just fine. Even as crowded as New York is, even as hard as they have to work—the young, the old, even many of the children—they all nod as they sit together, in their kitchens or on the stoops outside their tenements on steamy summer evenings, nod and say in the Russian that makes them feel at home, yes, they say, this is better.

Up and down the street, in other kitchens and on other stoops, people say the same thing. In Italian, in Yiddish, in Armenian, they all say, yes, no matter the hardship, no matter the suffering, this is better than what we left behind.

Elena does not agree. From the moment she landed in this alien place, where people crowd around her and talk too loud and smell bad and push and shove and talk about God but steal fruit from the corner grocery, she has wanted to go home. The buildings are too tall, not like the human-sized cottages in the village she loves and misses. And these awful buildings go on forever and ever, block after block in every direction, hiding the sun.

Where are the open fields? The trees that birds can sit in and sing? Where are the cows? She can't live without a cow. And where is the sun?

This isn't a loud, demonstrative campaign on her part. That isn't her way. It's a silent cloud of rebuke she carries around with her everywhere she goes. She does what she is told; she has too much sense of duty not to. But she has closed in on herself and rarely speaks and never smiles.

Her parents think at first that she will get over it, and so do the neighbors on both sides of their crowded little apartment and across the street. And so does her teacher. And so does the woman her mother works with, who knows more than anyone about suffering and having to adjust—this child's grumblings are nothing compared to what she's been through herself, and is still going through, truth be known, though you'll never hear a word of complaint from *her* lips, God as her witness. They've all said, all these friends and neighbors, they've said, "Give her time. She'll get over it."

But she hasn't. She is determined not to. She is determined to make everyone around her pay for what they are doing to her.

It works. How could it not? Such a heavy cloud she has brought into their lives, a cloud that never goes away, morning or night, ordinary day or holiday. In time, her parents give up, stop believing things are going to get better, and say yes, she can go home. Back to Russia, to the village she loves, to live with her grandmother. Elena is overjoyed. Now she can smile and talk, without it costing her anything. So she smiles and talks and does her best to show how grateful she is for this miracle. She goes to church every chance she gets to tell the Blessed Virgin how grateful she is. She can put up with anything now—the noise, the smells, the crowds—because she knows it won't be for much longer.

Oh, a *little* while longer, she understands that. Her father will have to save up the money for her passage on the ship, but she trusts him to do that as quickly as he can.

Then comes word from Russia. That terrible afternoon, when she arrives home from school and her mother, face swollen, red eyes full of tears, tells Elena her grandmother has died. Several months before, apparently, the letter has taken so long to get here. Her grandmother is dead. She won't be going back where she belongs.

She knows deep inside her that she will never forget. Or forgive. She isn't at all sure who it is she won't be forgiving. Not God certainly, Who has decided to take away her grandmother at such an inconvenient time. Even though she can't help thinking that He could have waited just a little while longer, until Elena could get back home. But even so. It isn't up to Elena to forgive or not forgive God for that. He's the one Who's in the forgiving business, should He be inclined to or have the time.

Nor is it her parents. They *had* decided to let her go, after all, though they might have done so sooner, if they'd really put their minds to it. No, she isn't sure whose fault it is, but it's *someone's*. And she will never forgive whoever that may be. A part of her goes far down inside herself and never comes out again.

29

Elena's father and mother make enough, barely, that she doesn't have to go out to work. She keeps on with her schooling, is attentive, learns to read and speak English, though she finds it thin and weak after the richness of the Russian she prefers. Less interesting even than the Polish she shifts into whenever it suits her. But she's going to be here in America, no way out of it now, so she'd better do what it takes to get along.

She is sixteen now, settled in, after her fashion. She has friends, not too many, but enough. One Saturday afternoon, she goes with two of them to a wedding. Even though she doesn't know the bride very well, it's a welcome alternative to sitting at home watching her father read the newspaper and her mother sew pieces of old clothes together to make a quilt. Her friends assure her there'll be plenty of food and music and interesting people. Elena puts on the new dress her mother has made her, braids her long thick shiny hair, pinches her cheeks to make them rosy, and off she goes.

The food is good, the music is loud, and the people are interesting. Especially the best man, a young Russian they all call Steve. The girl he's engaged to stays close by his side, but even so, he spends a lot of time looking at Elena. She's not experienced enough to be coy, so she looks right back. He parks his fiancée with a group of her friends and comes over to ask Elena—first in English, then in Russian when she simply stares at him—to dance. She says she doesn't know how to dance but she'd be very glad if they could talk a little.

Steve laughs and says, good. We'll talk. And they do, for quite a while. So long, in fact, that Steve's fiancée comes over and says she needs him. He says, later, can't you see I'm busy? She says right now. He says no and turns back to Elena. The fiancée huffs around for a while, being loudly offended, and then leaves. Steve doesn't seem to mind.

The next Saturday, Steve asks Elena to go out with him for a hamburger. Three months later they are married.

30

Deciding to marry Steve is easy for Elena, once she finds out he's willing to give her the two things she wants most—a large family and a home out in the country, away from all these noisy crowds. Where she can see the sun and have her own cow. Steve moves in with Elena's family, works hard, and saves all he can. Elena watches him do this and is pleased. The warmth and gratitude she feels toward him, she thinks, must be love.

After their first child, a daughter, is born, Steve works even harder. He sees as clearly as Elena that raising children—certainly as many as *she* wants—in a crowded apartment in the city is not a good idea. Late that fall, he takes the train out to Long Island. Fifty miles out, past the built-up areas to where the land is cheap. Elena is excited and wants to know all about the trip. He tells her about a farm he saw, four hundred acres, beautiful land. He's never farmed before, but he grew up among farmers in Russia, and he knows beautiful land when he sees it. If he can get his boss, the wealthy tailor, to back him, well, maybe . . .

His boss doesn't like the thought of losing Steve, who's now an assistant manager, but he's shrewd enough to understand that he's going to lose Steve anyway, so he might as well make the best of his loss by banking the interest on what he knows is a surefire loan. Steve goes out again to Long Island, and comes back a farmer.

"Let's move—right now," says Elena, in the English Steve insists they always use, even when they're alone like this and Elena is so fired up she finds the foreign words hard to come by.

"No," says Steve. "We must wait for the sale to be finished up. And I must fix things at my work, so to be easier for who comes after me. My boss, after all, is the one who makes this possible."

"I see," says Elena. But she doesn't. She doesn't see at all. They should go right away. Pack up tonight and leave tomorrow. A second child is on the way already, and she wants it born out there. Not here.

Late in February, Steve says it's time to go, to get the farm ready for the spring planting. They pack their few belongings, pay a man down the street who has a trash-hauling truck to help them, and move out to Long Island. Steve, as charming there as on the streets of the city, goes around to his neighbors. He spends days with them and with the local agriculture agent, and learns all he can about potatoes. Elena, heavy and uncomfortable but determined, works at bringing order to the run-down old farmhouse. She buys a few pieces of secondhand furniture, only the essentials at first, plants her vegetable garden out behind the house, and gets a bunch of chickens settled in and ready to lay.

The potato plants are up, rows and rows of them as far as she can see, when her second child, a son, is born. At home, in the bed she and Steve sleep in every night. The way it should be. By the end of the week, Elena is back milking her cow. The neighbor woman who helped out in exchange for half the milk only had to come over three days.

Once the potato harvest begins, Steve makes payments on his loan, religiously, on the first of every month. He sees himself, now, in a whole new way, as a man of substance. He's got a farm, a house, a family, a wife, and a huge barn to spend most of his time in, whenever he's not out in the fields. He isn't tied down anymore, to somebody else's rules and somebody else's routines. He has room to be on his own and freedom to choose. All this, he thinks, proud and satisfied, is just fine.

31

Life is very different for Elena.

As the years pass, the farm acquires a tractor and a harrow and a couple of trucks, but its primary machinery is 'the men,' a crew of six, eight, ten workers who do whatever is required to keep a four-hundred-acre potato farm running—plowing, planting, spraying, irrigating, harvesting. When she's not taking care of her five, then six, then seven children, Elena is in charge of fueling this machinery.

Before the sun is up, she is, peeling potatoes, slicing them, frying them, frying bacon, cooking sausage, slicing and toasting bread, scrambling, frying, or boiling eggs, making pancakes, being absolutely sure the huge pot of coffee is brewed and boiling hot before the first of 'the men' come in through the kitchen door. She barely has time to finish the dishes and bring what order she can to the kitchen before it's time for the mid-morning snack. More coffee, pastries, bread with jelly or peanut butter or both, which she lugs out to whichever field her husband and 'the men' are working in.

Back to the kitchen to fix lunch—an enormous meal of soup, meat, vegetables, always potatoes, often mashed, cole slaw, pickles, sliced tomatoes once they've ripened, glasses of milk fresh that morning, more bread, more coffee, more pastries, pie maybe, or a cake, topped with whipped cream or just-picked berries. Clean up fast, do as many other chores as she can, then take the mid-afternoon snack—sandwiches, lemonade, pieces of fruit—out to the fields, and start in on supper, an only slightly smaller version of lunch.

Day after day after day after day, Elena does her duty. Fuels the machinery that keeps the farm running. Only once does she fail. A neighbor woman, during one of their communal sauerkraut-making afternoons, has told Elena she should serve 'the men' fish. Fish are plentiful on Long Island, god knows, in these long-ago days when the ocean is still pure, fish are therefore cheap, and everyone knows fish are good for you. They don't call them brain food for nothing. Elena, nodding her babushka-covered braids, agrees.

So it is that one day in late summer, along about noontime, Steve is driving home from an early-morning run to the markets of Manhattan. There, on the road coming toward him, are 'the men.' *His* men. He slams to a halt and jumps from the truck, face red, eyes ablaze.

"Where the hell do you think you're going?" he asks.

"Into town, dammit," says one of 'the men.' "To get ourselves a decent lunch."

"What's up? Is my wife sick?"

'The men' glance at each other and laugh.

"Looks like it." They nod and laugh again.

Steve is flustered. "What's wrong with her? She's never sick."

"It's in her *head*," says one of 'the men,' pointing toward his own. "She tried to give us the *fish*." His mouth curls downward as he says the word.

"Fish!" says another.

"Hop in the back of the truck," says Steve. "I'll get to the bottom of this."

And he does, in an icy voice heavy with sarcasm. Elena protests. Steve insists.

"This is *my* house, and you'll do things *my* way," he says. "Or else."

Though she has never experienced that "or else," Elena knows she wouldn't like it.

She goes back into her kitchen. She fries a mound of pork chops, reheats the vegetables, slices more bread. As she serves it all in silence, eyes narrow and lips tight, she is carefully filing this day away. Among the things she will never forget. Or forgive.

32

Worse than this clash, though, by far, is the battle over the icebox. Elena sees one in a neighbor's kitchen and knows immediately that she has to have one. She almost laughs out loud when she thinks how much easier her life will be. Food will keep longer, things won't spoil. And she'll have what she needs right there in the kitchen, not way off around back in the root cellar. A man comes out twice a week to deliver ice, her neighbor tells her. He can just stop by the Marchak farm on his way to the O'Reilly's.

It's such an obviously good idea that Elena doesn't ask Steve if she can have one, she simply tells him to go buy her one. He stands frozen on the spot. He tilts his head, as if she has spoken to him in Swahili, and tells her to say that again. She does.

"No," he says

"Yes," she says.

"No."

"I slave hard in this kitchen every day . . . ," she says.

"No."

"You don't have any idea how . . ."

"No."

"For *once* in our lives," she shouts, "you are going to listen to me!"

He goes very still again, but the atmosphere around him quivers. He raises his hand, calmly and deliberately, and holds one finger in front of her face.

"You will never, *never* speak to me that way. Never."

She only stares at him.

"You will forget this foolish idea. I'm not spending my hard-earned money on foolishness. Do you hear me?"

She stares.

"Do you hear me?"

She stares.

He lowers his finger, goes out through the door, and slams it behind him.

That very day, Elena finds a big tin can, sticks it way in the back of the pantry, and starts filling it with nickels and dimes, pennies even. Whatever she can lay her hands on. She skims some out of the household money. She sells a few extra eggs. She finds a few coins behind the cushions of the sofa and of the easy chair over by the window. Slowly, very slowly, the can fills up.

Every month or so, on an evening when her husband is off 'visiting,' which means having a drink with someone somewhere, and none of the kids are at home, she takes the can out and painstakingly counts the coins. She's been to Sears Roebuck in town and knows exactly how much it will cost, including delivery—to the penny.

It takes her almost two years, but that's nothing, really. She'd've kept at it for *ten* years, if she'd had to. When she has enough, she walks into town to do her regular errands and orders the icebox. A few weeks later, a letter comes to say that it is here. She hides the letter in her apron pocket, walks into town again, and tells them the best day for delivery. It's the day Steve leaves early in the morning to take his potatoes into the city.

He gets home in the middle of the afternoon, goes to the kitchen for a glass of water, sees the icebox in its new place near the center of the back wall.

"Elena!" he yells.

"Elena!"

She hears him the first time, but doesn't go to the kitchen till he's called her four times. She walks slowly in through the door. He points at the icebox.

"You disobeyed me," he roars. She is sure 'the men' in the fields can hear him. "You intentionally disobeyed me!"

She says nothing.

"Are you listening to me?" he yells.

"Yes," she says.

"You will take that thing back."

"No."

"You will *take* that thing back."

"No. It stays, I stay." She lifts her chin. "It goes, I go."

He clenches his hand into a fist and raises it high over his shoulder. She stares at him.

"Go ahead," she says. She steps toward him. "Hit me. Go ahead."

He stands there, breathing hard, weighing his options, weighing her resolve. He lowers his arm, kicks the door of the icebox, says "Keep the damn thing then," and storms out.

She is glad to have the icebox. It *does* make things easier for her, the cooking and the storing. And yet . . . something is gone from her life. Some piece of the bond between her and her husband that she didn't know was there, until it wasn't anymore.

She has won. Of course she has. But she has also lost.

— 33 —

The consciousness of human frailty and its inevitable companion, guilt, are frequent visitors in the Marchak house. Almost permanent residents. When they haven't been around for a day or two, they are missed, as if the kitchen table or the piano in the parlor had up and disappeared. And if, by some inexplicable coming-together of good fortune and sunny days, they are gone for much longer than that, they are hastily summoned and invited back in.

Given a choice, the family would have been Russian Orthodox, the proper religion. But the only places of worship on Long Island are too far away—all right for christenings and funerals maybe, but too far for more than that—which means a bit of Roman Catholicism around the edges has had to do. Russian Orthodoxy's dim and brooding view of human nature mixed in with the strict, puritanical aspects of Catholicism have created a potent brew of negative emotions, whose aroma permeates the house and the lives of those within. Tony, the last of the Marchak children, has grown up with these feelings, absorbed them, and had special reason to believe they apply to him.

Even in the midst of such a large family and so many workers and neighbors coming and going, Tony is a lonely child. His six older sisters and brothers have paired off, two by two down the line, forming intense bonds held together as much by rivalry as by affection. When Tony comes along, four years after the sixth child, there is no one for him to forge a bond with. Elena fills the gap the best she can, although she's much too busy to spend the time she'd like to with her youngest son, her prize, with his quick temper and his sad eyes.

All the children have to help with the work on the farm. It's understood and unquestioned. Tony likes doing things for his mother— bringing carrots and parsnips and jars of sauerkraut in from the root cellar, picking green beans and squash from her garden out back.

When he's old enough, he starts sitting with her and the neighbor women who've come by to help cut seed potatoes. He learns quickly, true of everything he does, to cut across and down, with caution, of course, fingertips well out of the way, being sure to leave an eye in each small cube of potato. As they sit and cut, the women talk, in low voices, with pursed lips and sidelong glances at Tony, about dark deeds, injustices, sins that Tony now learns, to his surprise, are common occurrences not just in the outside world but close around him. Some he can recognize: drinking, gambling, slaps across the face that become too frequent. Others are mysterious, involving unspecified parts of the body Tony can only guess at.

Once he's older, stronger, Tony gets to go out to the fields, with his brothers and sisters, to help 'the men' plant and harvest potatoes. He's glad for the change. He feels free out here, free to breathe the clean air and free of the weight of the women's discontent. He likes the harvest best. The crispness, the earthy smells, occasional geese and ducks flying south. It's a poignant time that suits his view of the world.

Most of all about the harvest, he loves cooking and eating potatoes right out there in the fields. He does what the others do. He walks along behind the harrow, being pulled by a tractor, as it turns over the ground exposing the potatoes and also gathers up the dead plants. Every so often, the driver dumps a pile of dead leaves and stems. Tony tucks a few potatoes under one of the piles, lights it, and moves on down the row, bending over and putting potatoes into his basket. He goes to the end of that row, puts down his full basket, grabs an empty one, and heads back up the next row. By the time he reaches the smoldering pile, the potatoes underneath are cooked through. Steam rushes out when he squeezes and bursts the blackened, crunchy skin. Flaky, moist, hot inside. The most delicious thing he's ever tasted.

Tony works on the farm when he's not at school, but he also plays. There aren't many boys his age around, but some. Every once in a while, one of them will want to play a special game, out in the woods or high up in the hayloft of his father's barn. Wrestling that turns to exploration. Two little boys sliding down their shorts and touching. At first, it only tingles, feels good to both the toucher and the one being touched. Later on, when they're older, the toys become hard and do amazing things, giving such pleasure as Tony had never imagined.

He is certain all this figures prominently among the unnamed sins hinted at, ominously, heads nodding, by the women as they cut their potatoes. Guilt settles comfortably around Tony's shoulders—in this, he becomes a full-fledged member of his family—but the habit of finding pleasure, and companionship, in this way takes firm root nevertheless.

– 34 –

When Tony finishes college and finds a good job with an accounting firm in New York, he moves to the city and with little trouble discovers the gay subculture there—and its unending supply of sexual partners. Though he is shy and unsure of himself, he is, after all, a farm boy, he is tall and good-looking and his chest is broad and there is always someone eager to be with him and do those wonderful things.

At home, though, as the years go by, the pressure is relentless.

"Tony, my son. My *Kolya*. What is it with you? Thirty years old and not married. What is this?"

"What's the rush, Papa?" asks Tony.

"What's the rush?" says Steve. "I'm not getting any younger, that's the rush. I want to see my grandchildren."

"You've got hundreds of grandchildren already, Papa."

"Not hundreds, *Kolya*."

Tony counts quickly in his head. "Seventeen! What do you need with more?"

"It isn't a matter of 'need,' you goofy person. Need? It's 'want,' that's what it is. I *want* to see your children. *Your* children. What'sa matter? There aren't any nice young girls anymore? They've all gone away? Flown the coop? In my day, I coulda had my pick of twenty."

"Twenty, Papa?"

"*Thirty*. Don't gimme. They were dropping outa the trees. But no more? Some epidemic killed them all off? What?"

"No, Papa. It's just . . ."

"No 'just.' Don't gimme any 'just's. 'Just this.' 'Just that.' You young people gimme a pain. The only 'just' is, just go find yourself a nice girl and get married. Get some grandchildren on the way before I'm so old I have to go visit them in a wheelchair. 'Just!' Just go do it!

Thirty years old, you're practically middle-aged, and here you are rattling around all by yourself. No place to hang your hat. I'll tell you something. When *I* was thirty . . ."

"You had six children already. I know, Papa."

"And you, the last one, my baby, you came along when I was only thirty-four. You hear that? Seven kids by thirty-four. And where are yours, may I ask? Mr. 'Just This' and 'Just That'? Never mind seven. Where's your *one?*"

"I've been busy, you know, with school and then work . . ."

"Don't gimme 'busy.' For god's sake, don't gimme 'busy.' 'Busy' is worse than 'just.' 'Busy!' You don't *know* from 'busy.' Me? *I* know from 'busy.' Your mother? *She* knows from 'busy.' Your sisters? Your brothers? Kids. Jobs. Homes. Responsibilities. *They* know from 'busy.' *You?* You float around like Mr. Lah-di-dah. Nice clothes. Nice car. Your time's your own. Don't gimme 'busy.'"

"Okay, Papa. For you I'll try."

"I don't believe it. Now we got 'try.' I don't believe it. First it's 'just.' Then it's 'busy.' Now we got 'try.' You never learned a thing from me? Your own Papa? I'd'a come here with only 'try' in my pocket, I'd'a starved. They'd'a found me in a ditch someplace, starved to death. Not only did I make it once, I almost lost it all for good. Every bit. In the Great Depression, just after you were born, my little *Kolyichka,* my treasure—you somehow manage to forget all that? But then I made it all back again, and even more. You ever looked at this farm I got here?"

"Yes, Papa."

"Four hundred acres of prime potato land. You ever starve?"

"No, Papa."

"Ever in your life? Even during those bad times when most people didn't have two sticks to rub together? You ever starve, even then?"

"No, Papa."

"You go to college?"

"Yes, Papa."

"Your sisters and brothers go to college?"

"Yes, Papa."

"Help me here. Did I pay for that, or was it somebody else?"

"It was you, Papa."

"Well, I'll tell you a secret. Just between us. Don't tell another soul. Don't let it get out of this room." He leans forward and whispers. "I didn't do it by saying, 'I'll try.' I did it by *doing* it." He sits back up. "Isn't that amazing? You never thoughta that, it's clear. But it's true. It's *my* secret that nobody else ever thought of before. You want something, you go get it. *And* . . . Your *father* wants you to do something, you go do it. 'Try' doesn't come into it. 'Try' is for losers. Let all the losers of the world stick with their 'try' and their 'just' and their 'busy.' Not you, Tony. My *Kolya.* So close to my heart. You go do your duty. Go find a nice girl and get married. Gimme some grandchildren before my eyes go bad and my ears get where I can't hear a word they're saying."

— 35 —

Tony does find a nice girl. One Saturday while he's visiting his parents on Long Island, at a diner where he's gone with a friend for lunch, he bumps into a classmate from high school. He starts asking her out—occasionally at first, then more frequently—on those weekends he's at home. Marie hasn't married yet either, though she's thinking it's time if she hopes to have a family, which she does. That's assuming, of course, that she'll be lucky enough to meet the right man.

As the months slide by, Tony finds himself going less and less often to the gay bars in the city, spending more and more time with Marie. Dutiful and conscientious, like his mother, he does what he is supposed to do. The habit of obedience to his father's wishes is firmly entrenched in him.

Does he want to do this? No. He doesn't *want* to. But he understands this is what men do—when the time comes. And since he has to do it, he knows he is lucky to have found Marie. She's a quiet, attractive woman. Attentive. Good-hearted.

Tony likes Marie, they have fun together, and he is in awe of her brassy, classy mother, Lorraine, a buyer for Bergdorf Goodman. Tony has never known anyone like Lorraine, the opposite of her sensible, not to say staid, only child. The amount of care—and money, his accountant's eye tries to estimate—that Lorraine lavishes on herself astonishes him. Hair, eyes, eyelashes, fingernails, skin. And the adornments: skirts, blouses, sweaters, suits, hats, gloves, earrings, bracelets, rings. Never in the same combination, that he can remember. No babushkas or sensible, flat-heeled shoes for Lorraine.

Long divorced from her Italian husband and with time on her hands, she becomes a third, and almost equal, partner during the time Tony and Marie are courting. After they are married, she's around even more. The house Tony has bought on Long Island—in one of the developments going up on farms just like his father's—is only ten minutes from Lorraine's. She drops in whenever she isn't working. Marie is glad for the company, and Tony certainly doesn't mind. He and Marie deal with each other better when other people are around.

Five days a week, Tony takes the train into the city in the morning and rides it back out late in the afternoon. At first, Marie drives him to the station and returns to pick him up, but he finds after a while that he prefers walking.

"After all," he tells her, "twenty minutes each way isn't so much extra time. And the exercise is good for me."

What he doesn't tell her is how much he looks forward to this time alone.

He misses sex with men. Of course he does. Sometimes so much so that he feels little stabs of pain in his chest and in his groin. But he tries to put all that behind him. He's had his fun, and now he's got to shape up, do what's required of him. Follow the rules and regulations. He finds, to his relief, that Marie isn't much interested in sex, not with any real frequency. Occasionally, just not very often. She likes closeness, being held and touched, but not what she calls 'the rest.' Tony can manage that kind of closeness just fine.

Relieving his own needs as he sits in the bathroom or stands under the shower, with vivid memories of hard bodies and strong arms to excite him, keeps Tony's internal pressures down to a manageable level. Almost. He slips, though, a time or two. Well, three or four. He doesn't intend to, but he does. Men he meets at work. Bumps into at lunch. Finds too attractive to resist. But mostly—mostly—he's able to fight off temptation and stick to his resolve.

The Russian sense of martyrdom he's inherited from his family comes to his rescue here. Since he's unhappy so much of the time, he must be doing the right thing.

All of this changes when Laura is born. She's the joy of Tony's heart. And of her grandfather Marchak's. Everyone who sees her can easily understand why. She has black hair, dark dark eyes, and soft round white cheeks. And she adores Tony. Her daddy reads to her, bathes her, and takes her for walks in the park. She sits on his lap, pulls at his hair, squeezes his fingers, and hugs his neck.

One summer day when Laura is four, Lorraine takes all three of them out for a picnic by the shore. Laura runs around and laughs and splashes at the edge of the water. She eats most of a hamburger, pets a dog that wanders by, and chatters about her new dolly. They start home about mid-afternoon. Along the way, Laura, in the back seat with her mother, says she has a headache.

"It's okay, sweetheart," says Marie. "Too much sun and excitement, that's all it is. Just sit still. We'll be home soon."

A few minutes later, the convulsions start. Marie screams. Tony fights the panic that threatens to engulf him. Lorraine drives straight to the hospital.

They wait, distraught, for nearly an hour before a nurse finally comes out to see them. The doctors are unable to get away, she says, so they have sent her.

"What is it?" asks Tony. "What's wrong?"

"It's . . ." The nurse hesitates, which terrifies Tony.

"Please," he says. "What is it?"

"It's an aneurysm," she says. "In your daughter's brain."

Tony feels as if he can't move, but does manage to speak.

"What does that mean?" he asks. "Will she be all right?"

The nurse hesitates again. "You'll have to talk with one of the doctors about that, and they're all tied up right now."

Marie's face is white, her eyes wide.

"I want to see her," she says.

"She's unconscious," says the nurse. "The doctors are with her. Doing all that's humanly possible."

"Please. I have to see her."

"It's best if you don't. Not like this. You'll only distress yourself."

For hours they wait. Walking in the hall. Not talking much. The nurse comes back once to say there is no change. They listen. Nod. Say thank you. Just before midnight, a doctor comes into the waiting room and walks toward them. Lorraine moves to the next chair so he can sit beside Tony. She and Marie lean toward him.

"I'm sorry I couldn't get out here sooner," he says. "But we've been very busy. Doing everything we could."

"I understand," says Tony. "Please. Tell us what's happening."

"You know what an aneurysm is?"

"Sort of."

"They occur when the wall of a blood vessel becomes weakened. Your daughter's was deep inside her brain. It has ruptured, and there is no way we can reach it. No way to stop the bleeding."

"Bleeding?" says Tony. "Inside her brain?"

"Yes."

"Then . . . If you can't reach it, what can you do?"

"Nothing. She will die when the pressure of the blood on her brain becomes too great."

Tony is glad he's too tired to scream. He looks over at Marie. She is staring at the doctor. Numb. Barely reacting. Tony understands. This can't be happening. How could it be happening?

"She's not feeling any pain, is she?" asks Marie.

"None," says the doctor. "None at all."

"Can we see her? Just for a minute?"

"Yes," he says. "Of course."

The three of them follow him down the hall and into a room. Laura is lying there, pale, still, tiny. Tubes connect her to machines and bags of fluid. She is so tiny. So still. Tony puts his arms around Marie, and they both begin to cry. Lorraine sits in a chair, her head in her hands.

Back in the waiting room, Tony and Marie sit a little apart, not speaking, not touching. A short time after noon the doctor comes back. To say it is over.

After that, things are never the same. Marie blames herself. She should have known. A mother should have known. Tony grows impatient with the blaming. They try living apart, then together, then apart. Apart is better. Marie asks for a divorce.

All by himself in a bare apartment back in the city, Tony has too much time to think. No matter how hard he tries, he can't make any sense of it. He has done what he was supposed to do, he's been a good husband and a loving father, and still he's been punished. What kind of a God would kill a little girl to get back at a man for sins he's stopped committing? Has avoided since the day she was born?

Angry and confused and lonely, he starts committing them again. When a job in his firm's Washington branch opens up, he takes it.

36

For Adam, living with Tony is the best thing that's ever happened to him, although the apartment *is* little and they are both good-sized men. When they're on the move at the same time, they can't help bumping into each other.

Tony has been living in an efficiency on the eighth floor of a high-rise in southwest Washington. He doesn't have much to bring along— a mattress, which they put on top of Adam's; an Oriental rug they have to fold on one side to make it small enough for the living room; a big chair they squeeze in beside the fireplace; a television set that goes in a corner of the bedroom (Adam's smaller set is demoted to the back of the closet); some clothes; some books; and a beautiful, wildly healthy spider plant that they hang in the front window. These things fit in all right, but the apartment sometimes feels full to Adam now, not cozy like it was before.

What matters to Adam, though, is having Tony there with him. To care about every day and to make love to every night. It's exciting, and satisfying, for Adam—being with the same man each time, a man whose enthusiasm matches his own. He learns where to touch Tony, how to please him, the thrill of being inside Tony and then having Tony inside him.

It's later—after the orgasms, after they've lain together a while, their arms around each other, after the last endearments as they drift off to sleep—that the trouble comes. Not every night, but often enough. The noises pounding inside Adam's head. Explosions. Shouting. Machine guns that won't shut up. Shrieks. Crying. Shouting. And the blood. So much blood. Bloody stumps. Bloody limbs torn from bloody bodies. Adam has to wake up to save himself. Always sweating, sometimes screaming, trembling so hard he can't stop.

Tony reaches out and holds Adam as close as he can.

"It's all right," he says. "I'm here. I'm right here."

Crying would help, Adam knows it would. But he doesn't do it.

"Want to talk about it?" Tony always asks.

"No," says Adam. "It's too awful."

"All the more reason."

"No. Nobody wants to listen."

"I do. I want to listen."

Adam shakes his head. "I'd rather just forget it."

"But you're obviously *not* forgetting it. That's what this is all about. Maybe if you . . ."

"NO!" says Adam.

They lie there, side by side, staring at the ceiling.

It's Tony who breaks the pattern. Adam wakes up one night trembling, sweating, breathing hard. Tony holds him, says, "Want to talk about it?"

Adam says no.

This time Tony sits up, switches on the lamp beside him, folds his arms, and says, "I'm going to wait right here until you talk to me."

Adam wrinkles his forehead. "It's . . . too hard."

"You think what you're going through—what *we're* going through— is easy?"

Adam stares at him, looks away, looks back at him, all the while chewing on his bottom lip.

"I guess . . . ," he says. "If you think I . . . but if it . . . if I can't . . ."

"You can stop. Of course you can."

Adam sits up, facing Tony. The sight of Tony's face, his strong shoulders and bare chest, comforts Adam. A little. He doesn't know why, but it does.

"It's about . . . ," he says. "Oh, god. It's about being dead. Thinking you're going to be. Or that you *should* be. That whole year . . . that frigging year that wouldn't end . . . I knew I was going to die. I don't know how to make you understand. I *knew* it. I . . ." He closes his eyes for a couple of seconds, then opens them. "That's a whole lot different from thinking it or assuming it. Or even dreading it. I was just . . . certain . . . I was going to die. There, in those wretched jungles. Any day now. Any day. And I was terrified. You can't be any more frightened than that. I'm sure of it. Because . . . it's too soon. You know? It's much too soon. You've got places to go and things to learn, and you're never going to get the chance.

"Christ! You've barely gotten started. Just begun to figure out what things are about. *Everything* is out there in front of you, and you're not going to see one damn bit of it. You know that. Absolutely. Because what you *do* see is death. It's all around you. It's every-fucking-where. So many of the guys you've cared about are dead. Not 'passed away.' Not 'gone' to their goddamn 'reward.' They're dead. And I don't mean just some. I don't mean one here and one there. I mean lots of them. Ten of you go out on patrol, and five of you come back. You wake up in the morning and find out two of your buddies on guard duty got shot through the head.

"And . . . it's not just the ones you know and care about. You're back at the base on stand-down for a few days, and you start wandering around. It seems like the most miraculous thing on Earth to be able to mosey off anyplace you feel like going. And then you take a turn and by rotten goddamn luck you're right smack at the Graves Registration tent. Hundreds of long dark bags, all zipped up and laid out. Each one full of what's left of some sweet young guy. Some terrific kid who had the same hopes and dreams as you. But . . . it's over for him. For all of them. No more hopes. No more dreams. Just rows and rows of long dark bags. As far as you can see."

Adam stops, takes a deep breath. Then another. Tony waits.

"So," says Adam. "For these very good reasons, you come to the natural conclusion that you're gonna be dead, too. Why wouldn't you be? The only thing you don't know is when. Tonight, in your tent, when a mortar round falls on top of you? Tomorrow, when your idiot commander orders another idiot attack on the same goddamn hill you took last week, dead buddies all over the place, and then gave right back to Charlie? Oh, not then? Well, the next day, for sure.

"You live with that fear. Day and night. It doesn't go away when you're sleeping. If you can call that restless kind of tossing around sleep. No. It just keeps on eating away at you. You live with it, and it gets to be part of you, like your leg or your arm. Pretty soon it isn't something you actually think about. It's just something you know.

And this . . . certainty . . . works its way clear to the back of your brain. And just sits there, waiting. Waiting for what you *know* to finally come true.

"Then—oh, my god. You start counting down those last few days. Seven. Six. Five. Four. Could it be? Could you really . . .? You cut it off fast. You don't dare let that thought take any kind of form. Jesus! *Nobody's* stupid enough to tempt fate like that.

"Three. Two. One. Christ! What's happening? Don't think it! Don't dare think it! Then something screws up. The whole world goes haywire. All your certainty just spins around and flies out the window. You find yourself standing in a line at the airport, shooting the shit with a bunch of other guys. Don't think it! For god's sake, don't think it! It's not too late for the ground to open up and swallow you.

"Instead, you walk up the stairs. You sit down in a seat. The plane takes off. A big-chested blonde with a Hollywood smile serves you a Dr. Pepper, and you finally let it sink in. 'I'm alive,' you think. 'Holy god. It can't be, but it is.' You're alive, and you're headed home. And your mind can't get itself wrapped around that idea. Can't shift gears like that and stop believing what it's believed so . . . completely . . . for so long.

"I . . . Christ! I do all right, pretty much, when I'm awake. When other stuff—work, and you, and fixing supper or washing dishes— takes up all of my attention. But when I go to sleep, when my mind relaxes and my guard goes down, all those . . . visions . . . of things I couldn't leave behind come pouring back in. And while that's happening, I think it's true. That I *am* about to die. This time, for sure.

"And . . . it's not just fear, although god knows that's bad enough. It's guilt. For what I did. What we all were a part of. And . . . because I'm here. Isn't that a hell of a thing? I feel guilty because I'm alive. Because I've got you to love and a life to live, and they've got . . ."

Adam looks away. Tony waits, but Adam doesn't continue. He waits a while longer.

"I know a lot about guilt, Adam," he says at last. "A *lot*. I grew up on a steady diet of it. But, you know . . . I've looked at it, hard, recently. And I think now it's a trap. It makes you believe you can't accept any of the good things that come your way. Because you haven't paid enough for them. And I think . . . if you let it do that to you, you're sunk."

He hesitates.

"What if . . . ," he says. "What if you could see all this as a gift, this extra time, instead of a debt you owe? Like something unexpected that's been handed to you? I've done that with my daughter. With Laura. I hated losing her so much, I thought I'd never be happy again. That I *shouldn't* be happy again. Then I met you, and I am. And I'd be ungrateful if I let sadness for her affect my happiness with you. Do you know what I mean?"

Adam nods.

They're both quiet for a while.

"If . . . ," says Tony. "I don't know. If you had a consciousness after you were dead—which I'm not at all sure if we do or don't—but if we do . . . And if you'd died over there and could still see some other guy, who went through it all, just like you, but for some reason, some stroke of luck, or fate, *didn't* die, and when he got back home, he found himself someone to love, someone who loved him very much, too . . . wouldn't you be glad for him? Wouldn't that be part of why you died? So he wouldn't have to?"

Adam stares at the foot of the bed. Slowly at first, he begins to cry. That whole year's worth of sorrow, shoved far down inside him, starts to come out. And once it starts, he can't stop it. He cries for a long time, not only for the war, but for everything else that's been screwy or hard to understand. Tony just holds him. Rocks him a little and holds him.

"It's all right," Tony says. "I'm here. I'll always be here."

After a while, the crying slows down, and Adam's breathing becomes more regular. He reaches for a Kleenex from the bedside table, wipes his eyes and nose, and nestles back in beside Tony. He closes his eyes, thinking he could never sleep after all that. But he does.

37

So it is that when Irene calls to summon Adam home for Christmas, he says no. She has a hard time grasping what he is saying.

"But we've *always* had Christmas together," she says. "Except for last year, of course, when you were so far away. But always before. And I just assumed we pretty much always would."

"Not this year."

"*Especially* this year, sweetheart. Because of you being back home safe and all. I've made lots of plans already. You know me."

"I was just there, Mother."

"But not for *Christmas.* Christmas is special."

"I agree. That's why I want to spend it with Tony."

There's a silence at the other end of the line.

"Tony?" she finally says.

"The man who's moved into the apartment with me. You can't have forgotten."

"Of course I haven't for*got*ten. I just can't figure out why you'd rather spend Christmas with him than with your own family."

"Can't you?"

"Well . . . no. I can't."

"It's because he *is* my family now. At least I hope to god that's what's going to happen."

"Don't curse, Adam. Not with me."

"I'm not cursing, Mother. I'm *hoping.* There's a big difference."

"But . . . this doesn't make any sense. How could you think of a roommate as *family*?"

"Because . . ." He hesitates. Is he getting in over his head? Too bad if he is. He's not going to back off. Not this time. "Because I love him, Mother. And he loves me."

He hears a sharp intake of breath and presses on before he can waver.

"We're a couple now. Or, I guess I should say, we're trying awfully hard to be. And spending our first Christmas together, just us, seems like a good way to help make that happen."

It's Irene's turn to hesitate. But at least, Adam thinks, she hasn't hung up. Or gone running for her inhaler.

"I'm having a real hard time with this," she says at last.

"Which? Tony? Or my not coming home for Christmas?"

She laughs, a little nervously. God bless her, Adam thinks.

"Both, I guess," she says.

"But . . . ," says Adam. "It doesn't have to be hard. It is what it is, Mother. Whether it's hard or not is up to us. Isn't it?"

"I . . . guess so."

"Can you help me, then? To make it all right?"

She hesitates again. "I don't know," she says.

"Well, that's an honest answer."

"It is, as a matter of fact. I really *don't* know. I . . . I have to say, this is coming kind of out of nowhere for me. I mean, I'd thought *maybe* . . . a time or two. But then I'd decide it was something you'd grow out of."

"What was?"

"Well . . . being . . . you know."

"A sissy?"

She laughs again. "I guess so, yes."

"But I haven't. Grown out of it."

"No. Apparently not."

"And I'm happy about it. It's fine, Mother. It really is."

"Is it?"

"Yes."

"Well, that's good. Considering. But . . ."

"What?"

"Couldn't you come on down for Christmas, anyway? Surely he has a family he could spend it with. And then do all this sorting out after you get back?"

"I don't think so, Mother. I'd be sending him the wrong message."

"I'm not real happy about the one you're sending *me.*"

"No, I suppose not. But that's the way it is."

"Well . . . all I can say is, thank goodness your daddy's down at the golf course. I don't know what on earth I'll tell him. About you not coming."

"What do you mean? Just tell him the truth."

"Oh, I couldn't do that. It'd kill him."

"*Kill* him?"

"He's been so much better recently. Mentally. Now that you're back from over there, and his job here's going so well. But he's still . . . precarious. You know? And I'm afraid this would just . . . tip him over the edge again. We'll have to keep it from him as long as we can."

"But I don't *want* to. Keep it from him."

"Now, you're being selfish here, Adam. Thinking only of yourself and what *you* want. Try thinking about him for a change. You were right to confide in me. I can handle something like this, if I have to. But he . . . I just think it would make things worse again. I *know* it would. For him *and* for me."

Adam wants to object. He knows this is important, and he thinks his way is better. Maybe. But he isn't sure. She could be right. She knows his father a lot better than he does. There's that to consider.

"All right, Mother," he says. "Do what you think is best."

"Remember now," she says, "if you change your mind about Christmas, you just let me know. There's always room for you here."

38

That spring and summer are happy times for Adam and Tony. Adam's nightmares have been growing less frequent—and when they have come, they've been far less intense. At some point, without Adam's being conscious of it, they fade away and don't come anymore at all.

The first sunny weekend in April, they drive out to Shenandoah and check into the Lodge at Big Meadow. They explore the woods, just coming to life, light filtering down through tiny leaves that are a fragile but vivid green. They walk across the meadow, where flowers bloom in clusters of purple and yellow and pink. At the edge of one clearing, they come upon a herd of white-tailed deer and stand motionless watching them graze, until a sound from the road startles the herd and they leap away, tails erect.

After lunch, the two of them go down a narrow trail to Dark Hollow Falls, a torrent of clear water that tumbles and twists as it descends to meet the river's continuation far below. Small groups of hikers come toward them every now and then. Each one smiles and says hello. Toward the middle of the afternoon, they climb a sometimes-rugged trail to the top of Old Rag Mountain. From there, they can see for miles, the fresh carpet of blue-green and gray-green and yellow-green reaching down into the hollows and up the sides of the mountains beyond. As they sit there, saying very little, nobody else around, Tony reaches over and takes Adam's hand in his.

They climb back down and drive to an overlook from which they can see the sun setting behind the mountains on the far side of the valley. The clouds just above the mountain peaks turn bright orange and crimson as they catch the last rays of the sun. Adam and Tony wait quietly as the deep rose of the afterglow spreads across the sky, silhouetting the mountains darkly against it. The dining room at the Lodge is only half full, so they get a table by the windows, from which they watch the twinkling of the lights in the little towns scattered across the valley floor.

After dinner, they walk over to the outdoor amphitheater at the edge of the campground. A nervous young park ranger, a tall, thin-faced woman with a long brown pigtail, lights a bonfire up front and then stands beside it to give a talk, illustrated with slides, that she calls "The Shenandoah of Yesteryear." In a quivering voice, she talks about the old mountain families who lived rugged lives in the hollows all around.

They found the land, though beautiful, to be rocky and far from fertile. Coaxing crops and farm animals to grow was tough going, and they were often hungry and sick, humans and animals alike. But still, these people made cider and quilts, sang songs, and raised their children. Their lives were harsh but full. Having always lived precariously on the very edge of subsistence, they were pushed over into famine by the chestnut blight that swept the area in the 1930s. They were forced by circumstance to leave the mountains and hollows they loved to seek new lives in the flatlands they had always disdained. But they've left their mark, the ranger says. If you look closely as you walk through the woods, long since returned from cropland to forest, you'll see a stone foundation here, a few apple trees there. A piece of split-rail fence. "Their silent way of saying," she concludes, "'Don't forget us, for once we, too, were here.'"

The applause is polite, the children have sat too long and are itching to go, and the audience begins to disperse. Without conferring, Adam and Tony both head down against the crowd toward where the ranger is standing.

"Thank you," says Adam. "That was a wonderful program."

The ranger smiles. "You really think so?"

"Definitely," says Tony, nodding. "We learned a lot."

"It's my first one," she says, "so I wasn't sure."

"Well," says Adam, "you made those times come alive for all of us. You should be very proud."

"Gosh," she says, maybe blushing, maybe only reflecting the light of the bonfire. "I really appreciate that. It means a lot."

"Good luck," says Tony. "You're going to be a fine ranger."

"You bet," says Adam.

– 39 –

As that next Christmas approaches, Adam thinks, why not? He wants his parents to know Tony, and, of course, wants Tony to know them. He's feeling confident enough in the strength of their love for each other to risk it. Well, almost enough.

"But only five days," he tells Tony. "That's the limit. Any more than that, we're pressing our luck."

They fly down to San Antonio the day before Christmas Eve. The airports are jammed, the planes are packed solid, their connections are tight, and they're both feeling frazzled when they arrive in the early afternoon. But even thinking of taking a rest is out of the question. Irene is agog with excitement when she meets them at the airport. She tells them right off that she's got the tree all set up in the living room (an artificial one, Adam is sure; she discovered long ago that real ones just set off her asthma), and she's been waiting eagerly for 'you boys' to get here before even starting to decorate it.

She's in a super-cheerful, almost manic mood. Adam knows exactly where it's coming from. She's not sure how Sam is going to react to Tony's presence among them, and just in case he decides to be glum, she wants to pump the general atmosphere up to such a high level that even a lack of enthusiasm on Sam's part won't be able to pull it down *too* far.

As it happens, she needn't have worried. Sam is polite, almost cordial, as Tony gives his hand a hearty, manly shake. And Tony is splendid. He tells Sam that his accounting firm is renovating an old townhouse in Georgetown to create new office space, and he wants to ask Sam some structural questions that he's not sure those Washington engineers know the right answers to. If, that is, it isn't an intrusion. Sam, mightily pleased, says it is not.

131

As Tony passes through the living room, the things he notices and comments on—a painting by one of Irene's cousins, some Pueblo Indian pottery, a dried-flower arrangement she did herself—are, by some uncanny radar, those that mean the most to Irene. She beams and smiles and gives Tony a detailed history of each object, to which he listens intently.

Irene puts them in the room Adam and his brother Dwayne used to share, at the back of the house. Well, Adam thinks, I guess that's an acceptable compromise—same room, twin beds. He knows what Irene doesn't know. That, even though they're both big men, they'll sleep together in one bed or the other, being careful to mess up the unused bed before morning.

After the tree is decorated and the lights are lit and the appliquéd stockings that say 'Irene,' 'Sam,' 'Adam,' and 'Tony' are hung at the edge of a window sill, Tony goes and sits beside Sam in front of the TV and watches a stock car race with him. Although Adam is absolutely certain Tony cares very little, if anything, about the race, still he sits patiently and asks Sam apparently intelligent questions about weight and speed and carburetion ratios. Adam feels such a wave of love for Tony he can barely resist going over and hugging him.

As soon as Irene realizes that Tony is occupied, she pulls Adam into the kitchen. She takes cups of coffee out to Sam and Tony, then makes tea for her and Adam. They sit, cozily, at the kitchen table, Irene filling Adam in on family gossip. Adam has already heard a general outline of much of it, but it's the details, the kind that can be dwelt on during long chats over cups of tea, that warm Irene's heart.

She starts with Sam's side of the family, a misunderstanding she's had with Nathan's wife that kept her from going over to their annual Christmas party the week before. Sam went, but didn't stay long. Seemed to have enjoyed it all right, but didn't have much to say about it. Then, the question of whether to put Sam's mother into a nursing home or not. And, if not, just who's going to be willing to take care of her, off up there in Slaton.

Irene moves on, after a while, to things that are troubling her closer to home. She'd hoped they could've had a bigger gathering, since he and Tony were going to be here, like she'd been used to all her life.

Lots of her own family around. But Carolyn is off traveling in India, some sort of conference on healing by meditation, leaving her husband to take care of the kids. And Dwayne's second marriage seems to be a bit rocky these days. He thought this was going to be the one, but storm clouds are gathering.

At one point, she does take time out to say what a nice man Tony seems to be. So polite. And so good-looking. Tall and . . . solid.

"He is that," says Adam.

"And he and Sam appear to be enjoying each other's company," she says. "I can't tell you how relieved I am to see it."

Adam wants to say, "Yeah. I guess it's not going to kill Daddy, after all." But, he doesn't.

Christmas Eve is full. They go out to a steakhouse with a Gold Rush theme for dinner. They drive around town looking at the houses with the most extensive lights and the most elaborate decorations, Irene navigating with the help of a map she cut out of last Sunday's paper. They end up at the eleven o'clock candlelight service at the big Methodist church downtown. The church is full of evergreens and poinsettias, and a brass quintet plays along with the carols. At midnight, in the darkened church, as candles are being lit throughout the congregation, Adam feels Tony reach over and lightly rub the side of his leg.

Irene knocks on their door to wake them at seven the next morning so they can all gather in the living room before breakfast. The stockings hanging on the window sill are now bulging. In his, Adam finds an orange, an apple, a bag of peanuts, a tangerine, some Hershey kisses, and a tiny bottle of cologne.

The presents from Irene are exactly, evenly matched. A sweater for Adam, a sweater for Tony. A package of three white T-shirts for Adam, a package of three white T-shirts for Tony. A Mexican-food cookbook for Adam, a Russian-food cookbook for Tony.

"I hope I got your sizes right, Tony," Irene says, eagerly expectant. "From Adam's description."

"You did," says Tony, smiling. "Everything's perfect."

Sam's gifts are more eclectic. A wristwatch and a book of Maupassant stories for Adam, a necktie for Tony.

Two days later, while everybody is still smiling at each other, they all head out to the airport. After Adam has hugged and kissed both his parents, Tony kisses Irene's cheek and thanks her for all she's done. He holds out his hand to Sam. Sam hesitates, just a bit, then pulls Tony close to him and gives him a hug.

Late in June, Tony's accounting firm sends him to a conference in Chicago. He's gone only five days, but it feels much longer to Adam. When Tony gets back, they make love every chance they get.

Local farmers have started bringing their produce in from the country to the street outside Eastern Market, and a Saturday morning walk to buy fresh fruits and vegetables becomes a routine they both look forward to. One Saturday, though, on the way back, as they're passing the little park near 9th Street, Tony says, "Could we sit here for a minute? I've . . . got something to tell you."

"Why here?"

"I'm not sure. It just . . . seems better."

"All right," says Adam, trying to ignore the uneasy feeling that's pinching at his chest.

They sit side by side on a little bench, Tony staring at the sidewalk.

"Well?" says Adam. Although he'd much rather just forget the conversation and go on home.

"I . . ." Tony rubs his forehead. "You have to go see your doctor. Get a blood test right away."

"Why?" says Adam, absolutely certain he doesn't want to hear why.

"To see if you have syphilis or not."

Adam knows the answer before he asks, but he asks anyway. "Why would I have syphilis?"

"Because I do."

Adam nods. "Chicago. Right?"

"Right," says Tony. "Just some . . . guy, Adam. That last night we were there. I . . . well, that's what happened. But it's easy to cure, the doctor says. When you catch it this soon."

"Easy to cure," says Adam. "What a blessing."

He wants to hit Tony. It's the most violent feeling he's had since Vietnam. He wants to pick something up and hit Tony across the side of his head. But the only thing handy is the sack of groceries at his feet, and he'd just end up smashing the tomatoes.

How could he do this? thinks Adam. How could he ruin the wonderful thing they've built up between them? Well . . . there's only one way to find out. Ask him.

"How could you do this?" says Adam.

Tony is still staring at the sidewalk.

"Habit, I guess," he says. "It's what I did before. Just . . . take advantage of opportunities when they arose. He was . . . available. And you were a long ways away."

"Right. Sitting here loving you and missing you."

Tony doesn't respond.

Adam feels dirty inside. A rotten little bacteria has passed from some . . . *stranger,* through Tony, into him. Into *his* body. It's awful. Repulsive. Still . . . it's not like Adam hasn't been asking for it. He could have caught something from any one of that long line of guys before Tony. Any one of them. But that was different. None of them meant anything. Not really. This does.

Tony looks up.

"Would you have told me," asks Adam, "if it weren't for the syphilis?"

"I doubt it," says Tony. "No."

Adam sees the pain and confusion in Tony's eyes. He wants to reach out and touch him, make contact, renew the sense of oneness that's been so abruptly ripped apart. But he's too angry. My god. Too angry. That realization makes Adam glad, and gives him strength somehow. He's angry, not hurt. Aggrieved, not victimized. I've learned a lot from you, Tony, he thinks. You bastard.

"Will you forgive me?" asks Tony. "Do you think?"

Adam just stares. He knows the answer to that one, too. Of course he will. What other answer could there be? Lose Tony over some stupid one-night stand? Not likely. But he won't give that answer too easily. Or too soon.

"Probably," he says. "Eventually. But not right away."

Pain again fills Tony's eyes.

"You won't give up on me," he says. "Will you?"

"No," says Adam. "I won't do that."

— 41 —

Adam's blood test comes back negative. He has another test three weeks later, and it's negative, too. Tony finishes his regimen of penicillin shots and is pronounced cured. The only residue that's left is the tension between them and Adam's lingering disappointment.

Now, in mid-October, Tony is gone again. To a meeting in San Francisco.

San Francisco! thinks Adam, slamming a dish into the drainer. Gay heaven. Doesn't anybody ever meet in Des Moines?

"There's nothing I can do about it," Tony had said. "I have to go. It's my account."

"So go," Adam had said.

Last night's phone conversation was brief. Tony had arrived there late, after missing his connection in Dallas, and was cranky and irritable.

"Look, I'm really beat," he'd said. "I'll talk to you tomorrow night. I should be in a better mood by then. I *hope!*"

"What's a good time?"

"Well . . . midnight your time is nine here. I should be able to manage that all right. Unless it's too late for you?"

"No. That'll be fine."

Adam finishes his supper dishes, reads a while, writes a birthday card to a cousin, waters the spider plant, reads some more.

Midnight comes and goes. 12:15. 12:30. Adam takes off his clothes. Brushes his teeth. Washes his face. Turns on the TV. Flops on the bed. Everything is dumb. He turns it off. Picks up his book. Puts it down. 1:05.

I knew it, he thinks. Goddammit.

He puts his jeans and shirt back on. He slips on his shoes and jacket by the front door and looks at his watch. 1:15. The bastard, he thinks.

'I'll always be here.' Bullshit! He goes out the door. He drives straight down 8th Street, turns right toward the Lost and Found, and finds a parking place two blocks away.

At that relatively late hour on a weeknight, the bar is lively but not jammed. Adam orders a Coke, no rum, and stands beside the dance floor watching the couples gyrate.

What am I doing? he thinks, and turns to go.

The son of a bitch, he thinks, and turns back.

"Hi," says a voice to his right. He looks down at a young Hispanic man with beautiful brown skin, shiny black hair, deep-set black eyes, and a thin mustache.

Uh-oh, thinks Adam.

"My name is Salvador." Just a touch of an accent.

"Adam."

"Would you like to dance?"

"Sure."

The song that's playing is a fast one. They turn and sway, touching hands only occasionally. Each time they do, though, Adam feels a spark of electricity. When that song ends, a slow one begins. Without saying anything, Salvador moves close to Adam and wraps his arms around him. He rests his head on Adam's chest, and they move leisurely in slow, languid circles. Adam feels Salvador's erection pressing against his leg. His own, equally hard, presses back. Adam closes his eyes, lays his cheek on Salvador's head, and drifts. They could hardly be any closer, but Adam still tightens his arms around those strong shoulders and that slender waist. He slides his hand down past Salvador's belt onto a firm roundness that sends a tremor of desire up through him. Salvador murmurs something and moves his hips sideways across Adam's. Around they go, slowly, slowly, eyes closed, both breathing fast. Adam's erection has grown so full it hurts.

When the song ends, Salvador moves back a step and looks up. His lips are full and parted just a little. Adam leans down and kisses them.

"Will you come home with me?" asks Salvador.

"Yes."

Salvador reaches for Adam's hand and leads the way toward the door. In the light of the entryway, he stops and smiles up at Adam.

Adam feels a jolt and steps backward. Memories come flooding in. Same entryway. Different smile.

"Oh, god," he says. "I can't."

Salvador's eyes widen, and his smile goes away. "What do you mean?" he says.

"I can't go with you. Oh, it's not *you*. Please believe me. You're wonderful. I wish . . . you're wonderful."

"But . . . no?"

"No. I've got somebody at home, you see. Well, not *tonight*. That's the problem. But we're . . ."

"It's okay."

"Thanks. I don't want you to . . ."

"It's okay. Only . . ."

"What?"

"If you change your mind . . . sometime . . . will you come here? And look for me?"

Adam puts his hand on the side of Salvador's neck. The electricity is still crackling.

"Oh, yes," he says. "I can promise you that."

Halfway down the block, Adam turns around. Salvador has gone back inside.

The phone is ringing as Adam walks in through the front door.

"Tony?"

"Thank god you're there. I've been calling and calling."

"I'm fine."

"My boss wanted me to meet some people—wouldn't you know?—and we all went out for drinks. I just . . . I couldn't get away to look for a phone, till . . ."

"Don't worry. Everything's fine."

"Where were you?"

"I went out for a drive."

"So late?"

"Yeah. I just felt like it."

There's a pause.

"You were mad at me," says Tony. "Weren't you?"

"Yes."

"For not calling when I said I would."

"Yes. But it's all right now."

"I'm being good, Adam. I promise you. That stupid thing in Chicago scared the hell out of me, and I haven't even thought of . . ."

"I know, hon. Don't worry. It was just *my* turn to be a little stupid."

"Only a little?"

"Only a little."

"Just the drive?"

"Yeah. Just the drive. Well . . . plus a kind of a bonus."

"What's that?"

"Realizing you're it for me. For better or for worse, as they say."

"That's what they say, all right."

"You're back in your room now?"

"Finally."

"Well . . . we should both get some sleep, don't you think?"

"Good idea. I'll call you again in the morning."

"You'll have to get up awfully early, won't you? To catch me before I go off to work?"

"I'll set the alarm and go back to sleep."

"You're sure?"

"Positive."

"I don't . . . I mean, that's only a few hours from now."

"So?"

"But . . ." Adam stops. "You're right," he says. "So?"

They both laugh. A comfortable, easy laugh.

"Adam?"

"Yes?"

"You're *really* all right?"

"Couldn't be better."

The rest of that winter and into the spring, Adam and Tony walk
around Capitol Hill looking at houses. They're not picking out one to
buy, necessarily. They just enjoy discussing which ones they like and
why. Their tastes in this area, Adam is delighted to discover, are
very much the same. They both like old houses, the older the better.
They like two-story houses, porches out front, gingerbread trim.
They make a point of walking at night every now and then, so they
can see into rooms that are lighted up.

One Saturday morning late in March, on their way back from Eastern Market, they stop on the sidewalk at the same time. A 'For Sale'
sign has gone up in the yard of a house they've both admired. It's in
need of care and attention, it's true. The paint on the brick front is
peeling, and some of the wooden trim around the porch is missing,
but underneath all that, it's graceful and nicely proportioned. A faded
lady of dignity and breeding, just a little down on her luck, tempo-
rarily.

Tony calls the number on the sign, and an agent says she'll meet
them at the house at two-thirty. As soon as he walks in, Adam knows
he could be happy living here. It's a standard turn-of-the-century row
house—he's been in dozens of them around Capitol Hill. Entryway,
with stairs on the left that go up to the second floor, kitchen back behind, nice-sized living room through an archway to the right, dining
room behind that. Bathroom upstairs over the kitchen, big bedrooms
over the living room and dining room, a much smaller bedroom above
the entryway. Full basement down a stairway through a door in the
kitchen. Compact and efficient and comfortable.

But this house has some real pluses. A fireplace in the living room,
with an ornate, dark wood mantelpiece around it, carved wooden col-
umns down each side and a beveled mirror across the top. Floor-to-

ceiling bookcases to the right and left. A large backyard, large for Capitol Hill, where most yards are tiny. And, best of all, sunporches enclosed by a wall of windows across the back of both floors—the downstairs one a ready-made breakfast room and the upstairs one, just off the back bedroom, a perfect spot for more bookcases, a lamp, and a big overstuffed reading chair. Adam loves the place and, as the agent talks with Tony about plumbing and furnaces and electric panels, has already started placing furniture and listing in his mind the things they'll need to buy. Dining table and chairs. Larger sofa. Bed for the guest room (they already have an extra mattress). *And,* Tony's Oriental rug can be unfolded and laid out flat across the living room floor. Tony, the more practical of the two in most situations, certainly this one, sits down that evening with Adam to go over the pros and cons. Adam, stuck firmly in the pro column, listens patiently to the cons, nods while Tony talks about foundations and roofs and missing storm windows, as if those were things Adam cared the slightest bit about, and says at every opportunity, "I like it. I want us to live there."

What decides things for Tony, the accountant, is the price. This neighborhood, like so many others around it, is changing. Middle-class whites are moving in, a good many of them gay, buying these wonderful old houses, fixing them up, painting them, planting azaleas near the house and tulips and hyacinths out by the front sidewalk, displacing poorer black families in the process. Tony calculates what this upgrading will mean for the neighborhood over the next few years, and ends up seeing the house as a good investment. Adam thinks of long rainy Saturdays reading on that upstairs sunporch, maybe even doing a little writing, and sees the house as home.

They've been pooling all their money for months. Tony suggested it after he found the constant dividing up ("I bought the groceries, and you paid for the cleaning, so you owe me eight dollars and forty cents") to be a monumental irritation. Adam is grateful for the sense of unity this has brought to their lives. In any event, their combined assets—bank account, savings, investments—impress the mortgage company. Their application is approved with only a slight delay, and the house is theirs. Closing in three weeks, after which they can move in.

Adam and Tony, the only whites on the block so far, grow more and more fond of their neighbors as the weeks go by. On one side is Horace, a big, hearty black man who keeps a large collection of used appliances, mostly stoves and refrigerators, in his backyard. He moved to Washington from South Carolina with his wife and two children, got a good job as a janitor at the junior high school over on Pennsylvania Avenue, fathered another child, bought this house, had it made. He only took drugs for a little while, he says, just long enough to lose his job, and then his wife and kids. He got himself straightened out, but it was too late. All he managed to hold onto was his house, and even that is precarious. He does odd jobs all over Capitol Hill, whatever he can find, and takes in boarders, anywhere from two or three to sometimes seven or eight men and women who spend the night in sleeping bags scattered around the house and wander in and out during the day.

Horace likes Adam and Tony. Decides they're brothers and admires the fact that they get along well enough to live together like this, after they're grown up and all. You wouldn't catch him living with any of his brothers. Hell, no. Sisters neither. Too mean and sassy. He comes over to fill buckets with water whenever he misses too many payments and his gets cut off. He sees Tony doing fix-up chores around the house and starts bringing by things he's 'found.' Half-empty cans of paint. Scraps of lumber. A sack of nails of many sizes. Tony thanks him and uses as much of it as he can.

"You bof my frien's," Horace says proudly. "No sum'bitch gon' mess wif you while *I'm* aroun'."

On the other side of them are Mr. and Mrs. Tatum, an elderly black couple who've lived in that house for fifty years. Bought it after their second child was born and raised all four of their children there. She's a tiny woman, with a warm smile and genteel manners. She sits on her front porch most days, from early spring to late fall. She knows pretty much everybody who passes, many of whom stop to chat, some from down on the sidewalk, some up on the porch. Mr. Tatum is not much bigger than his wife, small and wrinkled. He, too, sits out on the porch whenever he can, saying very little, nodding to those who wave, smoking his pipe and an occasional cigar.

Across the street are the Jacksons, younger than the Tatums by ten or fifteen years. His father was a sharecropper in Georgia, he says, and look how far he's come. Retired from the local transit company, where he rose to be head of a maintenance crew. Top man. And not only that, shop steward for the union. His daddy woulda been *proud.* Now he looks out for the neighborhood, mostly, picking up stray cups and empty soda bottles and candy wrappers, carrying the Tatums' garbage out to the curb every Tuesday and Friday, telling the rowdy groups of teenagers who drift through to just keep moving along.

Mrs. Jackson, Mavis, is round and happy and full of life. She still works as a receptionist for a dentist up in Northeast and walks off every weekday morning toward the bus stop, laughing and waving and shouting advice to whoever is out at that hour. "Cut those petunias way back, and they'll keep bloomin' clear on till fall." "Don't be paintin' that trim till you got the old coat scraped off good. Might's well not bother if you're not gonna do it right." "Uh-*uhnh*. No, ma'am. You don't wanna be wearin' them high pointy heels. You'll be all crippled up, girl, b'fore you're thirty. You listen to me, now."

Next to the Jacksons are Esther Brown and her two boys, Tyrone and Gus, for Augustus. They're nine and seven, far younger than her three other children, now grown and gone. She worries about her babies, having to be by themselves after school for nearly three hours before she can get home from work. Across town at the DC government's office of personnel, where she's a file clerk. But the Tatums and Mr. Jackson keep an eye out for the boys, somebody checking each afternoon to be sure they're back from school all right and not getting into any mischief.

Adam and Tony get to know the boys gradually, Tyrone first, then the much shyer Gus. Tyrone is a pint-sized Mavis Jackson, full of assurance, his mouth never stopping.

"Want me to help you wash that car? I know all about how to wash cars. Just 'cause we don't have one don't mean I don't know how. We did have once—a Buick. Back when my pappy was alive. Blue an' silver. The silver was the chrome. All over. Snazzy car. You like that word? Snazzy? I know lotsa good words. Equanimity. Ain't that somethin'? Equanimity. An' munificent. Want me to spell it? M-U-N-I-F-I-... C'mon, man. Lemme show you how to use that sponge. You missin' places all over. See right here? An' that spot there?"

Gus all the time hanging back, watching with wide eyes, listening. Adam sits on the curb beside him sometimes and talks to him, while Tyrone and Tony do their verbal sparring.

"What grade are you in?" asks Adam.

"Second," says Gus, so softly Adam can barely hear him.

"Do you like it?"

"Some."

"What classes are you taking?"

"Things."

"Like what?"

He shrugs. "Things."

"What's your favorite?"

"Basketball."

It's Tony who suggests they take the boys places, show them the city. Adam is hesitant at first, unsure of how Esther will feel about letting her young sons spend so much time with the two of them. But, when he and Tony go over to ask, she smiles and claps her hands and says it's a fine idea. Think what adventures like that will mean to her babies. She seems, like Horace and the Tatums and the Jacksons, to appreciate the way Adam and Tony have entered into the life of the block. Seems to look on them as neighbors, whatever else they may or may not be.

They start taking the boys off on a Saturday or a Sunday, once a month for sure, sometimes twice. To places Tyrone and Gus have never been. Up to the zoo. Over to the Smithsonian. Out to the Arboretum. The boys love the Arboretum. Not the trees so much, they look just like trees to them, but the open spaces. Room to run and shriek and fall down and chase each other.

Tyrone has to be careful not to run as much as Gus, though. He has sickle cell anemia, which hurts him so bad sometimes he can't go to school. Has to stay home, calm in bed, so his blood can flow quietly and smoothly, his funny-shaped blood cells slipping past each other instead of getting all tangled up and causing that awful pain. He never complains. Just goes off to school whenever he can, and lies in bed at home when his mother says he has to.

Esther stays with him sometimes, but mostly she can't. She'd lose her job. So Mrs. Tatum goes over and sits with him. Or Mr. Jackson looks in. Or Tyrone's older sister comes by to check. Every now and then, Adam makes excuses at work—he never uses his sick leave any other way, so why not?—and spends the day with Tyrone. He reads to him (Tyrone loves *Kidnapped* and *Hiawatha*), helps him with his arithmetic, tries to keep him quiet, which isn't easy.

That next summer, on the Fourth of July, Adam and Tony take the boys to the Mall to watch the fireworks. They arrive early in the afternoon, with blankets and a cooler full of sandwiches, potato salad, and soda, so they can get a spot just down the hill from the Washington Monument, directly under the evening's main event. They all sit a while, take turns going off to look at the rest of the crowd, eat their picnic supper, and lie back on the blankets laughing and joking. A few of the people passing by stop and stare or turn to whisper to each other. Troubled by this casual, and congenial, mixing of blacks and whites, Adam figures. He'd like to say something to them, try to fluster them if he can. But he doesn't. Why bother? If Tyrone and Gus are noticing, they give no sign. Why call it to their attention? Adam just wishes jerks like that would stay in the suburbs where they belong.

Soon after nine, the show begins. Suddenly, with bursts of red, green, gold, high up. Bangs and whistles. Descending layers of color that explode, then explode again, and again. Tyrone can't stay still. He jumps, shouts, claps, wiggles, whistles, shouts some more. Tony tries to calm him down, but it's no use. Gus's reaction is more intense. He watches, eyes wide, mouth open, turning his head quickly toward the next burst.

On and on it goes. So many shapes. Such marvelous sounds. Fast, then slow, then fast again. When the finale begins, a rapid-fire sequence of uninterrupted noise and color, it's hard to say which of the kids—the two young novices or the two older veterans—are the more excited. They all shout and clap and whistle and wave their hands.

Then it's over. A second or two of silence, after which everybody starts cheering and applauding again. The four of them stand up and begin folding the blankets.

Tyrone is shaking his head.

"Would you just look," he says, "what we been missin'."

– 43 –

Both of them are happy with their work. Tony's intelligence—and diligence—are admired and rewarded by his bosses. He handles their most difficult, and therefore most lucrative, accounts, for which they pay him handsomely. He wishes, from time to time, that he could be doing something more creative, but, he tells Adam, he's not sure exactly what that might be.

Adam moves from news releases to advance work for the Secretary of Transportation to the department's quarterly magazine. These moves are accompanied by promotions that come with satisfying regularity. Adam finds that he loves everything about magazines—the research, the writing, laying out the pages, even proofreading, at which he is very good—but most enjoyable of all is the writing. It revives in him a long-dormant desire to write fiction, to create a real book of his own, like those he has loved since he was a child. He makes a stab at it once or twice, but can't quite figure out how to write magazine articles all day and then shift gears to something so completely different after he gets home.

Tony's diligence includes keeping an eye on his mother. He's gotten into the habit of driving up to Long Island to spend the weekend with her, not every month, usually, but every other month for sure. He's been handling her finances ever since his father died a few years back, and he also likes to see for himself that she is all right. Elena lives alone now, in a one-story, two-bedroom tract house that looks very much like its many neighbors. Their old potato farm, the southwest corner of which is only a couple of blocks away, is quickly being covered with other look-alike housing developments and little strip malls.

Once on the go from before sunup till long after dark, Elena now spends most of every day sitting beside her front window. She watches the neighbors going to and from work, the postman arriving between two and three, usually closer to three, the garbage men on Mondays and Thursdays, and an occasional UPS truck. Although she can't actually see what's left of the farm, she knows that it's not far away, and she can feel its presence, in a way.

Three of her children still live nearby, as do some of their children and, in the case of the eldest, some grandchildren. But when Tony comes, it's a special treat for her.

Adam goes up with Tony as often as he can. He loves Elena, and she makes it clear that she loves him. He's sure she doesn't know exactly what it is that he represents in Tony's life, but she can see that he cares a lot about Tony and tries to make him happy, and that's enough for her. She shows her appreciation by patting Adam's arm and nodding at him from time to time.

Elena fascinates Adam. He enjoys sitting with her, for hours sometimes, listening to her stories. About Russia. About coming to America. About the farm. About Tony.

"Did you ever go back to Russia?" Adam asks.

"No."

"Why not? Later, after the kids were grown and you could afford it."

"Where I've always wanted to go is Ireland," she says, answering instead a question that *wasn't* asked. "It's so beautiful. Green. Beautiful."

"But you've never actually gotten there either?"

"No."

"Why is that?"

"Did you ever see it? Ireland?"

"I haven't, no."

"I've seen it before, on the TV. Green. Beautiful."

Adam asked Tony once if they couldn't take her to Ireland sometime.

"No way," says Tony. "They wouldn't let her back in."

"Why not?"

"We can't get her a passport."

"*What?*"

"She's not a U.S. citizen. No citizenship, no passport."

"What do you mean she's not? She votes. She always tells me, proudly, who she's voted for."

"I know. That's why we can't ever tell her. That she's not a citizen. She thinks she is. She hasn't missed a vote for as long as I can remember. Since I was a little kid. Somehow, obviously, she got registered to vote. But when I checked, years ago, there was no record of her citizenship."

"Too busy cooking, I'll bet," says Adam.

Tony laughs. "I'll bet. But we can't tell her now. She'd be horrified. Doing something against the rules and regulations all those years. So . . . no Ireland."

Elena still cooks—whenever Tony and Adam are there, at any rate. Enormous quantities of food. Borscht, kielbasa, big roasts, and mounds of mashed potatoes, turkey-barley soup, pork chops with sauerkraut. And she worries about whether Tony and Adam are getting enough to eat. She's certain they are not.

She worries about so many things. Cold, rain, heat, damp, mildew, frozen pipes, snake bites where there are no snakes, rapacious squirrels that she's sure are going to eat through her electric wires and set fire to her house, the furnace in the basement, which could explode at any moment.

She worries about time, especially being *on* time, which to her means being early. Hours early. On Saturday night, without fail, she asks Tony what time he thinks he'll leave the next morning, so he'll be absolutely home well before dark.

"It's only five hours, Mama," Tony says. "If we leave at nine, we'll be there by two."

"Better to make it eight. For the safe side. You never know about the traffic."

"Okay, Mama. We'll leave at eight."

"So . . ." She nods. "You should be already on the road, then, by seven-thirty. Just to be sure."

The next morning, every next morning, Tony and Adam, sleeping together in the basement, hear the springs on Elena's bed, in the room above them, creak as she sits up. They hear the thud of her footsteps as she moves along the hall, into the kitchen, over to the door down to the basement. They hear the door open.

"Tony?" she yells.

"Yes, Mama."

"Five o'clock."

"We're not leaving till seven-thirty."

"Seven-thirty?"

"Yes, Mama. Go back to bed."

Back she goes. They fall asleep.

Creaks above them. Thuds. The door.

"Tony?"

"Yes, Mama."

"Five-thirty."

And she worries about her hair. It was long and thick once, and shiny. She'd been proud of it, and her husband had loved it. Loved to touch it. At the end, after his stroke when she knew he was going, he'd said, "Promise me one thing, Lanoushka. Promise me you'll never cut your hair."

"I promise," she'd said. And she hasn't. She's watched it get less thick, less shiny, a pathetic shadow of what it once was. But she hasn't cut it. It would be so much easier to take care of shorter. The way other women wear theirs. But she can't cut it, ever. She promised.

Adam sees her sitting, heavily, as if a huge magnet were pulling her down toward the floor, in front of her mirror. She slides her brush through the thinning, whitening hair, braids it, twists it into a bun, and sighs.

Occasionally, when the thought occurs to him, Adam tries to remember if he's ever seen Elena smile.

— 44 —

Tony's first depression comes as a huge shock to Adam. He's never experienced anything like it. Not his mother's quirky ups and downs. Not his father's moody silences. Those were fleeting and soon gone. Nothing has prepared him for the intensity of this. Tony retreats to a place that's unreachable, and won't come out.

Adam has no idea where it came from. They're on their way to the circus. At the DC Armory out by the stadium, not far from their house. Adam is like a kid about it. He hasn't been to a circus in years, and has never seen the biggest and best of them all. Ringling Brothers. He's been antsy with anticipation for weeks.

The night finally comes. Tony drives, and Adam chatters as they go. About work. About some old friends he's bumped into. About nothing, really. Then, as they're nearing the Armory, the atmosphere inside the car grows chilly, compressed into something thick and claustrophobic. Adam is confused. Is he imagining it?

"Tony?" he says.

No answer.

Adam looks over. Tony is staring straight ahead.

"Tony?" Adam says again.

No answer.

"What is it, hon?" says Adam. "What's happening?"

No answer. Tony stares straight ahead.

Adam is frantic. He can't bear the cold, unyielding silence, so he starts chattering again. Just look at all this traffic. Like rush hour. Wonder if we'll ever find a parking place. Quite a crowd over there at the door. But the chatter is even worse. Hollow. Foolish sounding. He lets the silence swallow them up again.

Tony stares, glancing at cars and pedestrians, never at Adam. The air around them feels so heavy Adam wonders how they can breathe.

Tony turns into one of the huge parking lots, follows the directions of policemen with flashlights and whistles, pulls into a parking place. He turns off the engine, still not looking at Adam.

"We might as well not go, hon," says Adam, "if you're not going to enjoy it."

No answer. Tony gets out, slams the door, locks it, starts walking away. Adam gets out, locks his door, runs to catch up with Tony. They wait in line, saying nothing. Tony asks for the tickets they've reserved, pays for them, hands one to Adam, walks away. Adam follows him. They find their seats, Adam sits in one of them, Tony goes back down the steps and disappears. Adam sits there, stunned, confused, beginning to tremble. He tenses his muscles, clenches his fists, wishes he were anywhere but here.

Twenty minutes till time to start. He looks in every direction for Tony but doesn't see him anywhere. He gets up, goes down the steps, wanders around. No Tony. Should he leave? How can he? He can't go home without Tony. He goes back to their seats, hoping. Tony's not there. The performance begins. Loud music. Bright lights. Brilliant colors and sparkling glitter fill the place.

The irony is overwhelming. Hilarity all around him. Clowns with huge grins slapping along in their enormous shoes, the band playing maniacally, sequined acrobats twirling and leaping high up near the ceiling, children screaming with delight. And Adam sitting in a daze, unable to comprehend what's going on.

There's nothing he can do. Nothing that he can think of. But he can't imagine just continuing to sit here like this. He wants to go home—the laughter is unbearable—but how can he go without Tony? And he has no idea where Tony might be.

Hours later, the performance mercifully comes to an end. Still no sign of Tony. Adam follows the crowd down the steps, out through the door, across the parking lot. Tony is standing beside the car. When he sees Adam coming, he opens his door, gets in, reaches over to unlock the other side. Adam gets in and closes the door. Tony starts the car and backs out.

"Did you watch it at all?" asks Adam.

No answer.

"I hated being there without you, hon," says Adam. "I wanted us to see it together."

No answer.

"I love you, don't you know that? I don't want there ever to be things like this between us."

No answer.

Tony parks just down the block from the house. They go inside. Tony walks up the stairs, goes into the guest room, and closes the door. Adam lies wide-eyed on their half-empty bed, unable to sleep.

The next morning, around seven-thirty, Adam gets up, knocks on the guest room door, hears no reply, pleads, cries a little, goes off to work. He comes home, knocks again, pleads. This time, when there is no response, he opens the door a crack. He has to know if Tony is still there, still alive.

"Go away," Tony says.

From then on, after he knocks and gets no answer, mornings and afternoons, Adam listens at the door, long enough to hear a cough or the creaking of the bed. These sounds are the only relief he gets.

The days go by—two, three, slowly, agonizingly—and Adam doesn't see Tony at all. He doesn't know if Tony has called his office, maybe even gone in while Adam is away. If he's eating or bathing. Adam sees no signs of either around the house. He's never been more miserable in his life.

On the fourth morning, when Adam knocks, Tony says, "Come in."

Adam opens the door. The curtains are closed, and the room is dark. Adam can barely see Tony lying on the bed, fully clothed. The air smells stale, sour.

"I'm hungry," says Tony.

Adam goes over, sits on the bed beside him, bends down and kisses him. He feels the prickles on Tony's cheeks.

"Are you all right?" asks Adam.

"Better," says Tony. "But . . . very hungry."

"I'll make you a nice breakfast, okay?"

"Okay."

"You'll be down soon?"

"Soon as I shower and shave. And brush my teeth."

Adam kisses him again, gets up, and goes downstairs.

Tony doesn't bring the matter up, and Adam is afraid to. He airs out the guest room, changes the sheets, puts in a little room deodorizer. He and Tony drift back toward normalcy. They laugh, they make love, they go off on Saturdays or Sundays to Baltimore, Annapolis, the National Gallery, sometimes taking Tyrone and Gus, sometimes not. They go up to Long Island for the weekend. Adam is happy to pretend it never happened.

Then it happens again, about ten months later, and it's just as bad. They're out to dinner with friends, a gay couple around the corner. Halfway through the meal, Adam can feel Tony retreating. Tony stares at his plate. Doesn't respond when he's spoken to. Adam and the hosts exchange glances and do their best to keep conversation going.

Soon after dessert, Adam says he thinks they'll head on home, which they do in total silence. Once again, Tony walks up the stairs, goes into the guest room, and closes the door. Once again, Adam knocks, pleads, cries, spends sleepless nights feeling helpless. This one lasts five days. Tony comes out. Nothing is said.

About a week later, though, one evening as Adam and Tony are sitting in easy chairs beside the fire in the living room reading, Tony closes his book and says, "We need to talk."

Oh, god, thinks Adam. I don't want to.

"About what?" he says.

"Me," says Tony. "My depressions. Will you help me? Please?"

"Of course, hon. You know I will. If I can."

"You can."

"How?"

Tony hesitates. "I thought maybe they were gone—*hoped* they were—when I went those couple of years without one. Hoped you wouldn't ever have to deal with them. But they're not gone. Obviously. So . . ."

He rubs his forehead.

"I can't handle them by myself," he says. "You have to help me."

"But how?" says Adam. "I don't know anything about this stuff."

"By . . . we have to grab them as soon as they start. That's the only thing that'll work. Don't let me slip away. *Make* me talk to you."

"But I tried to. Didn't I? Both times?"

"Not hard enough, no. Not the right way. That mousy, teary 'Please tell me what's wrong' baloney is never going to work. I hate that. It's so . . . wimpy."

Adam laughs. "Then what?" he asks.

"Be firm. *Make* me talk."

"Like you did me. About the nightmares."

"Exactly. You see, it's . . . I guess I . . . when one of these things hits me, it feels like I'm on some kind of . . . I don't know . . . like a spiral, sliding down in circles. Down and down. You—or whoever—you're up there on the surface getting fainter and fainter the further down I go. And the deeper I get, the harder it is to climb back out. You've got to stop me as soon as I start. Make me connect, so at least I don't keep sliding away from you."

"But . . . are these things *about* something? I mean, are you reacting to something I've said or done?"

"Not really," says Tony. "Not in the sense I think you mean. Something triggers it, of course. Usually something inconsequential. Like that dinner at Joe and Tom's. I thought you were all ignoring me. Having such a good time, the three of you. Or on the way to the circus that night. You were so busy talking about yourself. *Your* work. *Your* friends. You, you, you. All of a sudden, I got the idea you didn't care about me at all."

"Not *care* about you?" says Adam. "But that's . . . completely irrational. It doesn't make any sense."

Tony smiles, patiently.

"Of course it doesn't," he says. "We're not talking about rationality. If we were, I'd've found a way by now to get a grip on it myself. No. It's about as far from rationality as you can get. That's the problem."

Adam spends some time thinking about this, and when it happens again, he's ready. They're back out at Shenandoah, hiking through the vibrant colors of fall. Adam, walking beside Tony, is chattering

about something, he has no memory of what. He feels Tony closing
up, slipping away.

"Tony?" he says.

No answer. Tony just stares at the trail and keeps walking.

Adam stops.

"Oh, no, you don't," he says. "I'm not going through this again, you
understand me? You come back here and tell me what's happening."

Tony keeps walking.

"Go ahead, you asshole," Adam shouts. Two hikers coming toward
him, a young man and woman, glance at him, startled, and move
quickly up the trail.

"Go find a good spot to feel sorry for yourself," Adam yells, "you
selfish bastard. I'll be here waiting if you want to come back, but I'm
not going down there after you."

Tony stops, but doesn't turn around.

"You can wander off and sulk all you like," Adam yells. "Be my
guest. Or you can come back here and work it out. It's your own
fucking choice."

Adam sits on a large rock beside a tree. Tony disappears down the
trail.

Oh, dear god, thinks Adam. What have I done? He said make him
talk, not beat up on him like that. Adam wants nothing more than to
run down that trail, find Tony, hug him, plead with him. But he
doesn't do it. He sits on his rock, feeling wretched.

Each time he hears footsteps, he looks up. Hikers pass by in both
directions. Some of them say hello. Others, less willing to break the silence, only wave. Adam waves back. Thirty minutes. Forty-five.
Adam waits. He goes over in his mind what he said. What he *should*
have said. How long he ought to wait. Over and over. Footsteps from
down the trail. He looks up. It's Tony, coming slowly toward him. He
waits. Tony stops beside him, face immobile, the barest hint of a twin-
kle in his eyes.

"You've got a dirty mouth," says Tony. "You know that?"

Adam laughs. "Only when I have to."

"Want to go get some lunch?"

"Do *you*?"

"Yeah."

Adam gets up, and they start off together.

"Are we . . . reconnected now?" asks Adam. "Or do I need to make you talk about it some more?"

"We're reconnected," says Tony. He walks along for a while without speaking.

What am I supposed to be doing? Adam wonders. Talking? Waiting? Asking questions? What?

"I expected you to come after me," says Tony. "When you didn't, after I'd waited and waited, I got scared."

"But . . . you told me *not* to be so . . . wimpy . . . when this happens. Didn't you?"

"I did."

"Well, what could be more *wimpy* than running off after you, saying I'm sorry for I have no idea what?"

"I don't know. But . . . your sitting up here *not* coming after me seemed like you couldn't've cared less."

"Holy sweet Jesus," says Adam. He stops, grabs Tony's arm to stop him too, and turns him around.

"Look at me," says Adam.

Tony does.

"Do you hear yourself? What you just said? You're making it so I can't win no matter *what* I do, and I don't like that one little bit. I go all meek and misty-eyed and come running after you, and you think I'm ignoring what you told me to do, therefore I don't care. I sit down and *don't* come after you, and you decide I'm only thinking about myself. Therefore I don't care. Is that it?"

"Something like that."

"Well, you can't have it both ways."

"Why not?"

"Because you'll drive me crazy if you try, that's why."

"Good," says Tony. "I don't see why *I* should be the only one who's crazy."

Adam smiles. "You're not crazy. You're just weird."

"Do you love me? Anyway?"

"More than I can say."

Adam and Tony are lying in bed, late at night, watching television. They hear three small pops, then two more. Faint little sounds.

"Was that the TV?" asks Adam.

"I don't think so," says Tony. "Sounded more like next door. At Horace's."

Three more pops. Screams. Yelling. The sound of feet running. Loud knocks on one of the windows in their guest room.

"What the hell is *that*?" asks Adam.

"Somebody knocking on the front window," says Tony.

"Of course it is, you dope. That's not what I meant. I meant, who could it be?"

"I have no idea. But we sure won't know if we don't go look."

More knocks, louder than before.

"I'm scared," says Adam.

"So am I," says Tony. "But I think we'd better go see."

The knocks, hard and heavy, stop for a second or two, then continue. Adam and Tony both pull on a pair of pants and go into the guest room and over near the window.

"Who is it?" Tony yells.

The knocking stops.

"Horace, goddammit. Gimme a little help here."

Adam pulls back one of the curtains. Horace is there, kneeling on the porch roof, his face pressed against the window. Tony turns the key in the window lock and raises the window about six inches.

"Lemme in there," says Horace in a loud whisper.

"Was that shooting?" asks Tony.

"Goddamn right. Still is, for all I know. Lemme in there."

"Was it you doing the shooting?"

"Hell, no. Some damn goons. Now, lemme on in there."

"I don't know . . . ," says Tony.

"For god's sake, I'm a sittin' duck up here. Lemme in first, then go figurin' 'bout what you do or don' know."

Tony looks over at Adam, who nods. Tony looks back at Horace, pushes up the window, then the screen. Horace bursts inside. Tony lowers the screen and the window, turns the key in the lock, and closes the curtains.

"Damn fool Rodney and his gamblin' debts," says Horace. "I tol' him an' I tol' him."

"Is that who they've shot?" asks Adam, his voice trembling.

"It's who they come for, shoutin' his name soon's they got inside the door. But they're takin' out ever'body in the place, looks like. So's there's no witnesses, I reckon."

Tony goes to the phone in the hallway.

"Do they know you're over here?" asks Adam.

"Don' think so," says Horace, struggling to get his breath. "I was settin' out on my porch downstairs when I seen these two guys under the streetlight, a-comin' our way. An' I knew jus' who they was, I sure did. An' what they was comin' for. Instinc'. Save my sorry ol' black ass many a time. I scooted myself inside and right up them stairs, a-yellin' at the others as I went, but they wouldn't pay me no mind. Damn fools. One of 'em even went and opened the door." He stares at Adam, clicks his tongue, and shakes his head. "*Opened* the door! Soon's the shootin' started downstairs, I come out my upstairs porch window and straight across to here."

Tony walks back into the room. "The police are already on their way," he says. "Mine was the third call."

Adam hears sirens. He pulls the curtains back again and looks down at the street. Lights are flashing all over. Police are rushing out of their cars. Groups of people have gathered on the sidewalk.

"We'd better get out there," says Tony. "Now that help has arrived."

He heads down the stairs first, then Horace, then Adam. Tony goes with Horace to talk with the police. Adam stays on the porch, thinking about sudden death. And about the war. Far behind him at last.

Far enough that he's reacting now just to what's happening here. Only this. Not that. In an odd, disconnected way, he's grateful.

Sheet-covered bodies on stretchers start coming out of Horace's house. Three. Four. Five in all. One a gambler, thinks Adam, the others just people who needed a place to sleep. Dear god.

A policeman comes up the steps toward Adam.

"Did you catch them?" Adam asks.

"No way," says the cop, a nice looking young black man. "They were in and out and long gone before we got here."

"Sounds like they knew what they were doing," says Adam.

The man nods. "You can bet they did," he says.

He takes out a little spiral notebook and a pen. He asks Adam what he's seen and heard, what Horace said, what the people next door were like. He nods a number of times, writes it all down, says, "Thank you, we may want to get back to you," and heads across the street toward the Jacksons'. Horace gets into the back seat of a police car. Tony comes up the porch steps. He squeezes Adam's arm. They stand watching until the ambulances and police cars have all gone.

"I feel like we've walked right inside the TV set," says Tony.

Adam laughs, a nervous laugh. "I guess we have," he says. "In a way."

"How do you feel?" asks Tony.

"Numb. And very sad. How about you?"

"About the same. I don't know when I've been so scared. Jesus. Right next door."

"Just think, though, how much worse it's been for Horace," says Adam. "Those people were his friends."

"I can't even imagine. Well . . ."

They go inside and lock the door.

Tony looks at his watch. "Twelve-forty-five," he says. "Think we'll get any sleep?"

Adam shakes his head.

"I doubt it," he says.

— 46 —

Horace comes to the back door of their house, one evening while they're eating supper. His shoulders are slumped, and his face is sad.

"I give up," he says. "I cain't fight no more. I jus' cain't. Ever' goddamn thing's agains' me, seem like. I'm goin' on back where I b'long. Back down to Carolina."

"Will you be all right?" asks Tony.

"Cain't say. All I know is I shore ain' all right here."

"We'll do anything we can to help," says Tony. "Anything."

"I know that," says Horace. "I known it all along."

"Most of all," says Adam, "we'll miss you. A lot."

"I 'preciate you sayin' that. Ol' blackass no-good like me. Truth is, I'll miss you, too."

"What are your plans?" asks Tony. "I mean, what all do you need to do?"

"Sell my damn house, mos' important thing," says Horace. "If they's anybody aroun' want th' ol' wreck. You reckon they'll be?"

Tony looks at Adam. Adam raises his eyebrows, thinks for a second, then nods.

"I do reckon," says Tony. "We'll buy it. Adam and me."

"You kiddin' wif me here?" says Horace. "You got yourselfs a house. What'chu be needin' wif another one?"

"We'll rent it," says Tony. "Fix it up and rent it out."

"Good luck's all I gotta say. Takin' in renters what done me in."

"Even so," says Tony. "We'll take our chances."

He and Adam spend a while conferring, then go over to Horace's to negotiate. Adam realizes as he walks in just how much work the place is going to require. He tries not to think about bodies lying around on the floor.

"You sit on them two chairs," says Horace. "I'll bring in the stool from the kitchen."

After they're all settled, Tony says, "Shall we get started then?"

"Got to some time," says Horace.

"So . . . what's a fair price?" Tony asks. "Do you think?"

"I been studyin' 'bout that," says Horace. "Axin' aroun' some. Mebbe . . . thirty thousan'?"

"Thirty-five," says Tony.

Horace laughs.

"Hol' on a minute," he says. "You goin' the wrong damn way. You *suppose* to be talkin' me *down,* not up."

"This house is your only real asset," says Tony. "Right?"

"All I got."

"The way we figure it, you're going to need enough money to get started again in Carolina. Thirty-five thousand. Not a penny less."

Horace looks at Tony, then at Adam, then at Tony.

"'Member what I tol' you when you firs' come here?" he says. "That bof you was my frien's? I never said a truer word."

To make things fair, Horace decides, he gets some guys he knows to come by with a truck and empty the backyard of its washers, dryers, freezers, and refrigerators. They come on a Saturday, and Adam gets up from his reading chair every now and then to watch from the upstairs sunporch. They have to make three trips, and it's a *big* truck.

Then one day Horace isn't there. Leaving a hole, Adam thinks, that nobody is ever likely to fill.

Tony locates a carpenter, who comes in with another worker and attacks Horace's house. The two of them rip out badly cracked old plaster walls, rip up faded and torn linoleum, nail up new plaster board, new kitchen cabinets. Electricians put in new wiring. Plumbers put in new plumbing and a heating and air-conditioning system. The carpenters strip layers of paint from beautiful old woodwork, replace or repaint what can't be salvaged, refinish the floor, and paint all the walls.

Adam and Tony go off every Saturday and most Sundays looking at bathtubs, sinks, kitchen appliances, water heaters, and venetian blinds. They have a great time choosing colors and models, looking for bargains whenever they can find them. They plant some grass in the backyard, and a couple of trees. When the front of the house and the patched-up porch have been painted, the place unrecognizable now in its new glory, the neighbors all come by to take a look. They pronounce it just fine.

An ad in the Sunday paper brings a good many phone calls. Adam sets up appointments with those callers who seem most promising, interviews them, and confers with Tony. They end up renting the house to three young black women—a lawyer, a psychiatric nurse, and a graphic designer for an advertising agency. Attractive, energetic, impressive women, who are thrilled to be moving into a brand-new house. Inside, at least. Adam and Tony hope nobody ever tells them about the murders in their living room, dining room, and front hall.

As soon as these tenants have moved in and the rent starts arriving regularly, the carpenter and his helper begin converting the damp old cellar into a basement apartment. They work the same magic as before, and another parade of prospective tenants comes to look it over. This time, Adam and Tony choose a young white legislative assistant to a congressman from Connecticut. He is polite but keeps mostly to himself. He brings young women by, a different one each time so far as Adam can tell, with reliable frequency.

Adam and Tony are so pleased with their success they decide to convert their own basement the same way. When it's time to rent this apartment, the first applicant to come for an interview is a young Puerto Rican named Luis, who is just moving up to Washington to work for the Environmental Protection Agency. Adam shows him around the apartment, and he says, "Very nice," with a slight accent that Adam finds charming. "I will take it."

Adam shakes his head.

"We have quite a few other people lined up to come by," he says. "After we've seen them all, we'll let you know what we've decided."

"There is no need for that," says Luis. "I will take it now. Tell the others to look elsewhere."

"But that's not the way we're used to doing things. We like to talk with as many people as we can, and then pick . . ."

"There is no need. I will have a good salary. I can show you the amount, if you like. I am very tidy. *Very* tidy. I do not smoke. I have no pets. I will not entertain loud people. There is nothing you can object to. And I like the apartment. I will take it."

"But I think . . ."

"Please listen. I will take this apartment."

Adam smiles, feeling helpless.

"All right," he says. "You will take it, apparently. Let's go upstairs and sign the lease."

Soon the three rent checks are paying for all the construction loans and the mortgage on Horace's house, with some left over to go into their investment account. This account has been growing right along, ever since they started living on Adam's salary and putting all of Tony's into stocks, bonds, utilities, mutual funds, and even a little gold and silver.

— 47 —

They first hear about the strange new illness from friends. Friends of *theirs,* in New York and San Francisco primarily, are falling ill, wasting away, dying. All of them gay. Nobody has the least idea what it could be.

Soon, Adam begins to read reports in the newspapers. Small at first, buried in the back, then more detailed and full of alarm right on the front page. A pattern is developing among gay men. Those who've had frequent sex with a great many partners. The ones, Adam thinks ruefully, who rushed headlong through the doors so recently flung open. As many as half of them may die.

Before Adam can adjust to this terrifying onslaught out there somewhere, the epidemic hits Washington. His and Tony's own friends are being diagnosed with maladies whose names have been dug up out of footnotes in dusty old medical textbooks. Pneumocystis pneumonia. Kaposi's sarcoma. The experts are stumped. Speculation in the papers becomes even more dismaying. Multiple exposures may not be required after all; one may be enough. Predictions of the mortality rate have been far too optimistic. Everybody who gets it is dying. *Everybody.*

'It' is now being referred to in shorthand. Like a kind of voodoo, Adam thinks. A necklace of garlic to ward off the full horror of the lengthy multisyllable official titles. The virus that infects is called HIV. The illness—or set of illnesses—that kills is called AIDS. Like cozy names for old friends. Alex, when Alexander takes too long to say. Peg for the more austere Margaret.

The most appalling attribute of the disease, for Adam, is the length of the incubation period. Three years, he hears at first. Then five. Then ten. He won't be absolutely sure he and Tony are safe for a long,

long time. A decade after either of them last had sex with somebody else.

The toll becomes relentless. Funerals. Memorial services. Evenings consoling lovers left behind. So many friends now gone. Adam stops counting at thirty.

Their tenant downstairs finds out abruptly, brutally.

Luis has come to their front door often in the year and a half he's lived here. Mostly with something to ask—about the dishwasher or the subway schedule. Other times with something he's brought—a picture of his nieces and nephews or a plate of plantains he's just finished mashing and frying. Adam is convinced the real reason lies elsewhere: a need to be talking. As soon as the door is open, he begins, the thousands of words trapped just inside his mouth pouring out, making room for new ones already piling up right behind. The telephone, Adam suspects, is a poor substitute. Face-to-face is far more satisfying.

This evening, though, Luis is wide-eyed, barely able to speak. He's just gotten home from work, he manages to say, and opened his mail. He holds out a letter. Adam takes it. It's from the Red Cross.

"We will be unable to accept any more blood from you in the future," Adam reads aloud, "as your most recent donation has tested positive for HIV. Please consult with your physician."

No warning. Just this brief, efficient message out of nowhere. Luis sits with Adam and Tony, talking and crying. Adam puts his arm around him. Tony holds his hand. Infection be damned.

"It could be a mistake," says Luis. "Couldn't it be?"

"Of course it could," says Tony.

"I have read in the papers they are unreliable, these tests," says Luis. "Isn't that what they say?"

"Yes," says Adam. "I've read that, too." Although his memory is that the danger is false negatives more than false positives.

"I should have another test," says Luis. "Shouldn't I?"

The report from the second test, though, is exactly the same. The night after they hear this news, Adam is lying in bed in Tony's arms.

"Should we get tested ourselves," he asks, "do you think?"

"What's the point of knowing?" says Tony. "Really. They can't cure it. They can't prevent it from happening. Eventually, once you've been infected. They're not even sure they can put it off for long, after it decides to strike. I guess . . . I mean, if there was a danger we might infect somebody else, maybe. But there isn't. I'm certainly not sleeping with anybody but you. Haven't for years and years, not since . . . and I can't imagine that you are either."

"Not a chance."

"So . . . either we both have it already or we don't. All those tests are, for us, is a death sentence, if you ask me. I'd rather live for however long we've got with*out* knowing—happy years with some peace of mind—and then find out. Wouldn't you?"

"Absolutely," says Adam.

Luis still talks, every chance he gets. His one subject now, however, the obsession that drives all other thoughts from his mind, is his illness. He talks about every aspect of it, over and over. Possible treatments for pneumocystis and their likelihood of success, what researchers are beginning to find out, what the experts are saying, opinion, speculation, straws to be grasped and held onto for dear life. Luis catches Adam on the front steps, in the backyard, in the laundry room downstairs they all share, and talks and talks and talks.

This time, he's using words as a weapon, Adam thinks. If he can just throw enough of them at the menace that's threatening him, maybe he can drive it away. Or create a thick cloud of words in which to hide.

It doesn't work. The disease, instead, progresses more quickly in him than in many others. He gets steadily weaker, loses weight, spends a week in the hospital, comes home, goes back to the hospital. His mother arrives from Puerto Rico. She introduces herself to Adam and Tony, moves into Luis's apartment, and spends most of every day in his hospital room.

Marta is short, slender, bursting with energy. She talks as much as her son, only faster, and her hands are never still. Her defense is cleanliness. Unwilling to rely on the hospital staff, she scrubs Luis's room every day herself. Adam and Tony see her at it, and even when she isn't scouring, the smell of Clorox hangs in the air. If infections are the enemy, Marta will keep them at a distance, far away from her son. When people come to visit, she hands them a surgical mask at the door. She tries as hard as she can, but she doesn't succeed. Luis gets worse.

Then, miraculously, he gets better. Much better.

"You see," says Marta triumphantly, "what my prayers, and my Clorox, have done!"

The doctors begin to talk about sending Luis home. Marta scrubs every inch of his apartment. Adam hears her down there, moving furniture, vacuuming, running water, vacuuming again. She invites Adam and Tony down to see the result. They take off their shoes at the door and walk through the spotless rooms, nodding and smiling. A large bouquet of spring flowers sits in a vase on the dining table.

"It will be so good to have him here," says Marta. "Where I can look after him myself. I will make myself a bed there on the sofa. Cook and clean and look after him. I will make him well again. You will see."

Luis is to arrive home on a Thursday afternoon. Marta calls Adam at work that morning to say Luis is much worse. Suddenly, during the night. Specialists have been sent for, but she is so worried. Can Adam come?

He calls Tony at his office, and they meet in the hospital lobby. Marta is sitting beside her son's bed, holding his hand. She doesn't bother to give them a mask. Adam and Tony bend down to kiss her. Luis lies very still, eyes closed, an oxygen tube leading into his nose.

"How is he?" Tony whispers.

"Bad," she says. Her face is composed, but her lips are trembling.

"What do the doctors say?" asks Adam.

"That it will be soon. They think he cannot recover. Not this time. His lungs are too weak."

"Is there anybody we can call?" asks Tony.

"I have called them all," she says. "But they have not enough notice to come so far."

Adam and Tony go back to the hospital the next night. And again on Saturday afternoon. They sit with Marta. Nurses come in to check vital signs. Doctors arrive, and Adam and Tony wait in the hall while they confer. Injections are given. Oxygen flows. Luis opens his eyes a couple of times while they are there, smiles weakly, but does not rally. Sunday morning, as they are finishing the breakfast dishes, Marta calls to say that he has left her.

She takes Luis home to San Juan, to be buried with the rest of the family. She comes back to make arrangements for a memorial mass at St. Matthew's Cathedral, attended by his friends and co-workers in Washington. She spends almost a week packing and cleaning the apartment.

Adam and Tony visit with her most evenings, giving her a chance to talk about Luis. His childhood. His talents. His awards. What a good son he always was. She doesn't cry while they're with her, but they hear her after they've gone back upstairs. She cooks for them in the apartment a couple of times. They have her up for dinner the night before she leaves. And then she is gone.

They wait a couple of months, out of respect and affection, before they put an ad in the paper. Quite a few people come by, but one, a woman in her late thirties who works for AARP, is so taken with the apartment she calls twice to say she just *has* to have it. On the theory that an eager tenant is a happy tenant, they tell her yes.

When she comes by to sign the lease, she and Adam chat a while, about the neighborhood, the convenience of the subway down the street, that kind of thing.

"By the way," she says. "I've been wondering. What happened to the last tenant? I mean, I can't imagine anybody leaving such a great place unless they had to."

Adam has been dreading such a question. The fear of this disease is so irrational. People go to such lengths not to be anywhere near it. If he tells her, will she back out? Too bad if she does.

"He died of AIDS," says Adam. "Three months ago."

"Oh, my goodness," she says, her eyes sad. "Bless his heart. I'll take real good care of the apartment for him, you can be sure of that. It's the least I can do."

48

Sam and Irene's visit to Washington is not a great success. They enjoy the city well enough, but the neighborhood makes Sam nervous. Irene comes by herself when she can get away and has a much better time. Adam and Tony go down to Texas every few years. In the spring once and a couple of Christmases. Never in the summer.

They also drive up to Maine whenever they can. Tony has property there, fifty acres of woods down a country road, on a hill overlooking a bay. The minute Adam sees the hill, the woods, the bay, he knows he's come home. Never mind that he grew up in Texas, hours from the shore; the connection he feels to the ocean is immediate and deep. Maybe even primordial. The yearning of a creature that came from the sea to return to the place of its origin.

The emotion he feels for the woods—part companionship, part reverence—is equally intense. They surround him, holding him safe. The peaks that fill the horizon on the other side of the bay are much shorter than the mountains he's been used to on vacations out West, but too abrupt a change from the surrounding landscape to be no more than hills. Then he realizes it doesn't matter what he calls them. They are what they are. Friendlier, cozier, more accessible than the forbidding Rockies. You could climb to the top of these and back in an afternoon, and he and Tony often do.

They go to Maine for a week or two in the summer, for a weekend at least most autumns, and once for Thanksgiving, in a year when snow has already begun to fall and everything, trees, bay, and mountains, shimmers under a distant sun that hangs low in the southern sky. To his surprise, Adam sees around him infinite variations, pale and luminous, of what he's always thought of before as nothing but white.

At first they stay with Tony's older sister, Barbara, retired now from nursing in New York to an old farmhouse just down the road from Tony's property. Tony and Barbara learned about Maine from their father, Steve, the Long Island potato farmer with itchy feet who was always eager to see new parts of his adopted country, but also liked there to be a purpose to his wanderings. Going around New England and ending up talking with longtime potato farmers in Aroostook County seemed to him like an ideal way to do both.

In time, Tony and Adam pick a spot on their hill near the main road, have it cleared, and start building a house. They've talked about it for years and have agreed on a plan they both like. The house is made entirely of wood—board-and-batten on the outside that soon weathers to gray, long wooden clapboards of pine, spruce, and tamarack lining the walls and ceilings of the rooms inside. The heavy beams that hold up the second floor, as well as much of the paneling, have come from trees in their own woods out back. From the deck off the living room, they can see—and smell—the bay. A wonderfully tangy, woodsy, salty smell.

Whenever they're at the house in the summer or early fall, Adam goes off into the woods to clear paths through the dense undergrowth. He puts on leather gloves, takes a small saw and a pair of long-handled clippers, and loses himself for hours. He wanders around looking for a spot that appeals to him—a clearing, a little pond, a stand of maples. When he finds one, he snips, saws, and hauls brush away until a pathway to that place is unobstructed. Then he finds another spot deeper in the woods and starts snipping, sawing, and hauling again.

One fall afternoon, Adam heads back to the house, puts the clippers and saw in the shed, and comes and sits beside Tony out on the deck. They both rock a while in the big wicker rockers, looking down at the bay.

"It's hard to believe any place could be this beautiful," says Adam.

"You really love it here," says Tony. "Don't you?"

"I do."

"Ever think about living here?"

"Of course. All the time. You know what a dreamer I am."

"If we can work it out, financially, for us to quit our jobs, would you like to come on up? Maybe do some of that writing you keep putting off?"

Adam stares at Tony.

"You're pulling my leg," he says. "Right?"

Tony smiles.

"Not about this. Not about something that means so much to you."

"But, then . . . are you saying *you* want to come here, too?"

"Yes," says Tony. "I do. I'm tired of the hassle. It's wearing me down. So much noise down there. So many people around us all the time. So many people *dying*. That's probably what made me start thinking about it. All those friends, just . . . gone. They thought they had their whole lives ahead of them, to do the stuff they'd always wanted to do. And now they're gone. We ought to make sure that doesn't happen to us. We ought to come here now. As soon as we can. While we're still young enough—and healthy enough—to enjoy it."

"Can we really *do* it, though?" Adam asks. "Have we got enough to carry us through?"

"I think so, yes. The houses in Washington are paid for. We can keep them and have all that income from the rent. And our investments are doing well. I think we'll be fine. If not, we can always go back to work—later on."

"You're amazing," says Adam.

Tony smiles.

"Probably," he says.

49

They move to Maine in the spring, as soon as things have begun to thaw. Adam gets up every morning and goes to his study off the second-floor bedroom to write. Some short stories at first, then the beginning of a novel. Tony paints out in the studio he's built at the top of their road. He used to paint, back on the farm, but somehow he let it slip away. Now he's bringing it back. He paints haunting landscapes. Marshes with waving grass and streams that meander. The stark shapes of bare branches in winter.

They meet people, other artists, other writers, other couples, gay and not. Have them over for supper. Go to their houses. Talk. Laugh. Drink wine. Relax.

That next summer, Elena comes to Maine for a visit. She sleeps in the guest room on the first floor. Tony makes breakfast. Adam fixes lunch. Elena cooks supper. She visits with her daughter Barbara down the road. She sits by the window and watches the birds chattering and fluttering around the bird feeder. She reads large-print books from the library, tracing each line with her finger. Most of all, she enjoys their walks, after supper, along the rocky shore. She is content.

Until a cat walks out of the woods and decides she will live here, too.

The cat is small and seems, at first glance, to be somewhat dainty. Until you look into her eyes. They are tough, wise, unyielding. Tony has a feeling she's part Maine coon cat, but says she isn't nearly big enough to be purebred. She has black and dark gray mottled fur. Her ears are little, round, shaped like cup handles. She walks out of the woods behind the house, sits down on the deck, and stays there.

Elena wrinkles her brow.

"No cat in the house," she says.

When she takes this tone, no one, certainly not Tony or Adam, contradicts her. Tony rigs up a shelter, a tentlike affair with a plastic sheet and a blanket on the ground, out by the woodpile. He and Adam vie for who gets to take out food and water.

"Don't keep feeding that cat," says Elena.

"Yes, Mama," they both say. And they both keep sneaking out to do it. Not bring her into the house? Okay. Leave her to fend for herself? Never. Each of them has looked into her eyes and found himself smitten.

Tony names her Fuzzy Bobo. He never says why. Adam doesn't care. It suits her.

She is every inch a lady. But a formidable one. No one messes with her. Not twice, at any rate. She looks up sedately and bats her eyelids. She allows Tony and Adam to pet her, gently, on her back and to scratch behind her little ears. Any movement toward her underbelly, however, brings a snarl and a hiss. They stick with her back and her ears.

Each time Adam heads for the woods with his saw and clippers, she runs along beside him. She sniffs at leaves and bark and lichens as she goes, wanders off, comes back, sits near a tree while Adam works, trots beside him as he heads home.

When Tony gets out of his pickup and calls, "Fuzzy Bobo, come over here and see me," she runs to where he is, does her little dance with her two front paws, and allows Tony to reach down and pet her.

At the end of August, Tony takes Elena back to Long Island. Adam says he won't go this time. Too much to do, he says. But as soon as the car turns off their road and starts south, he opens the door and Fuzzy Bobo comes inside.

It's as if she's always lived here. Reigned here. "Contessa Principessa Marquesa," Adam calls her when she's in this mood. And she does walk regally from room to room, floor to floor, surveying her realm.

Adam drives right away to the pet store to bring back a litter box and a bag of litter. He gets it all set up in the second-floor bathroom and goes off to find Fuzzy Bobo, to show her where it is and what it's for.

Fat chance.

While he's looking for her down in the living room, he hears her upstairs. Scratch-scratch-scratch. Scratch-scratch-scratch in the litter box. Her real message, of course, is "You have absolutely nothing to teach *me*."

Adam also buys a cat carrier, so he can take Fuzzy Bobo to the vet for shots and a checkup.

Ha!

The minute she sees it, she disappears and doesn't come out for two days. Adam puts the carrier in the basement and waits for Tony to get back.

Early one morning, Adam goes up to the room at the back of the second floor where Fuzzy Bobo spends many an hour sprawled in the sunshine. Tony sneaks down to the basement to bring up the carrier. Adam talks softly, sweetly. "Pretty girl. Are you my pretty girl?"

Fuzzy Bobo cocks her head, alert and suspicious.

Adam reaches out, strokes her back, rubs her ears, picks her up, one hand holding her front legs together, the other holding the back two. Immediately she starts to twist and spit and snarl. Adam heads down the stairs.

"Get ready, Tony," he yells. "I can't hold her for long."

As Adam gets to the first floor, Tony is standing at the foot of the stairs, carrier aimed upward, door open. Adam shoves her in and closes the door.

Fuzzy Bobo is irate. She spits. Snarls. Hisses. When they get her to the car, though, she begins to cry. All the way to the vet, fifteen long minutes, she cries without letup. Fear. Pain. Betrayal. They're all in her cries.

The vet will give her the necessary shots, open her up to spay her, watch her for a while. They should come back late in the afternoon. Throughout that day, the house seems unbearably empty.

When they go back to bring her home, the vet tells them shocking news. When he opened her up, he found she'd already been spayed. She's been someone's pet. But he also found that her internal organs were badly scarred. Someone has beaten her, more than once. And her cute little rounded ears? They've been frostbitten. The tips froze at some point and fell off, so she has to have been out in the woods for at least part of a bitter Maine winter.

"I'll tell you what I think," says the vet. "I think she just said, 'Enough of this,' and wandered off to find a better place to live."

"She's found it," says Tony.

"Good," says the vet.

She cries all the way home, but forgives them in time. They discover, as the weeks go by, that she is firmly in control. Now, when Adam gets ready to work back in the woods, and says, "Want to come, Fuzzy?" she simply glances up and goes back to sleep.

When Tony calls, "Fuzzy Bobo, come here," her look clearly says, "You've *got* to be kidding."

– 50 –

Along about now, Adam's mother decides she's had enough. Irene's weekly calls become twice-weekly, then daily. She's going to leave Sam, this time for sure. Now that they're both retired and he's around so much, she just can't handle it anymore.

Tony has grown fond of Adam's mother through the years, in spite of her quirks, so he joins Adam in talking with Irene, for hours, on the phone. Listening to her, that is, more often than not, putting in a "yes" or a "sure" or an "I know" now and then—though, when pressed, both do, in fact, offer their opinions. Since Tony likes talking on the phone more than Adam, he's the one who usually answers. He gets the full rundown of Irene's discontent, after which Adam sits through the same story all over again.

She's got to find herself, she says, adopting the terminology as well as the tactics of her children's generation. She needs her own space, in which to get in touch with the real Irene—submerged all these years under the needs of others—from whom she'll learn the secrets of contentment and tranquility. She will also go places, see the world the way she's always wanted to, live, do all the things Sam's intransigence has kept her from doing. She doesn't talk about time running out, but Adam reads that message between the lines.

Then, she finally does it. She packs up and leaves San Antonio. After forty-six years of marriage, she's talking seriously with a lawyer about divorce. She moves to Weatherford, to the house her parents left her, the house she grew up in, five hours and two hundred and fifty miles from her husband, soon to be ex-. She is back in East Texas. Home at last, in a way she hasn't been for almost fifty years; her future is secure. But she can't help worrying about him, *his* future.

"Be sure to call your daddy, now, at least once a week," she tells Adam after she's settled in, signaling her intention to continue ar-

ranging things where Sam is concerned by long distance. "I'm afraid
he'll . . . you know . . . do something rash."

Euphemisms have been the official language of Adam's growing
up. "You don't mean, kill himself?" he says.

"Well . . . yes," she says. "He might. He's certainly capable of it.
And you can't be too careful . . . under the circumstances."

"What circumstances are those?"

"Why, his mental condition, of course. You know very well what
I'm talking about. He's never been exactly stable, for heaven's sake.
Don't forget all those shock treatments he's had."

"What do you mean 'all'? There weren't so very many, seems
to me."

"More than you knew, dear, believe me. More than you knew.
I didn't want to burden you with *every*thing, after all."

Coulda fooled me, Adam thinks, but he doesn't say that. He may
be well past forty by now, but he still reverts easily to habits acquired
in childhood. Don't say anything unpleasant. Be respectful of your
parents. And, whatever you do, don't set off one of your mother's
asthma attacks. So he backs off and says what she wants to hear: "Yes.
I know."

"He's never cooked a meal for himself in his whole life" (not quite
true, thinks Adam) "and I just know he won't be eating right. And
the washing and ironing! What on earth's he going to do about that?
He knows where the washer and dryer *are,* of course, but as for *using*
them . . . he's never so much as *looked* at either one, so far as I know."

Exasperation gives Adam courage. "What possible good does it do
you to worry about things like that, Mother?" he says. "You should either go on back and take care of them yourself, or just put them out of
your mind."

"Go *back!*" The pitch of her voice rises ominously. Adam can hear
the telltale tightening of her vocal cords, the faint vibrations of a
wheeze that will soon choke off her words entirely. "But you *said* I was
right." A labored breath. "We've talked about this . . . for months . . .
and you *said* you understood. You *said* . . ."

"Yes, Mother." A full retreat is called for here. "I only meant . . ." He hears coughs and those tight half breaths that break his heart. "Look, I just . . . don't be upset."

"Up*set*!" She can barely spit it out. "Of course I'm up*set*. I . . . I'm hanging up now. I've got to go take care of this."

The line goes dead.

"Trouble?" asks Tony, who has come in from the kitchen and is leaning against the doorway.

"The usual," says Adam. "Although . . . I don't know . . . she sounded pretty bad this time. I'd better call her back."

"Jesus, Adam! You *always* give in."

"Do I?"

"Always. Let her stew a little this time. It'll do her good."

"Maybe," says Adam. He is drumming his finger on the back of the receiver. "I . . . no, I'd better call her back."

He begins to dial.

Tony slams his hand against the wall. "Honest to god, you're enough to drive me to drink. I tell you what I think, and you go right ahead and do exactly as you damn well please."

Adam doesn't look up and continues to dial.

"Dammit!" says Tony. He goes back toward the kitchen.

Adam leans forward and listens to the ringing. The voice that answers isn't his mother's.

"Is Irene there?" he asks.

"Gone," says the voice. "That you, Adam?"

"Yes, ma'am."

"It's Miz Hardy, Adam. From next door?"

"Yes, ma'am."

"Listen, my husband, Fred? He's taken your mother on down t' the 'mergency room. I couldn't make out much of what she was tryin' to say, but I got the idea it was *you* set her off, some way or another?"

Adam sighs. "Yes, Mrs. Hardy. I'm afraid I did. Could you leave her a note, do you think? Tell her I called to see how she was?"

"No, I couldn't. I'm stayin' right here till they get back, so I'll tell her myself. *I'm* not *about* to leave her all alone over here. Not when she's as bad off as this."

"Yes, Mrs. Hardy. I appreciate that. Thanks very much."

He hangs up and stares at the phone. He heaves himself out of the chair and walks to the kitchen. Tony is chopping onions, his lips tight, his knife coming down hard on the cutting board. Adam goes over, kisses him on the cheek, and rubs one hand up and down his back.

"What's for supper?" Adam asks.

"Pork chops and sauerkraut. If we're lucky."

Adam smiles. He knows this mood well and feels an odd kind of relief. He can handle these bursts of irritation, soon gone. They beat the hell out of those terrifying depressions, which keep trying, now and then, to make a comeback but haven't quite succeeded for years.

"What can I do to help?" he asks.

Tony looks around.

"Well . . . ," he says. "If you'll deal with the garlic, and get the pork chops ready, I'll take care of the vegetables."

Adam gets the other chopping block and the knife he likes to use and takes them to the counter beside Tony.

"Want this whole head of garlic?" Adam asks. "Or will that be too much?"

"Are you serious?" says Tony. "There's no such thing as too much garlic."

Adam laughs.

They chop a while in silence.

"Look," says Adam, resting his knife on the counter. "I'm sorry. I don't mean to ignore what you say. I'm just . . . having a hard time dealing with all this."

"I know," says Tony. "Of course you are. And I shouldn't be making it any worse. I know that. So from now on, I'll try to . . ."

"It's all right," says Adam. "Really. We'll be fine."

"Daddy?" says Adam. "How're you doing down there?"

"All by myself, you mean?" says his father. "Not too bad."

"What about meals? Are you eating all right?"

Sam chuckles. "Your mother put you up to asking that, didn't she?"

"Well . . . I . . ."

"C'mon, son. Give me a little credit here. I didn't fall off the turnip truck this morning, you know."

It's Adam's turn to laugh. "I'll say you didn't. But . . . well, I don't see why Mother's getting involved should mean I can't be concerned about how you are. Should it?"

"No. You're right, it shouldn't. I'm eating just fine, thank you. I've got a big pot of soup on the stove right now."

"Soup? I didn't realize you knew how to make soup."

Adam feels a tenseness at the other end of the line.

"You might want to consider the possibility," says his father, "that there are a great many things you don't know. About me, in particular."

And vice versa, thinks Adam, but what he says is "I'm sorry, Daddy. I'm sure there are."

"One thing I've never understood is why people make such a big deal about all these little chores around the house" (which you've spent fifty years not doing, thinks Adam). "Cooking. Washing dishes. Vacuuming, for heaven's sake. As if there were some great mystery involved. I mean, you look to see where the dirt is on the floor, you aim the hose at it, and, lo and behold, the vacuum cleaner sucks it up. You don't need a degree in engineering to manage *that*.

"And the washing machine! Your mother called up to tell me how to make it work. I told her I'd already done three loads and managed just fine, thank you very much."

"I'm sure she was just trying to be helpful."

Another pause, more tense than the last.

"I'll tell you what *I'm* sure of, Adam. I'm sure I don't need you calling up here to apologize for your mother. Or to check up on me just because she told you to. Now, if you want to see how I'm doing because it's important to you, well, that's a different story. We haven't had much opportunity for talking, just the two of us, without your mother camped out on the other extension, and I have to say I'd welcome that. But I've been checked up on enough to last a lifetime, and I don't want you trying to fill in where your mother left off. Fair enough?"

"Fair enough," says Adam. "And . . . next time I call, I'll get off to a better start. I promise."

"We both will," says his father.

Adam hangs up and sits a while, holding the phone in his lap.

– 52 –

Their third winter in Maine begins to seem long. Adam and Tony talk about going to Mexico for a week or so.

"Go ahead," says Barbara. "I'll look after the house—and Fuzzy Bobo. Feed her and change her litter box. She's at home here by now. She'll be fine."

They order their passports, buy their tickets, fly down to Cancun, and pick up the rental car they've reserved. Neither is interested in seeing the city—a trumped-up copy of Miami Beach, they've heard—so they head west out of town toward Chichen Itza. Adam, the navigator, checks the map of the Yucatan he brought along and helps Tony find the road they want, a narrow two-lane highway with what looks like mostly local traffic.

Excited to be here, Adam watches the land go by. He thinks at first that the scenery is not very interesting. Flat for as far as he can see, with no rises at all and few trees taller than ten or fifteen feet. But the more carefully he looks, the more fascinating it becomes. What had appeared to be uninterrupted stretches of identical vegetation turns out to be a wide variety of shrubs, bushes, deciduous trees, and palmettos. Some are flowering, in bright shades of yellow and orange and red and softer shades of lavender and pink. The barks, far from being all the same, are dark brown, light brown, gray, brownish-gray, grayish-brown.

Fairly often along the way, they come to small villages. Many of the houses are built in the Mayan style Adam recognizes from the books he's read. Upright sticks placed close together form oblong structures, with wide doorways left open on both sides for cross-ventilation. Dried palmetto leaves thatched together cover the high-pitched roofs. Inside the houses Adam can see hammocks of bright colors strung from wall to wall. More often than not, people are lying in them, swinging slowly back and forth.

Low rock walls outline the boundaries of each family's property. Within these walls, children are playing, chickens peck at the ground, pigs walk around looking for food, and skinny dogs with alert eyes and lively tails stand guard. Many of the houses are shaded by large bougainvillea bushes, whose red, orange, and magenta blossoms are so vivid they startle Adam's eyes.

He and Tony have a late lunch in the little town of Valladolid. Pork cooked in a banana leaf, which they both find delicious. Just past the far side of town, Adam sees the sign he's looking for. It says 'Dzitnup' and points to the left.

"That's it," he says.

Tony turns off the main road onto a much smaller one.

Adam wants to see as many things having to do with the Maya as he can, and this *cenote* is high on his list. Most of these pools of water sacred to the Maya, he knows from his books, were formed when the earth above an underground stream caved in, leaving what then looked like a deep circular well. The *cenote* called Dzitnup is quite different. Here, the pool is at the bottom of a large cavern.

Tony turns left again into a parking lot.

"No other cars," says Adam. "Thank god."

They pay their entrance fees, go through a door, and climb down steep winding steps carved into the rock, holding on to a rope as they go. They walk out into an amazing room, with nobody else in sight. The ceiling soars high above their heads. Light coming in through a small hole at its center is augmented by three or four bulbs strung on wires across the cavern. From the ceiling hang stalactites of many shapes and sizes. Some are rounded masses that look like enormous bunches of petrified grapes. Others are slender and pointed. A few of these touch the pool on the floor of the grotto. Most only reach toward it, growing nearer at a pace too slow for Adam to comprehend.

The water is a luminous turquoise color, paler in the shallow parts near the edge, rich and radiant out where it deepens. It's so clear the fish moving past seem to be flying rather than swimming. Then one of them snaps at an insect, and a flash of silver marks the surface where the water touches the air.

At first, the silence presses down on Adam. Then he begins to hear the sounds of the cave itself. Gentle plinks as drops of water completing their slow journey down from the surface fall from the tip of a stalactite into the pool below. The softly flapping wings of a lone bat circling the hole in the ceiling. Random splashes as fish flip the surface of the water.

Adam feels a kinship with the Maya who worshipped here, and an intuitive understanding of their view of the world. This is as sacred a place as he has ever been near.

They arrive at Chichen Itza after five, when the gates are closed. The verandah of their bungalow at the Hacienda Chichen faces the jungle out of which the Maya carved their ancient city. They sit outside for a while, rocking, listening to the calls of birds and frogs. At dinner on the terrace of the Hacienda, their waiter is a slender, elegant man dressed all in white. He has a stunning Maya face, with honey-brown skin, deep-set black eyes, and a regal, arching nose. Adam tries not to stare as the man comes and goes.

He and Tony are at the gate just down the road when it opens at eight the next morning. Only a few other groups of twos and threes follow them in and quickly disappear. At the end of the path, a pyramid rises suddenly high above them. Silence as thick as the stones it's made of surrounds it. Adam moves onto the central plain and looks around, awestruck. None of the photographs he's seen have prepared him for this grandeur. He and Tony walk from structure to structure with a kind of reverence.

They sit on the steps of the Temple of the Warriors, and Adam talks about what he knows of the Maya from his reading. Time was at the heart of their religion, he tells Tony. Their priests studied the intricate movements of the stars as a way of comprehending the mysteries of time itself. They invented complex methods of counting so they could calculate the exact moments when the various wheels of time, circling above and around them, would touch each other. For at those precise moments, blood must be shed in sacred rituals that would ensure the continuation of life.

This blood—small amounts from their rulers, large amounts from captured warriors—must be offered back to the universe, to feed the forces of creation and nourish them. It was the responsibility of the Maya, their special burden, to keep the count, to mark the passing of the days. If they failed in this—if the count was not accurate and blood was not offered at the proper moment—the wheels would stop turning, life would cease, and time would be no more.

Tony wrinkles his forehead.

"All that blood," he says. "It sounds barbaric."

"Does it?" asks Adam. "Really? More barbaric than guys like me getting blown apart in Asian jungles?"

"But . . . wait a minute. I don't see how you can compare the two."

"No? Think about it, then. The blood's the same. It flows out just the same. And when it's gone, you die. Besides . . ."

"What?"

"The Maya, at least, knew why they were doing it. The blood they shed was to keep life going. All of life. Ours is so we can hang on to what we've got. I like their reason better. It's more . . . honest . . . and straightforward. Everybody understood what it was *for.*"

"Come on. That doesn't make any sense. You were fighting a *war,* for god's sake. For your country."

Adam shakes his head. "You can talk about it like that because you weren't there. 'Fighting a war' is too . . . abstract and heroic a way to describe it. What we were doing was wandering around in jungles getting ripped to pieces. For no reason, that I can see. But . . . for the Maya, for what they did, there was a *purpose.*"

"Well . . . ," says Tony. "They thought there was, I guess."

"They *believed* there was. It's not the same thing."

"How do you mean?"

Adam is silent for a minute or two, staring across at the pyramid. Tony waits.

"So many people," Adam says, "we Americans in particular, have the idea that the world simply *is* what we think it is. All we have to do is look around and nod and agree about what's out there. Grass is green. Yep. The sky is blue. See there? Water's wet, you're taller than I am. But that's not it at all. Not at all. We've been taught, from the time we're born, to see things a certain way—the way our parents, and their parents, saw them.

"Animals don't talk. Of course not. Spirits don't live inside trees, gods don't appear among us, the cosmos spins along on its way without any help from us. We get it into our heads that that's the way things *are,* so of course what we see when we look at something is exactly what we expected to be there. No more, no less. If an animal talked to us, we wouldn't hear it. If a god appeared, we wouldn't even know it was there. And the universe . . . well, it's on its own. Good luck to it."

He reaches over and takes Tony's hand.

"It's just . . . the Maya saw things very differently, but what they saw made as much sense to them as what we see does to us, I'm sure of that. They believed that when their king shed blood from his penis into a clay dish, the gods were made manifest—the same way I believe that . . . what? That protons and electrons whirling around in empty space make up . . . my arm. Or your brain. I can't see that, and I never will. But I believe it."

He looks down the long plain toward the Ball Court.

"What's important is the Maya were looking at their lives from the *inside,*" he says. "To them, what they did wasn't bizarre, or exotic. It was just . . . necessary. So for us to sit here, on the outside, judging something we know nothing about . . . what does that get us? We end up right where we started."

He squeezes Tony's hand.

"There are a lot more ways of seeing, and a lot more things to be seen, than we have any idea of. I believe."

They sit for a while, not speaking. Adam lets go of Tony's hand, stands up, stretches, and says, "Want to go up to the top of the pyramid?"

"Great idea," says Tony.

As they climb, Adam counts the narrow steps. Ninety-one. Four times ninety-one. Three hundred sixty-four. And one for the temple on top. The representation of a year in stone. Systematic. Methodical. Exact.

The sky is clear, and the sun is hot. The pyramid shimmers beneath them. Adam looks out over the flat jungle toward the flat horizon. Off to the southeast, a grove of imported palms surrounding a large hotel rises above the much lower tree line of the native vegetation. Nothing else alters the sameness of the view. Adam feels the silent, orderly passing of time.

He hears noises from the plain below. He looks down and sees people moving onto it from all directions. The tour buses are beginning to arrive. Groups break away and start scrambling up the pyramid toward him.

"Let's go back to the Hacienda," he says. "Take a swim, maybe. Come again later on, after they've gone."

Tony nods.

54

The next morning, they are back as soon as the gates open and again have the place pretty much to themselves. The few other people who came in with them wander off out of sight. Tony heads down toward the Ball Court. Adam goes and sits on the steps of the Platform of Venus, from which he has a clear view of the pyramid. Its symmetry is pleasing and majestic at the same time. The play of light and shadow on the raised stone patterns of the terraces is hypnotic. Adam leans back and closes his eyes.

From somewhere off to his left, near the Temple of the Warriors, comes the sound of drums. Slow and insistent. Adam sits up. Groups of short dark people are moving toward him from the right. They are simply dressed, and their heads are bowed. They gather at the base of the pyramid. As the drums grow louder, they turn to face the Temple of the Warriors. Down its steps come ordered rows of men in magnificent attire. Elaborate headdresses in the shapes of birds and animals. Feather capes around their shoulders. Jaguar skins around their waists.

They walk slowly across the open plain toward the stairway on the near side of the pyramid. As they move, they form two lines. They climb the steps, one line on each side of the stairway. When the first warrior reaches the top step, he halts. The next warrior does the same on the step below. This continues until a warrior stands guard at each side of every step. The drums stop. The crowd looks up.

From inside the temple at the top of the pyramid comes another group of men, even more splendidly dressed. The sound of their chanting drifts down to where Adam is sitting. They form a wedge from the central door of the temple out toward the sides of the stairway where the guardian warriors are standing. The chanting stops.

A tall man walks out from the temple and stands at the head of the stairs. He wears a flowing cape of yellow and red feathers and a towering headdress of iridescent green plumes. At his side is a young man wearing only a simple white cloth around his waist. The crowd on the plain shouts. The tall man chants. The crowd shouts. The man chants. The crowd shouts.

The young man starts down the center of the stairway, followed by the tall man and the others from the temple. They cross the plain toward Adam, heading for the wide roadway that leads to the sacred *cenote* off to the north. The guardian warriors come down the steps and follow behind.

Drumbeats begin again. The young man, at the head of the procession, walks steadily toward Adam. As he nears, Adam can see that his only adornment is a small necklace of gold and jade. His head is held high, and his face is radiant.

The procession passes to Adam's right, the pace slow and steady, the mood jubilant. The crowd of commoners brings up the rear. When the last of them has disappeared up the roadway, the drumming stops. The plain is empty once more.

55

"We're back from Mexico, Mother," says Adam. "And I just wanted to call and see how you are."

"You had a nice time, then?" says Irene.

"Very nice. Wonderful places."

"I'm so glad for that. And so glad you called. It always makes me feel less lonesome."

"For heaven's sake. *Are* you lonesome?"

"A little bit, yes."

"I thought you were all settled in and happy there in Weatherford. Getting involved in all kinds of things."

"I thought so, too. But I've had kind of a setback that's really thrown me for a loop."

"What's happened?"

"It's a long story."

"I've got time."

"You're sure?"

"Yes. I'm sure."

"Well . . . about a month or so ago, one day when I was driving by Miz Rothrock's house on the way home from the beauty parlor, it hit me that the Presbyterian church here didn't have a visitation program any more, not a regular, organized one like there always used to be. And I thought we needed to start one up again. Go by to see shut-ins. People who're old and don't get out much, or sick, or just need to know every so often that somebody cares. Take by a few flowers or a casserole. Or just sit and visit for a while. Bring a little sparkle into their lives. You know?"

"I do know. It's what you do best."

"Reverend Riley sure didn't think so."

"What do you mean?"

"He was all for the *idea,* when I went in and proposed it to him. He thought *that* was fine and should definitely be done. Of course. Should have thought of it himself. But when I said I'd love to get it organized, head it up, he said he thought not."

"Why on earth would he say that?"

"He figured it should have been obvious to me. That a divorced woman, especially a *recently* divorced woman of my age, wasn't quite the right representative for the church to be sending out into the community."

"He said that?"

"He said that. The whole time smiling the most patronizing, *Christian*-looking smile you ever saw."

"Oh, Mother," says Adam. "I'm sorry. I'm so sorry."

"Well . . . so am I. What's that saying about you can't go home again? I guess I thought I could."

"It's their loss, Mother. You'd've been wonderful. And people would've loved your visits."

"Well. We'll never know, will we? Now."

"So what are you planning to do?"

"I'm not sure. I don't see how I can stick around here. Not after this. I feel so . . . left out."

She sighs.

"I may go out to Albuquerque for a while," she says. "You know how much I've always loved it out there. And how well your daddy's cousin and I get along. A friend of hers is going on sabbatical and needs somebody to look after her house for the year she'll be gone. So I'm thinking about agreeing to do it. I've always wanted to spend a whole year out there. See all the ceremonial dances at the pueblos. And the luminarias at Christmas, and such. Just talking to you about it gets me all excited. I think I'll call up Billie June right away. Soon as we hang up. Tell her to let her friend know I'll do it. For as long as she needs me."

56

Adam flies down to San Antonio to visit his father. Tony says he won't go, so the two of them can have a chance to get acquainted. He'll stay home with Fuzzy Bobo. He calls after Adam arrives and has an easy, comfortable chat with Sam.

Adam and his father have such a good time with each other Adam goes back, once in the spring, again in the fall, for three years. Every other time or so, he flies out to Albuquerque, coming or going, to see his mother. She decides to stay and gets herself an apartment there. She buzzes around, has started taking ceramics classes, volunteers at the hospital.

In San Antonio, Sam takes Adam to his favorite places. They walk around a beautiful garden that covers an entire hillside. They go to the zoo. They drive past the golf course in Breckenridge Park, where Sam no longer plays.

"Do you see much of your brother?" asks Adam, one day as they're leaving the park.

"Not much," says Sam.

"But you used to do so many things together. Golfing and bowling. You had fun."

"We did."

"So what happened?"

"It's not important."

"Of course it's important. He was always such a big part of your life. And he only lives twenty minutes away."

Sam turns and looks at Adam steadily, then back at the road.

"Did you learn this from your mother?" he asks.

"Ah," says Adam, and he drops the subject.

At least once every trip, they take a picnic lunch and drive out into the hill country, where live oak and mesquite and scrubby pines dot the rock-strewn slopes. In the springtime, bluebonnets and other wildflowers, red and orange mostly, cover the hillsides and valleys.

They watch *Jeopardy* every evening, without fail, Adam shouting out the questions when he knows them, which is often.

"How come you're up on so many different things?" Sam asks.

"I don't know," says Adam. "I never realized I *was*."

As time goes by, Sam begins to rewrite their mutual history. He's always been so proud of Adam, he says. *Proud?* thinks Adam. Of that skinny little kid who dropped every ball ever thrown at him and read all the time? Well, maybe he was. Who's to say?

They go once a week, sometimes twice, to eat Mexican food, a passion they *have* always shared. Sam has a favorite restaurant, a branch of Casa Rio not far from his house, where the smiling waitresses flutter around this still-handsome regular customer, who comes in most often to eat alone. Sam always orders the same thing—cheese enchilada, rice, and beans. One beer before the meal, a second beer with. Adam drinks ginger ale and eats everything in sight.

One evening, as they are finishing, Sam says, "There's something I want to be sure you know."

He takes a sip of his beer.

"I've wrestled a lot with this," he says. "With what the Bible tells us about people like you."

Adam winces, but says nothing.

"And I've concluded," says Sam, "that God made you the way you are, just as sure as He made me the way I am. You didn't have any say-so about *what* you were going to be. All you could do was decide *how* you'd live your life. And I can't tell you how well I think you've done that."

He sips his beer again and wipes his mouth.

"I don't just love you very much," he says. "That's the easy part. I also respect and admire you more than anybody else I've ever known."

By the spring of that third year, Sam has grown noticeably weaker. He doesn't meet Adam at the airport this time; Adam rents a car.

They don't go out for Mexican food; Adam calls in an order and brings it home.

Sam's mind is still strong, he wills it to be, but his body is not. Adam's love for him is so intense it's like another person sitting here in the room with them.

"Are you all right?" Adam asks.

"I'm fine," says Sam. "Just not quite the man I used to be."

57

The full weight of mortality, Adam discovers, can arrive through as simple and unobtrusive a messenger as a small drop of blood. On the floor of your father's kitchen, right in front of the refrigerator. Neat. Round. Tidy in its symmetry. Outside, on this balmy October morning, the world goes on its way. Inside, a small drop of blood sits on the floor.

Adam stares at it, transfixed. It's little, about the size of a nickel. And bright red. Fresh. Recently fallen. The brightest red Adam can ever remember seeing. He's suddenly angry, irrationally angry at the defenseless little drop, lying so foolishly out here in the open. If it's going to do that, it should have the sense to be less red. Less tempting to the gods.

He can't stop looking at it. Can't move. Can't focus his attention on anything else. He just stands, staring at it. His father's blood. The blood he came from. He knows how it got here. He doesn't know how he knows, but he does. It's not a nosebleed. Not a cut. It's blood dislodged from someplace inside his father, pulled along by gravity, down through his father's penis and out onto the floor. Out into the intense light of a Texas morning. Out into the sunlight where it ought not to be.

Adam wants to put it back. Lift it carefully up off the floor, cup it gently in the palm of his hand, tiptoe into his father's bedroom, and slip it back in. Back where it belongs. Back where it can do what it's supposed to do. Give strength and wholeness to the body it's a part of. Not desert it. Not go dropping around on kitchen floors where it has no business being.

Adam bends toward it and sees another drop. And another. And another. A trail of them. He follows it. From the refrigerator past the sink, across the living room and in through his father's bedroom door.

Too many of them. He can't collect them all. Cradle them in his hand. Put them back where they belong. There are too many of them. He looks down at his father, sleeping on his side. There, in the crotch of his boxer shorts, is the evidence. Three drops of blood, close together. Adam was right. His vision of where it came from was right.

He goes to the kitchen. Over by the refrigerator. He stares again at the first drop, lying beside the big toe of his left foot. Bright red next to the gray of his sock. Blood from his father's penis. Blood to nourish the universe. But no gods are made manifest. None that Adam can see. The sacrifice has been made, but the gods haven't shown up. Where are they? What good are they? Blood has been let, but they are nowhere to be seen.

Back in his old room, the room his mother stayed in after she and Sam started sleeping apart, he hears the television set go on. Sam is up from his morning nap. Adam walks down the hallway, across the shiny clean floor of the kitchen to the living room, where the floor between the rugs is equally shiny. The top half of Sam's head pokes up above the cushion of his brown fake-leather recliner. The hair on that head was thick and black like Adam's until recently, but now it's gray and sparse. Adam smiles, in spite of himself, looking at the sparse, gray top of his father's head. He can't think of a reason in the world why he should be smiling, but he is.

Across the room, a tennis match is under way. Adam hears the soothing thwock, thwock of the ball and the quietly resonant whispers of the announcer. Whisper, whisper, whisper. Thwock. Thwock. Whisper. Thwock. Applause. He goes around, waves hello, and sits beside Sam, in the green fake-leather recliner his mother used to sit in, though not for tennis matches. He looks over and sees that his father has on a clean pair of shorts. He stares at the screen. Whisper, whisper. Thwock. Thwock. Thwock. Applause. The two players, holding their rackets in one hand and wiping their faces with towels they've been handed, change ends of the court.

"You were bleeding this morning," says Adam, still looking at the flickers on the screen.

"A little," says Sam, eyes on the match.

Thwock. Thwock. Whisper. Thwock. Thwock.

"More than a little," says Adam. "I mopped up quite a bit."

Out of the corner of his eye, Adam sees his father glance over at him, then quickly back at the television set. "Not so much. It's okay."

"It's not okay," says Adam. "Losing blood is never okay."

"It happens, though. I don't pay much attention to it."

"How often? How often does it happen?"

Sam reaches for the remote control and switches off the television. He puts the control back on the credenza beside him, folds his hands together, and stares straight ahead.

"There's something wrong inside of me, son," he says. "Has been for a while now. I'm not sure what, but probably cancer."

Adam wants to cry out, throw the lamp at the floor and break it, cover his ears, anything. Instead, he sits quietly, looking at the near side of his father's face.

"What do you intend to do about it?" he asks.

"Not see a doctor, that's for sure," says Sam. "I haven't been to one for going on ten years, and I have no intention of starting in again now."

"Even for this?"

"Especially for this. They'll want to do something outrageous. Just because they can. Show me who's in charge. Chemo. Radiation. Maybe both. They think they know best, but they don't. What they'll do is kill me. They'll charge me a fortune first and end up killing me. But I'm not going to let them. The cancer can do that just fine all by itself."

It's all Adam can do to keep from grabbing his father and shaking him. *No!!* he wants to shout. *No!!* But he doesn't move.

"You're just going to sit here and die?" he asks.

"Of course I am. We all are. We've been sitting here dying from the second we were born. You know that. I'm just a bit closer than I was—than you are—that's all."

Adam reaches over and puts his hand on his father's arm. Sam puts his hand on top of Adam's and pats it.

"You'll have to do me a favor, though, son," he says.

"What's that?"

"I don't want you telling your mother about this. Any of it. Or anybody else who might tell her. Do you hear me?"

"Why not?"

"Because she'd be all over me, that's why. Full of care and concern. And I just couldn't handle that. Not now."

"I'm sure she'd *want* to come."

"Yes. I'm sure she would, too. That's what I'm saying. But . . . that's no good, don't you see? Coming back like that out of pity. Or remorse. It's no good."

"I don't understand. Care and concern are exactly what you need, seems to me."

"And I'm going to have them."

"How?"

"I've hired a young man to come take care of me."

"When?"

"As soon as you've left. He'll move into your room back there and be around all the time. Do what needs doing. I'll ask him to come by before you go, so you can meet him."

"But . . . wait. Who is this man?"

"His name's Victor Ochoa. And this is his specialty. Taking care of people who are . . ." Sam shrugs.

Adam feels a rush of anger. And jealousy. And relief.

"How did you find him?" asks Adam.

"Didn't. He found me. Herminia, that waitress from Casa Rio who's been buying my groceries for me? She knows his mother. He heard about how I'm doing and called me up."

"But . . . I would've come, if I'd known. Come and stayed for a while."

"I know you would. That's why I hired Victor. You have a life. I have a life. They're not the same. You go look after Tony. Victor can look after me."

58

Adam walks out of the gate into the airport but doesn't see Tony anywhere.

Damn, he thinks.

He walks toward the escalator down to baggage claim.

"Boo," says a voice behind him.

He turns. Tony grabs him and gives him a hug.

"Hi, sailor," says Tony. "New in town?"

Adam laughs.

"You clown," he says. "I thought you weren't here."

"Where else would I be?"

On the way home, on an icy road that's just been sanded, Tony asks, "How's your father?"

"Pretty bad," says Adam. "Weak. Some kind of internal bleeding."

"What do the doctors say?"

"He won't go."

"*What?* What are you talking about, 'He won't go'?"

"It's a perfectly good English sentence. He . . . won't . . . go. He's always been suspicious of doctors. Never been sure they knew what they were doing, really. And he doesn't want them messing with him now."

"And you didn't *make* him go? You didn't just put him in the car and *take* him there?"

"No, Tony. I didn't."

"Jesus H. Christ! He's *bleeding* inside. What kind of son *are* you?"

"Just hold it right there. Don't you dare go sticking your nose into this."

"Dare? You've got a nerve. Of course I dare. After twenty-how-many years? Of course I dare. He could die, you know."

"Good god, Tony. You're really hitting below the belt. I *know* he could die. I'm scared to death he could die."

"Then why don't you do something to prevent it? Or at least postpone it?"

"Because he asked me not to. We spent a whole lifetime barely knowing each other, and now we're friends. Good friends. He trusts me. He asked me not to interfere, and he trusts me to respect his wishes."

"I think you're making a big mistake."

"Be that as it may."

"I should've gone down with you. This last time, for sure. He might've listened to me."

"Or *not*. More likely, he'd've clammed up, denied the whole thing, and we'd be right where we are now. Except he and I wouldn't be so close. He wouldn't have somebody he knows he can rely on."

"And that's more important to you than keeping him alive?"

Adam hesitates.

"Yes," he says. "I think it is."

They drive the rest of the way in silence. The road gets worse. A light snow begins to fall.

As Tony turns off toward their house, he says, "So what does this mean? Are we still going back to Mexico, or not?"

"We're going," says Adam.

− 59 −

The flight to Merida is tense. The pleasure Adam has felt on every other trip they've taken together is missing. Tony's insistence on interfering, his need to control and meddle and judge, continue to irritate Adam. Adam could make things all right again by giving in, apologizing, the way he always does. Well, not this time, he thinks. I'm tired of it. I've been doing that for much too long. The one who needs to learn about apologizing is Tony. Let *him* make things all right again for a change.

As soon as the plane takes off, Adam opens his book, a copy of *Pride and Prejudice* he found in a secondhand bookstore. He turns a little toward the aisle, away from Tony, and begins to read. Pretending at first, so he doesn't have to talk, then getting engrossed in the story. Even when the meal comes, Adam keeps his book open, ignoring Tony. He feels Tony withdrawing, not liking this treatment one bit. So let him, thinks Adam. He could use a taste of his own medicine.

They land, get their bags, clear customs, take a taxi to the hotel, downtown near the plaza. They exchange a few words at the airport, the necessary ones about getting where they're going, but Adam is careful not to go beyond that. The ride into town is completely silent, Adam staring out the window into the darkness.

After they check in and unpack, they go back down and take a walk around the plaza. The night is warm and clear, and the plaza is crowded. Normally, they would both be excited about seeing a new place and would want to compare first impressions. This time they only walk and look.

They go upstairs, brush their teeth, crawl into bed. The same bed. Adam isn't *that* angry. He is just drifting off when the phone on the bedside table rings, harsh and loud. He sits straight up, his heart beating fast.

"Oh, my god," he says.

Tony answers the phone and turns to Adam.

"It's for you."

Adam goes around, takes the phone, sits on the other bed.

"Hello?"

"Adam? It's Victor. Victor Ochoa?"

"Yes?"

"I'm sorry to call so late, but . . . your father just passed away. Just now. And I . . . I wanted you to know as soon as I could."

"Thanks. It . . . you were . . ." Adam stops, feeling stunned. He knew as soon as the phone rang, but he still feels stunned. Outside himself looking back in. What can he say? He has to ask. He wants to know more, but he also wants *not* to know. If he doesn't hear about it, maybe it won't be true.

"Adam?" says Victor.

"I'm here. I just . . . was it . . . difficult?"

"Not so very. I've seen worse. He had some pain, yesterday and today. Tonight, as I was getting ready for bed, it was the most, so he called me. I had nothing to give him, you know, prescription stuff. He wouldn't let me. So I just went in and held his hand. 'Is it time?' he asked me. I said, 'Maybe it is, before it gets too bad. If it is, let go. Just let go,' I said, 'and pass on over. It'll be fine there.' He squeezed my hand, had some more pain, made a little noise in his throat, and . . . he was gone."

"Oh, my god," says Adam.

"I straightened him out, gave him a little hug, and went to call the number I had. For the medical school. A man said somebody will come right over. I'm waiting now."

"Thank you, Victor. For everything you've done. I can't tell you . . ."

"It's okay. You don't have to. I loved him, too, you know."

"I know. Do you need anything? Should I come there?"

"No, no. Everything's fine. Sam had everything all taken care of. You know how he was."

"I do."

"Somebody will come and take him away. Just like he wanted. No services or nothing. He didn't want that. He's gone away now, and what's left behind will help young doctors to learn. That's what he kept saying. They need to learn. So . . . you just keep on with your trip. That's what he wanted."

"You'll be calling the others?"

"Of course. I have a list he gave me. Your name is the first."

"Thanks. I . . . I'll be in touch after we get back."

Adam hangs up and stares at the wall.

"Daddy's dead," he says.

"I figured that," says Tony.

The greatest sadness Adam has ever known presses down on him. He thinks it's more than he can bear. Far from relieving the pressure, his crying only makes it worse. Each ragged breath brings a memory, each memory a new sense of loss. He cries uncontrollably for a long time, he has no idea how long. Tony sits beside him, an arm around his shoulder, the other hand on his leg, patting, soothing, in time calming him. Thankfully, Tony doesn't speak, doesn't try to make it better, doesn't ask what he can do. Being there is what he can do.

Instead of rushing out as before, the tears now only slide down Adam's cheek. Tony wipes the cheek nearest him and kisses it. He gets up, goes to the bottle on the table, and brings Adam a glass of water. Adam drinks it.

"I'm sorry, hon," he says. "I really am. I was being such a jerk."

"I know," says Tony.

"That I was being a jerk?"

Tony smiles. "No. That you're sorry. So am I. Sorry I made you mad and really sorry about your father. We'll both miss him. He was a wonderful man."

The ceiling of their hotel room grows lighter. Imperceptibly at first, then more quickly, as a bit of gold begins to mix with the gray. If anyone were to ask, Adam would say he hasn't slept at all, though he probably has. Fitfully, off and on. The sadness pushing down on him is like a weight on his chest, and he's felt tears moving along the sides of his face through most of the night.

Around 6:30, after the noise of the morning traffic has begun to build, Adam gets up and puts on his clothes. Tony, who was awake with him a good bit of the time, letting him talk when he felt like it and just holding him when he didn't, is sleeping soundly now. Adam leaves a note on the bedside table, takes the key, and slips out the door.

Even at this early hour, the air in the street is beginning to be hot and heavy. He walks to the main plaza. There, where it's more open and the air has room to move, a breeze ruffles the leaves of the trees and folds and unfolds the flag at the top of the pole in the center. Each time the breeze dies down, the heat moves in and settles around Adam. But soon another breeze comes along to push it away again.

Adam sits on a bench near the street, fanning himself with his straw hat. The traffic gets thicker by the minute. A bus with a faulty muffler shakes the bench as it passes. Then a motorcycle with no muffler at all roars by and ups the ante. Fumes from all the vehicles drift from the street into the plaza and hang in the air. The trunks of the trees around the plaza are painted white from the ground about five feet up. Bugs? Adam wonders. Decoration? What? Healthy-looking vines climb most of the trees, their dark green serrated leaves a stark contrast to the white of the trunks.

Vendors are beginning to gather in the plaza. Mayan women in white dresses edged top and bottom with elaborate many-colored embroidery arrange their pottery and leather belts and painted tin ornaments. Young Mayan men sort out their string hammocks and Panama hats. Old Mayan men with creased faces set up their shoe-shine stands. Small boys and girls in shorts and T-shirts take boxes of the Chiclets they will sell from a man in a truck. Several well-dressed men carrying briefcases walk quickly along the sidewalks. One beautifully made-up woman in a stylish suit trails a cloud of perfume as she passes.

A bell in the cathedral tower rings the quarter hour. It sounds cracked and has very little resonance, but Adam feels drawn to it nonetheless. He walks around the plaza and across the street into the cathedral. It's dark inside. And cool. And empty. Nobody else is around. Although the decor is simpler than other cathedrals Adam has seen, still there is a sense of quiet majesty. Something to do with the height of the ceiling, Adam decides.

Each brightly painted plaster saint, standing in a niche along the wall, has its own devoted supplicants. Candles of many heights crowd the wrought-iron pedestals, flickering out the prayers of the faithful. The bunches of real flowers tucked into the niches have all faded and dried up, but the plastic ones retain their shapes and most of their colors.

Adam is at a loss. His Protestant upbringing has left him unfamiliar with saints. The Virgin Mary, of course, is unmistakable. A shawl of light blue plaster covers her head, and her face is kind and serene. The saint pierced with arrows has to be Sebastian, but Adam has no way of recognizing the others.

Near the front of the cathedral is a bowl of water. Adam dips his fingers in and makes what he hopes is a proper cross. The statue of Christ to his left is a tragic sight. Blood pours from the circle of his thorny crown and out of a gaping wound in his side. His kneecaps are bloody and bare where all the flesh has been torn away. Heavy nails hold his hands and feet tight against the cross. His body slumps sideways, his chin resting on his chest.

"Does it hurt?" Adam asks.

Jesus raises his head. "Not any more," he says. "It did for a while. For hundreds of years. But . . . not any more."

"Are you sorry?"

His blood-stained face is puzzled. "Sorry for what?"

"That you had to die in such an awful way."

"Only what led up to it was awful. The dying was not so bad."

"Looks to me like you suffered quite a lot."

"No more than many others."

"But . . . it seems so unfair. You came to show us how to live, and look what we did to you."

"Life *is* unfair. You must know that by now. The important thing is what you do with that fact."

"Do." Adam shakes his head. "But what if I get it wrong? My father did, and now he's gone and it's too late."

"Did he? Did he get it wrong?"

"He thought so. At the end, when he was so alone."

"But you loved him. You know you did. And he loved you. How can that be getting it wrong?"

"Wait a minute. That *can't* be all that matters. Can it? Loving people?"

"You tell me."

"No," says Adam. "I want to hear it from you. So I can be sure."

But Jesus just smiles.

"Please. Help me be sure."

He smiles again and bows his head. His chin is resting on his chest. He doesn't look up.

− 61 −

Adam is home only long enough to do some laundry and repack before he flies out to Albuquerque to see his mother. Irene meets him at the airport. As he walks through the gate toward her, he sees that her eyes are red, her face streaked. He puts his arms around her and holds her close. She leans her head against his chest, then hugs him and moves away to blow her nose and catch her breath.

"Let's sit here for a minute," says Adam. "I'm in no hurry."

They sit, and Irene rummages in her purse for more Kleenex and her inhaler.

"I just feel so bad about your daddy," she says.

"I know," says Adam. "I do, too."

"And no service! That's the hardest thing of all. I knew he wanted to give his body to that medical school. Fine. I understood that. But no service? No place to . . . I don't know."

"Comfort ourselves?"

"I guess so, yes. It all seems so sudden, somehow. I just never thought . . . well, I know I said those things about . . . you know, about him . . ."

"Doing himself in?"

She flinches.

"But I never thought . . . I never thought he'd actually be *gone* like this. So soon."

"I didn't either," says Adam. "He was bad that last time I saw him. But I didn't realize . . . if I had, I would never have left him."

Irene flinches again.

"'Left him,'" she says. "Oh, my."

She dabs at her eyes.

"You blame me, don't you?" she says. "For what I did. Moving out, and going ahead with the divorce."

Adam hesitates. He does, in fact, but can he tell her that? Should he? He looks at the pleading in her eyes. This is no time, he concludes, for that kind of honesty.

"No, Mother. You did what you thought you had to. Or wanted to."

"*Had* to," she says. "Let's stick with 'had to'."

"All right. Had to. We all do that, all the time. It's just that . . . sometimes it works out better than others."

"*This* didn't work out very well, did it? My leaving."

"That's for you to say."

She takes a deep breath, dabs at her eyes, coughs, spits into the Kleenex.

"It didn't," she says. "He was . . . so exasperating sometimes! He just . . . made me crazy. He wouldn't *do* things. Wouldn't *go* anywhere. We had that one trip. One trip! To Hawaii. Right after he retired. I just loved it so much." She blows her nose. "Six weeks of sun and sand. And the music! Ukuleles and hulas. Flowers everywhere. I just loved it. And he did, too!"

She looks at Adam, a bit fiercely.

"You can't tell me he didn't. He loved it. We both loved it together. And then he . . ." She struggles for a breath. "He just went home, sat down in that chair of his, turned on the TV, and watched ball games from then on. Wouldn't budge. Baseball season, then football season, then basketball. With golf and bowling and tennis thrown in there somewhere. I thought I'd just scream.

"I tried to get him out. Make him take an interest in things. For his own good. You know? But he just wouldn't . . ."

Adam squeezes her hand.

"I love you, Mother," he says.

She looks up at him quickly.

"Is that what we're talking about?" she asks.

"It's what *I'm* talking about. It's what matters. Between you and me. I love you more than I can ever tell you."

Irene gets out another Kleenex.

"So many of the good things in my life," he says, "came from you. I always knew you loved me. Always. There was never the slightest doubt. And that made everything else all right. Problems. Confusions. Disappointments. They had no power so long as I knew you loved me that much."

His father had done this for him, given him this extraordinary gift, before he died. The least Adam can do is pass it on to her.

"Thank you, Adam," she says, swallowing hard. "I can't tell you how much that means to me."

He squeezes her hand again.

"You don't have to," he says. "But all the rest of it . . . just forget it. It's gone. It's over. *You* did what you did. Daddy did what he did. I did what I did. And that's that. Could we have done it better? Oh, dear lord, yes."

He hears her sharp intake of breath.

"Sorry, Mother. 'Oh, *my goodness,* yes.' But you know what I mean . . . we struggle along. We do stupid things. Occasionally we do okay things. We just have to hope it all averages out in the end."

"Do you think it will," she asks, "for me?"

"It already has. You've loved so much, and given so much, that the other stuff . . ."

"Selfishness. Impatience. Stubbornness."

He puts his arm around her shoulder.

"Don't be so hard on yourself," he says. "Feel as bad as you have to about Daddy, and then move on. That's what he did. Things didn't turn out the way he expected. Hardly ever, seems to me. But he just kept on moving on. Hoping the next time would be a little better."

She smiles.

"Hoping," she says. "He did a lot of that, didn't he?"

"Yes. He did."

She blows her nose and smiles again.

"I'm glad you got to spend so much time with him," she says. "There at the end."

"Me, too. We had a good time."

"I'm glad."

He squeezes her shoulder and kisses her cheek.

"Why don't *we* do that?" he says. "You and me. Have a good time while I'm here."

She smiles again.

"We could do that," she says.

She stands up.

"Let's go get your bags. There's a wonderful Mexican restaurant right on our way home. They make the *best* tamales! I know how much you love *them*."

– 62 –

Tony walks back into the waiting room. Adam jumps up and goes over to him.

"What happened?" asks Adam. "You were in there so long. Did they give you the stress test after all?"

"Yes."

"And what do they say?"

"I'll tell you on the way home."

As Tony pulls the car out of the parking lot, Adam says, "Tell me now."

"They found some kind of 'anomaly'," says Tony.

"What does that mean, exactly?"

"Something's not right with my heart."

"But . . . they don't know what?"

"No."

"How will they find out?"

"I have to go to the hospital for an angiogram. Next Tuesday."

God, I'm so scared, thinks Adam. But I can't tell him that. It'll just make things worse for him. No, it won't, you idiot. It'll make him feel less alone.

"I'm scared," says Adam.

Tony looks over, smiles, and reaches for Adam's hand.

"Me, too. A little. No, a lot. It's all so unexpected. But we can handle it. Together. Right?"

"Right," says Adam.

The angiogram is scheduled for nine o'clock Tuesday morning. The hospital is in Bangor, more than an hour from their house. Tony will have to stay there overnight, to be sure the incision has healed and there's no internal bleeding. Adam makes a reservation at the hotel, a former nurses' dormitory, attached to one end of the hospital.

Tuesday morning, they check Adam into the hotel, then start the process of getting Tony registered, computerized, weighed, blood-pressured, into the proper room, changed into a hospital gown, and laid out on the bed ready to go. "Adam here is my lover," Tony says to each new person they encounter, "so I'd like him to be with me as much as he can." The answer, each time, is "Of course" or "No problem." At first, Adam is surprised by the response, but soon begins to expect it.

A doctor comes in to explain the procedure. A very thin tube will be inserted through an incision in Tony's thigh near his groin. It will pass through arteries all the way up to Tony's heart, where it will release an amount of dye. As the dye spreads, an X-ray machine will show where blood is flowing and where it isn't. Tony can watch all this on a video screen, if he likes.

"Will it take long?" asks Adam.

"Not long," says the doctor. "An hour or so."

Adam looks over at Tony.

"It's an easy procedure," says the doctor. "Routine."

'Routine'! thinks Adam. Not in my life it's not.

A little after 9:00, a gurney rolls up to the doorway. Tony gets on it, waves at Adam, and is rolled away.

"You can wait here in the room," says a nurse. "He won't be long."

"Thanks," says Adam.

He's fine till about 10:00. He reads a little, closes his eyes and rests a little. Reads some more. By 10:30, he's getting nervous. At 10:45, he walks to the nurses' station.

"Any word on Mr. Marchak?" he asks.

A nurse types on a keyboard, looks at the computer screen, looks up.

"He'll be back soon," she says.

"Is there a problem?"

She smiles. "They're just finishing up now. He'll be back soon."

At 11:20, a different nurse comes to the door.

"Mr. Hunter?"

"Yes."

"Mr. Marchak is being taken to Room 412, on the cardiac ward. You can meet him there."

Something's wrong, thinks Adam.

"Shall I take up his clothes and things?" he asks.

"If you don't mind, that would be a big help."

When Adam gets there, Tony is just settling into the bed near the door. An elderly man is asleep in the one nearer the windows. Tony is giddy and appears to be drunk.

"What's up with him?" Adam asks the nurse who's helping Tony. She laughs.

"They use a strong narcotic for this procedure. To ease the tension. They always tell the patients if they're feeling apprehensive, they can ask for more." She laughs again. "He obviously asked for plenty."

Adam smiles.

"What's the cure?" he asks.

"Rest," she says. "He'll fall asleep and be fine when he wakes up."

"When will we know the results?"

"Someone will be by to talk with you."

"When?"

"As soon as they can."

Tony does fall asleep. Adam goes down to the cafeteria to get some lunch. Just before 3:00, Tony wakes up. The man in the other bed is still sleeping, so Tony and Adam talk quietly.

"How do you feel?" asks Adam.

"Great," says Tony, stretching. "What a trip!"

"You were really flying."

"Was I ever. I've got to find out the name of that stuff and see about getting some more."

"You planning on becoming an addict?"

"Well . . . I might consider it."

"How was the test? Did you watch the dye go through your heart?"

"No, darn it. I missed the whole thing. I really *was* apprehensive—I mean, strange contraptions wandering around in your body up by your heart—so I kept asking for more. And they kept giving it. By the time the pictures came on, I was somewhere else entirely."

They chat a while. Tony takes another nap. Adam reads. Tony's supper comes in on a tray. The man in the other bed wakes up, says hello, and starts eating, too. Adam goes back down to the cafeteria.

Later, a little after 7:00, two men come into the room.

"Mr. Marchak?" says one. "I'm Dr. Forrester, head of cardiology here. This is my assistant, Dr. Ramirez. And you're Mr. Hunter?"

"Yes," says Adam.

"Well, then, let me tell you both what's happening." He pulls the cloth screen between the two beds along its track and then sits on the edge of Tony's bed. "You have some serious blockages, Mr. Marchak. So serious we don't dare wait. We've scheduled you for surgery tomorrow morning. I'll be operating, and it looks like I'll be doing four bypasses. Dr. Ramirez will assist."

He pulls out a piece of paper.

"Here, let me show you both on this diagram."

Adam goes around and looks over his shoulder.

"These solid lines are the blockages—ninety-eight percent, ninety-five percent, ninety percent, eighty percent. As you can see, not much blood has been getting through."

Tony looks up at Adam, his eyes wide. He reaches for Adam's hand.

Oh, dear god, thinks Adam.

"There's no question of not doing it this way. So in that respect, you're lucky. No decisions about the advisability of angioplasty or anything else. This is what it has to be. And the sooner the better. I would've been up earlier this afternoon, but I wanted to get all the arrangements made first. Any questions?"

Tony looks up at Adam again. "I guess not," he says. "Adam?"

"That diagram is . . . pretty dramatic," says Adam, "so . . . looks like that's it."

"Good," says Dr. Forrester. "One more thing. We're moving you down to ICU. It's just a precaution. We can monitor everything very closely down there, and we just don't want to take any chances, this close to surgery."

He stands up.

"Well," he says. "Dr. Ramirez and I will go home and get some sleep, and we'll see you tomorrow morning."

Hands are shaken all around, and the two doctors are gone.

Adam sits down.

"Dear god," he says.

"I feel like I've been hit by a truck," says Tony.

"Me, too," says Adam. He reaches for Tony's hand. "Think we could ask for some of that stuff you took this morning?"

Tony laughs.

"Or else a nice big quart of vodka," he says.

"Why not?" says Adam. "Although I guess there *are* some things to be grateful for. I mean . . . having it so soon doesn't give us much time to worry."

"Good theory. But . . ."

"Yeah," says Adam.

They sit, staring at nothing, Adam finding it impossible to think of anything else to talk about.

"Guess we'd better make some phone calls," he says at last.

"Guess so," says Tony.

They call Tony's sister, Barbara. She says she'll call Elena and the rest of the family. They call a few friends, who say they'll spread the word. They call Irene in Albuquerque.

A nurse comes in with a wheelchair.

"They're ready for you in ICU," she says.

By the time Tony is in his bed and hooked up to oxygen through his nose, heart monitors on his chest, and an IV into his arm, it's after 9:00.

"Should he be getting some rest?" Adam asks Jennifer, the night nurse.

"He really should, if you don't mind."

"How early can I come back in the morning?"

"They'll be prepping him by five or so. Five-thirty? Six?"

"I'll be here. You have my number at the hotel?"

"Yes, we do."

"And you'll call if anything . . ."

"We will."

She goes out.

Adam bends down and kisses Tony.

"Sleep well, honey," he says. "I'll see you tomorrow. Early."

Tony nods.

Adam stops by the desk at the hotel to say he won't be checking out tomorrow after all. He goes up to his room, brushes his teeth, and climbs into bed.

– 63 –

Adam's alarm goes off at 5:15, and he's in the ICU by 5:30. The door to Tony's room is closed. Panic hits Adam like a blow to the chest. He turns toward the nurses' station. Nobody's there. He turns back toward the room in time to see the door open and Jennifer, the night nurse, come out. She closes the door behind her, then smiles.

"He's fine," she says. "We gave him a shot last night, and he managed to sleep a little. Did you?"

"Not much," says Adam.

"Well . . . at least we didn't need to call you. He had some discomfort, off and on, but not a lot."

"That's good."

She smiles again.

"He talked about you last night," she says. "After you left, and before he drifted off. You're a lucky man. To be loved that much."

Holding himself together takes all of Adam's strength.

"I know," he says. He glances at the door to Tony's room. "What's happening now?"

"They're just finishing up the prepping. Washing and shaving. Things like that."

"What time does he have to go?"

"Around seven. So you still have lots of time."

"Yeah," says Adam.

She puts her hand on his arm. "I'll go see how they're doing. As soon as they've finished, you can go on in. Okay?"

"Okay."

About five minutes later, she swings the door back and props it open. Two women and a man come out, carrying pans and towels.

"He's all yours," says Jennifer. "We may be in and out a couple of times, but we'll let you be alone with him as much as we can."

"Thanks," says Adam.

As he walks in, he forces himself to smile.

"Hi, honey," he says.

"Hi," says Tony. He's still hooked up to the oxygen, the monitors, and the IV, and the fear is still in his eyes. Adam takes his hand, bends down to kiss his mouth, which seems dry and cold, and sits in the chair beside the bed, still holding on to Tony's hand.

"Remember the night we met?" asks Adam.

"Of course I do. Saturday night at the Lost and Found."

"What I remember most clearly," says Adam, "is standing just outside the doorway. We introduced ourselves and shook hands, and I remember not wanting to let go. Ever. I thought, right then, that nothing in the world could make me happier than to just keep holding on to that wonderful hand for . . ."

Adam turns away and fights to keep back his tears. Tony squeezes his hand hard.

"Look at me, Adam," he says.

Adam does.

"Go ahead and say it," says Tony. "'Hold onto my hand . . .'"

"For the rest of our lives."

"And if this should be it," says Tony, "we've had a damn good run for our money, don't you think?"

Adam, still fighting for control, says, "Yes."

Tony smiles. "I think so, too."

They sit, holding hands, not saying much, watching the open doorway as if it were a television screen. A male nurse strolls past. A phone rings, and a female nurse comes out of a room across the way to answer it. Then someone lying unconscious in a bed, surrounded by attendants with anxious faces, is wheeled rapidly by. They push the bed into a room off to the left, and a flurry of activity follows. People move quickly back and forth past Tony's door. Gradually, the tension subsides, and those going by move at a slower pace.

At 6:50, a nurse they haven't seen before comes into the room.

"Mr. Marchak?" she says.

Tony nods, still holding on to Adam's hand.

"My name's Mimi. I'll be taking care of you till seven tonight."

"Hi," says Tony. "This is Adam Hunter."

"Mr. Hunter," she says. "Just let me get your vital signs here, Mr. Marchak, and then we'll start putting some of the anesthetic through your IV. All right?"

"All right," says Tony.

Adam lets go of Tony's hand, stands up, and moves toward the door so she can get to the blood pressure machine. She puts a thermometer into Tony's mouth, writes, takes the thermometer out, writes some more. Then she fiddles a while with the IV.

"There," she says.

Through the door come two muscular young men with a gurney clattering along between them.

"Marchak?" says the shorter one.

"Yes," says Mimi.

Tony looks over at Adam. Adam swallows hard and then smiles.

The young men are brisk and efficient. They adjust the gurney to the height of Tony's bed and use the extra sheet on his bed to pull him across toward them. They unhook the oxygen tube from the wall and attach it to a canister strapped to the gurney. They wheel the monitor and the IV stand around beside them.

"Ready, Mr. Marchak?" says the taller one.

Tony turns again toward Adam. "Kiss me goodbye," he says.

Adam sees the shorter man flinch and look quickly across at the other. Adam walks over, bends down, and kisses Tony's mouth.

"I love you, honey," he says.

"I love you, too," says Tony. "You take care of yourself."

Adam nods.

The two men wheel the gurney out through the door and around the corner. Adam stares at the empty doorway.

"Try not to worry too much," says Mimi. "Dr. Forrester is an excellent surgeon, and the staff he's got in the operating room with him are all crackerjack. Your friend's in very good hands."

Adam turns and stares at her.

"Thank you," he says.

He knows he's supposed to go sit in the waiting room just down the hall, and he works hard at summoning up enough strength to start moving in that direction.

"You know where to go?" asks Mimi.

"Yes," says Adam.

He walks slowly out through the door, into the hallway, and down to the waiting room. A few people are sitting in little clusters around the edges. A large man with a beard has pulled a recliner out into the center of the room and is sprawled out horizontally, snoring loudly. A tiny elderly woman sits alone in one corner, eyes closed, lips moving as she progresses methodically around her rosary.

Adam finds a seat beside a table with a lamp on it. He takes the book he's reading out of his backpack and sets in on his lap. *Everything That Rises Must Converge.* Flannery O'Connor. He chuckles to himself. What a choice. He should've brought *Black Beauty* or *Lassie, Come Home.* No, he shouldn't. They're about loss, too. It turns out not to matter, because all he does is sit and stare at the unopened book.

Before long, Tony's sister Barbara comes in, hugs Adam, and sits in the chair beside him.

"Sorry I'm late," she says. "I went by to feed your cat, and just as I was on my way out the door, she slipped past me and ran off into the woods."

"Wouldn't you know," says Adam.

"I had to track her down and get her back inside before I could leave. That fox that's been sneaking around would've had her for lunch long before I could get over there again."

Adam smiles. "Or she'd have eaten him," he says. "But it's okay. Nothing's happened here yet. That I know of."

"He went off at seven?"

"On the dot."

"You all right?"

"No. I'm a wreck."

"Me, too. So we make a good pair."

Adam laughs. The elderly woman looks up, startled, from her rosary. Adam winks and waves. She smiles, bows her head, and starts in again on her beads.

"How's Elena holding up?" Adam asks.

"All right, I guess," says Barbara. "She can't believe it's happening to her baby, though."

"Neither can I."

"She'd be here if we'd had more notice."

"I'm sure she would."

"She sends you her love and says be sure to call her 'after.' When she can talk to Tony herself."

Adam nods. "I will."

Barbara talks quietly then—about the awful night she had, how she couldn't sleep, the weird programs that were all she could find on cable TV at 3:00 in the morning. One was a cooking program, conducted by two very large women in hippie dresses. A clip at the beginning showed them arriving on motorcycles.

"What was *that* all about?" asks Barbara.

"I have no idea," says Adam.

"And their *oven*. One of them opened it up to put in a leg of lamb, and it was the dirtiest thing you've ever seen. I couldn't believe it! I was *dying* to get up there and scrub it for her."

Adam laughs again, this time more quietly.

A little later, two friends, Barry and Jim, come and sit a while, asking Adam for details about what happened yesterday, last night, and this morning. The room is now about half full, the man in the recliner is still snoring, and the elderly woman is still whispering to her beads.

"Adam Hunter?" says the young woman at the desk. "Telephone."

Adam glances at his watch: 10:25. He runs to the desk and picks up the phone.

"Mr. Hunter?" says a woman's voice.

"Yes?"

"Mr. Marchak is safely on the heart-lung machine. He's doing fine. We just wanted to let you know."

"Thank you," says Adam. He hangs up and starts to cry. Good, he thinks. He hasn't been conscious of holding it in, but it's a relief to be letting it out.

Barbara walks over to him.

"What is it?" she says. "Bad news?"

"No," says Adam. "He's fine. It's . . . he's fine."

She leads him back to his seat and pats his shoulder as he continues to cry. He calms down, smiles, and says, "I'm all right now. Really. I just . . ." He shrugs. "I just . . ."

The others chat among themselves. It's good news, says Barbara. That was the hardest part, getting him on the machine. Lucky thing he's so strong, the others say, nodding. Adam tries to focus on what they're talking about. He wishes he could keep the vision of Tony's open chest and motionless heart out of his head.

After a while, Barry and Jim say they have to leave, get back to their shop, but be sure to let them know how it goes. Adam says he will.

By noon, Adam is starving. He realizes he didn't have any breakfast and hasn't eaten since supper last night. Three to four hours, the surgeon said. He's got time for some lunch, hasn't he? Barbara says sure. He goes over and talks with the receptionist. Of course, she says. If you go to the cafeteria here in the hospital, we can get word to you there. Should there be any change.

Adam and Barbara are sitting at a table in the cafeteria, Adam wondering about the fat content of his fish chowder, when the loud-speaker says, "Adam Hunter. Phone call in ICU waiting room. Adam Hunter. Phone call in . . ."

Adam is out the door and running down the stairs. In the waiting room, the receptionist looks up, smiles, hands Adam the phone.

"This is Adam Hunter."

"Mr. Marchak is off the heart-lung machine and resting comfortably. Everything went well, and you'll be able to see him in a couple of hours."

When Adam turns from the phone, Barbara is right behind him.

"What?" she says.

"It's okay. Oh, my god. He's off the heart-lung machine. It's okay."

They find two empty chairs. Adam looks around the room. The man in the recliner is sitting up, leafing through a magazine. The tiny elderly woman is gone. Adam goes over to the receptionist.

"The lady who was sitting in that corner," he says. "Has she left?"

"I'm afraid so, yes."

"Was it . . . bad news?"

"I'm not permitted to say."

Adam nods and goes back to his seat.

"I probably ought to be heading back now," says Barbara. "I need to get some groceries and stop by the drug store on the way home. If you think you'll be all right, that is."

"Of course I will," he says.

"You'll call me tonight? Let me know how he's doing?"

"Yes. I will."

"Don't worry about Fuzzy Bobo. I'll keep an eye on her."

Adam smiles.

"Thanks," he says.

He hugs her, and she leaves. Adam sits there alone, feeling numb. He opens his book, reads a few lines, closes it. A walk would feel good right now, he thinks. But he doesn't move. He just sits.

"Mr. Hunter?"

He looks up. The receptionist motions to him. He runs over to her.

"Dr. Forrester would like to talk with you. Through those doors there on the left."

Adam finds the surgeon in one of a row of offices, standing beside a desk flipping through a chart. He looks up and smiles.

"Mr. Marchak came through it all beautifully," he says. "We ended up doing five bypasses, though, instead of the four we expected. A place toward the back of his heart that didn't show up clearly on the angiogram. But they're all in place now. No complications during surgery. So we're hopeful."

"Thank you, Doctor," says Adam. "Where is he now?"

"Through those doors over there. He's still asleep, and will be for quite a while. But you can go in and see him for a minute, if you like."

"I'd love it. Thanks. And thank you, for everything."

"Not at all," says the doctor. He shakes Adam's hand.

Adam goes through the next room into the ICU. He sees Mimi standing in the doorway of a room straight ahead. He goes in. Tony is lying on the bed, absolutely still, face white, eyes closed. A huge plastic tube, taped to his face, comes out of his mouth and disappears over the side of the bed. A thick, reddish liquid moves along two other tubes poking out from under the bottom of his gown. On his left leg is a heavy white stocking. His chest rises almost imperceptibly, then falls. Rises, then falls. Waves of love, relief, and apprehension battle inside Adam. He looks up at Mimi.

"Is it all right to touch him?" he asks.

"Of course."

Adam puts one hand on Tony's arm. No response. Tony's eyes stay closed. His chest rises, such a tiny little bit. Drops of clear liquid slide down the IV tube into his other arm. Adam bends down and kisses Tony's forehead.

"How much longer, do you think?" Adam asks. "Till he wakes up?"

"Oh, a couple of hours, at least."

Adam looks at his watch: 2:10.

"Why don't you go on back to your hotel room," says Mimi. "You could use some rest yourself."

"Yeah," says Adam. "I could."

"I'll call you there as soon as he's awake."

"You promise?"

She smiles. "I promise."

Adam goes to get his backpack and book from the waiting room, then walks through the maze of corridors and tunnels that lead to the hotel. He takes the elevator up to his room. He's sure he could never sleep, but thinks he might just rest his eyes.

The phone rings. He sits straight up and looks at his watch. 3:30.

"Hello?" he says.

"It's Mimi, Mr. Hunter. Could you come right over?"

Adam feels a stabbing in his chest.

"Is he all right?" he asks.

"He's fine," she says. "He's just fine. But come as soon as you can."

Adam runs through the corridors, misses a turn, doubles back, slows down as he approaches the ICU. He's breathless, though, as he walks into Tony's room. Tony's eyes are still closed. The tube is still taped into his mouth. He's still that ghostly white. Mimi is standing on the far side of the bed.

"I thought you'd like to be here when he wakes up," she says. "It'll be just a few more minutes."

If she weren't so far away, he would hug her.

Tony's left arm begins to twitch. He moves his shoulders. He slides his right leg back and forth, moves his shoulders again. He opens his eyes and looks straight at Adam. Adam puts his hand on Tony's arm.

"Hi, honey," he says. "You made it."

Tony nods. His eyes are wide and full of pain. He puts one hand up to the tube sticking out of his mouth. Mimi moves his hand gently back down onto the bed.

"That's what's helping you breathe, Mr. Marchak," she says. He looks over at her. "And keeping you from being able to talk. We have to leave it in, for another hour or so. Till we get your oxygen level back up. Okay?"

Tony nods. He looks back at Adam.

"I love you, honey," says Adam.

Tony nods again. A jolt of pain hits his eyes. He slides his arms up and down, moves his legs from side to side. He looks up at Adam, his eyes pleading.

"Can't you give him something?" Adam asks Mimi. "He's really hurting."

"I'm afraid I can't, no. Not for a while." Tony looks over at her. "We have to get things inside him awake and functioning before we can sedate him again." Tony looks back at Adam.

"They can't give you anything just yet," says Adam. "They would if they could, but they can't. Do you understand me?"

Tony nods.

"Can you bear it all right?"

Tony shakes his head. He moves his arms and legs again, clearly struggling for relief but not finding any.

Adam pulls a chair over beside the bed, rests his hand on Tony's arm, and chatters mindlessly. About Barbara and Barry and Jim. About the women on their motorcycles and the cooking show with the dirty oven. About Fuzzy Bobo and the fox. About the fish chowder in the cafeteria. Anything. Dear god. Anything. All the while,

Tony is moving his arms and legs, clenching and unclenching his fists. He looks from Adam to Mimi to Adam, his eyes pleading.

"Can't you help him?" Adam asks her. "Please?"

"Not quite yet," she says. "Soon."

Machines by the head of the bed register Tony's heartbeat and blood pressure. Periodically, Mimi checks his oxygen level by slipping a clothespin-like device onto the end of one finger. At last, she leans down toward Tony and says, "We can take your breathing tube out now, if you're ready."

Tony widens his eyes and nods.

Mimi leaves the room and comes back with another nurse. They take the tape off Tony's face and, very slowly, pull the tube out of his mouth. It keeps on coming.

Jesus, thinks Adam. How long *is* it?

Finally it's all out, and the other nurse unhooks it from a machine over by the wall and takes it away. Tony coughs and winces.

"Ahhhhhh!" he says.

"How do you feel?" asks Mimi.

"Hurts," says Tony, in a kind of croak.

"I know," she says. "We can start giving you something to help now. All right?"

Tony nods.

"Water?" he says.

"Of course," says Mimi.

"May I?" asks Adam.

"By all means."

Adam pours water from a pitcher into a glass, unwraps a flexible straw, sticks it in the glass and bends it over, and puts the straw near Tony's mouth. Tony sips. Waits. Sips again.

"Thank you," he says.

Adam smiles.

The painkiller starts to take effect, and Tony relaxes. The other tubes come out of his chest, and he drinks more water. Adam goes out just long enough to make a few phone calls and comes right back.

At suppertime, Mimi asks Adam if he's planning to go to the cafeteria.

"Not on your life," he says.

"I can have something brought in."

"Would you? That would be wonderful."

Mimi's shift ends, and another nurse comes on duty. Tony naps a little and wakes up with a bit less pain in his eyes.

Around 8:30, the new nurse, whose name is Helen, comes in to say she thinks Tony might want to try getting some real sleep.

"I'll be going then," says Adam.

"Take your time," says Helen, and she goes back out.

"When I . . . ," says Tony. He coughs and winces. "When I woke up and saw you there, I was so glad."

"Me, too," says Adam.

Tony squeezes Adam's hand.

"Who'd've thought?" says Tony.

"Thought what?"

"That we'd be the ones to make it. You and me."

"I would," says Adam. "I'd've thought."

ABOUT THE AUTHOR

Robert Taylor is the author of *All We Have Is Now* and *Whose Eye Is on Which Sparrow?,* the winner of the 2005 Independent Publisher Book Award for best book of the year with a gay or lesbian theme both fiction and nonfiction, and also named the Best Gay Romance of 2004 by the InsightOut Book Club (both from Haworth). He is also author of *The Innocent* and *Revelation and Other Stories*. A longtime magazine writer and editor, he is an Affiliate Scholar at Oberlin College in Ohio and a member of the Board of Trustees of the Bill Long Foundation and the Pierre Monteux Foundation.